JOY AND PAIN

JOY AND PAIN

John P. Burdi

LUMINARE PRESS
WWW.LUMINAREPRESS.COM

Printed in the United States of America

Cover Design: Franchesca Malaga

Book Layout: Melissa K. Thomas

Author Photo by: Tim Anderson Jr

Luminare Press
442 Charnelton St.
Eugene, OR 97401
www.luminarepress.com

ISBN: 978-1-64388-210-9
LCCN: 2019916004

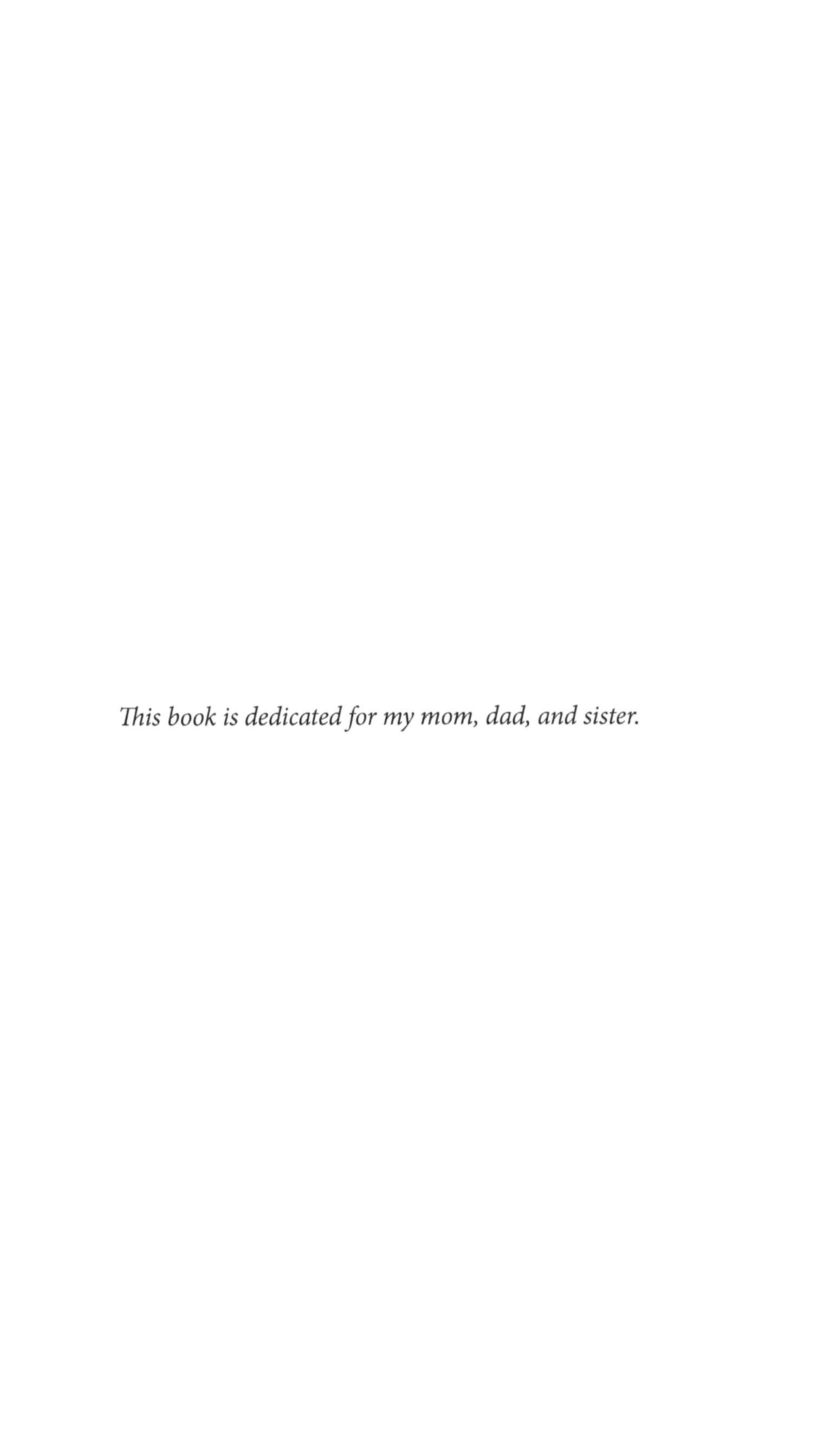

This book is dedicated for my mom, dad, and sister.

1.

THE MALL

"WHAT DO YOU MEAN THE CHOCOLATE IS STILL NOT working? It's been broken for over two months. This is getting ridiculous!" the woman exclaimed.

Perry, not thoughtful of his measly part-time job, was trying to figure out why a customer was getting so emotional over ice cream. He reasoned that if the chocolate had been broken for over two months, why would the customer bother to go back? Most of the customers came back even when they had a bad experience, which confused him, but the lack of reason behind that infuriated him. He felt like the customer was doing this just to prove that the customer was always right, which he thought was untrue, but he rarely stood up to a customer, because he was making barely above minimum wage, and there were other factors about the mall that scared him more than any customer. He insisted that the previous statement was nonsense.

"I have no idea when the machine will be fixed. They don't tell me anything about this place," he said, which was the truth in his mind.

The woman, who rolled her eyes in the manner of a teacher not liking a very poor answer from a student, said, "I do not like your attitude, and I want to know when it will be fixed. Give me corporate's number."

"I don't have that number, we don't have any numbers here, and we don't have a phone."

He did not work at an actual store; it was a small kiosk that had half of what the actual store of the ice cream company had. There was no need for a phone. He was working at an ice cream shop, which he felt was the bane of his existence. He was beginning to lose his patience with the customer as each word he said was slightly louder.

"What is your manager's name? I want to speak to somebody in charge!" The customer was frustrated that there was no chocolate, but now she was letting Perry know that she was in charge of the conversation. Other customers and mall workers were beginning to view the spectacle taking place.

"I don't have to give you my manager's name. That's ridiculous." He never responded this way to a customer. He was usually unconcerned with them. Once his shift was over, he forgot most of the customers and transactions, or he made himself forget. He loathed everything about his measly job at the mall, but something was different this day. For the first time, he was truly irritated with the customers. "Look, it's not my fault that the machine broke. It's not my responsibility to fix it or inform you when it will be fixed." He wanted to say to "inform rude animals," but he didn't want his manager, who was also the owner of the ice cream kiosk, to get in trouble with the management that ran the mall as a mass of unjustifiable oppressors.

"Did I say anything about it being your fault?"

Perry knew exactly what she was doing: she was rationalizing with herself and with him that she was not being rude and was clearly playing the victim in this unnecessary battle.

The woman became calm, which made Perry even angrier but made him realize the customer was incompetent.

"I'll ask again for the number to call corporate."

He wanted to jump over the counter and insult her so that she would never come back to the mall again. The rage inside him was rising. His legs grew heavy, his hands began to shake, and perspiration was showing on his forehead. The real kicker of this situation was that his shift was over in about twenty minutes. A stingy twenty minutes, and now he had to deal with this lunatic.

"I'm sorry, but I do not have any numbers here. The mall office might have the number." He had to bite his lip and close his eyes to come up with a response.

"Where is your name tag? You're supposed to have a name tag on."

Perry lost all patience. This occurred because the store did not have the product that the customer desired. He said, "What do you care? Are you corporate, and is this a bullshit secret test?" As much as she was surprised by his question, he was even more surprised. He never talked like that to a customer. He was one who barely stood up for himself, but he felt different during this exchange.

Her eyebrows went up so much that they were touching her hair. "Well, you wouldn't know, would you? And watch your language."

"If you were corporate, you would know that our machine was broken. Also you wouldn't dress like a complete slob with your leggings that you should clearly only wear if you were like fifty pounds lighter and that might be a stretch." Unconcerned about the consequences of this exchange, he felt a jubilation in standing up for himself. He felt proud even though it was in the walls of the mall.

"This is outrageous. I'm going to the coffee shop."

Not thinking and fueled with rage, he said, "Good. Now more chickens can live, because without your business and the quarts of ice cream you consume, more eggs will be saved."

"I am putting in a complaint about you." She looked as if the insult meant nothing to her. She had wanted to file a complaint at the beginning of the conversation, and this was just an excuse to do it.

He yelled, "Good. Tell them Perry says ``hello."

The customer left, but the affair was not over.

He was engulfed with anger. Never before had a customer put up such a fight for something as useless as chocolate ice cream. Granted, the store should have had the product, but he was concerned about why the customer cared so much. He thought, *People are suffering every day, but that fat ass only cared what else she can eat and spend her money on. Why do they care so much?*

He had worked there since he was sixteen, and now at twenty-four, he had had enough. He graduated from college two months before but was still figuring himself out. He did not have a career yet. The part-time job at the mall did not pay well, but he didn't need to pay off his student loans yet. He was in the grace period.

He was overweight but not fat. He wanted to lose some pounds. He stood at five feet seven inches and had a Napoleon complex, especially since his father was well over six feet. He had a pair of big glasses and was constantly pushing them up against his nose, and he had a dark brown haircut combed back. With an unusual first name, he had a chip on his shoulder. He wanted to do more with his life. He wanted to be of importance. He was intelligent, but he never had a full plan of what he wanted to do. Not knowing what to do was a big reason why, and not getting a big break in life was the cherry on top.

He had aspirations of being a psychologist, but he could not go to graduate school before he had his undergraduate loans taken care of, and with the grace period lasting only a couple months, time was of the essence to make a plan. Living with his parents created an undesirable living environment, but he did not have a choice. Some days he wanted to pack up everything and never come back, but that would have been too cliché. Sometimes he liked to do things untraditionally, but the yearning to leave the mall grew with every shift.

He was a simple young man, never big into the popular crowd. He had a small group of good friends, George being his best. George was a moral and smart friend, one who drove Perry in the right direction. George graduated from college a couple years earlier and already had a career, but Perry was not jealous. He knew that one day he would do something, but he did not have a strategy for how to do it.

He had one serious relationship, with whom he thought was the love of his life, Samantha, but the breakup derailed him. His relationship ended a couple weeks before his senior year in college. His girlfriend had already graduated, but he needed an extra year. They were going in different directions, but he wanted to be with her. She wanted to follow her career path, which meant additional schooling. The breakup was inevitable, but he did not want to accept it, and it was an ugly breakup, to say the least, but he knew everyone went through situations like that. Ever since then, he had a sense of loneliness and uselessness. He had good days and bad days.

There was nothing outrageous or extraordinary about Perry.

He did not have an answer to the question he had before no matter how much he thought about it. Did the customer's entire day revolve around her eating ice cream? *All the beauty and goodness in the world, and she had to act like a complete animal to me*, he thought. The twenty minutes until the end of his shift turned into fifteen, but he was still fuming. He wanted to punch something or throw whatever he could get his hands on. He was sweating; his face turned beet red, mainly because it was always so hot in the mall. He was staring straight ahead, not looking at anyone, even the girl across at the other store who he had feelings for but left bottled because he did not want to hear "no" or his least favorite answer, "I'm talking to somebody."

Julia worked at the toy store across from the kiosk. She was an energetic girl, and when she worked, he was pleased. She sometimes left her store and stood in front of the entrance to try and get customers to come in, especially when she was bored. Dancing was one of her favorite methods, and it was his favorite too. When she was standing in front of her store, he left the kiosk and went over to talk to her. It made his nights go by faster, but more importantly, he was attracted to her. Not just her physical looks. He enjoyed talking to her. She was sweet, never letting on too much. He liked her enough to consider asking her out, but at this moment, he was not thinking about her or looking at her. The fifteen minutes passed without a single customer as another associate came on to relieve him.

"Hey, how's it going, Perry?" said Tara, a kind girl but too young for him.

"I'm doing pretty well." This was a lie. He did not want to tell her about the argument with the customer. He told her all the flavors in the cases and what needed to be done to close for the night.

"Have a good night," she said.

As he was leaving the kiosk, he noticed the customer out of the corner of his eye and began to follow her. He had no idea what his intention was. He did not know if he was going to approach her or just follow her. He had never felt this rage before. He had few arguments in his life, and this was the first time he had a major argument with a customer. His hands began to shake, sweat was pouring down his face, and he needed to take his glasses off. He detected that his legs were getting heavier. Each step took longer and more effort. He was gaining on the customer as she went into an entertainment store, which happened to be his favorite store in the mall. "Of course, she has to go in there," he said softly.

He did not see where the customer went after she walked in, but he knew she could not go far, and the store was not the biggest in the mall. Avoiding the music section was tough, as it was something that he enjoyed. He had one mission—confront the customer—but then what? He had no idea what he would do once he saw her. Yell at her some more? He was not going to hit her. That could turn into more problems, so he relaxed, trying to figure out what to do. He went to the music section but kept a close eye on the exits so she would not leave before he said something. Remorse began to trickle into his head—not remorse for what happened but for what would happen. Deep down, he knew he would probably do nothing. He was wasting his time. He could have been in his car driving home, but instead he was contemplating yelling at the woman.

He realized that if he was to yell at her, he would go down to her level. *I can't make another scene. There is really nothing I can do.*

He walked out of the store and behind the food court, where he needed to clock out. As he pulled the timecard out, he noticed the time was 5:09. He had wasted nine minutes standing in a store. Another thought raced into his head. Instead of making the time a complete waste, he should go back and say goodbye to Julia.

The last few times that he and Julia talked, it was about television shows they watched when they were younger. He figured he would lead the conversation with that, but every time they talked, he was so jittery that it was hard to be composed in front of her. He was getting closer to his kiosk when he felt a tap on his shoulder. He turned around. To his astonishment, it was Julia.

"Hey, friend."

As soon as he heard the "f" word, he closed his eyes. This really was not his day. He did not want to respond to her. He knew she must think that he liked her on a deeper level than as a friend. *Julia is single, and I'm pretty sure she isn't talking to anybody, so for her to call me friend without it leading to something more is a slap in my face. Maybe I'm overanalyzing this.*

"Hey, Julia. My shift just ended. I'm going back, because I forgot my phone." He had his phone in his pocket. This was an excuse to talk to her.

"I hate when I lose my phone. My break is over, so I'm heading back over there anyway."

"Great. I'll walk you back." He had to pretend that he forgot his phone in the kiosk. *Why can't I just ask her out to dinner?* The reasoning was more than getting the courage. Did he want to hear her say no? He had little confidence that she would say yes at this point, and why would she? *I have been so awkward around her, I never know what to say, and she's probably not attracted to me anyway.*

 John P. Burdi

"So how is your day going?" she said.

"It's okay. How good can it be if I worked here today?" *Well, it's better now that I'm talking to you.* He was angry for not saying that, but it would be too obvious that he liked her. *You're overthinking this.* "How is your day?"

"It's not bad. I have been applying to a few places so I can leave here."

Of course she would leave without me saying anything to her. God, I'm a complete failure. "What kind of places did you apply to?"

"Honestly, anyplace that isn't here. I'm not sure what I want to do, but I can leave all this drama behind. I pretty much applied to any full-time job."

What drama? Should I ask that? It's not drama from me, is it? "What kind of drama are you talking about?"

"The people are crazy here, and I'm not talking about the customers. Did you notice how violent the security has been with shoplifters or even teenagers on a Friday night? They will escort them out now. They're making me uncomfortable here. Sometimes they hit on me in the most obvious way."

"Oh geez. You don't need that. People are stupid sometimes."

"Yeah, they are. Some people don't know when to speak up or have good timing, but I guess you can't expect too much from people."

Ignoring the obvious attempt she made about how his timing was so wrong, he thought, *Do it now. If she goes to another place, this is your last chance.* He whispered, "Julia?"

"Yeah?"

"I would like to know that if you ever had the time, would you like to grab a cup of coffee with me?" He asked in the faintest of voices, his throat dried up, his eyes closed.

By the time she responded, it seemed like years had passed. "Yeah. Of course I would love to grab some coffee."

He looked at her with his mouth wide open, but no words came out. He could not think of anything. He nodded and took out his phone. "Hey, I guess I had it on me the entire time. I don't have your number. How will I contact you for this coffee?"

She took out her phone and gave it to him so he could put in his number, and she did the same to his. "Well, your number is saved."

"Cool. I would love to grab coffee."

He needed to end the conversation on a good note and bring some joyfulness to his day. "Have a good night. Hopefully I see you in a couple days when I have to come back to this hell hole."

Laughing, she said, "Okay. Have a good night."

The exchange gave him excitement and self-confidence for the night, especially after his terrible shift. He turned and walked to the food court. He parked his van in the employee parking lot on the outside of the food court, but before he could go home, he saw someone out of the corner of his eye and delayed leaving to go home again.

The customer was walking toward the food court. He composed himself, because he wanted to get his question answered. Why did she care so much? She was going to the Chinese restaurant; he knew the owners and often got free food. He cut her off.

"Couldn't get the chocolate ice cream, so you're replacing it with Chinese. What are you going to order, the entire menu?" He faintly heard carnival music coming from the small carousel near the edge of the food court. The carousel had a large sign at the top saying, "Brine County Mall, Home of the Thompsons." The mall owner's picture was on the right of the sign, looking down at everybody as they walked past it.

The customer, looking baffled, was embarrassed, because now he was talking to her in front of other people. "Well, at least they'll have everything on the menu, and their employee isn't a little runt."

He cut to his question. "Why did you care so much about if we had chocolate ice cream?" He waited for the answer nervously. The carnival music seemed to get louder.

"Because I do. Now if you say one more word to me, you know who I will call on you, and it will get messy."

Knowing full well the severity of the threat, he had to walk away. He never had any altercation with the security there, but he knew how they would get. The carnival music was extremely loud, but he knew everybody else could barely hear it. He closed his eyes and walked away, but he felt something he had never felt before.

He wanted to kill this customer. The answer was not the one he was looking for. She had just given him a hard time, but he wanted to take her life. He had no idea why. The argument did not warrant murder, but that was what he wanted. He wanted to take the customer's life. He desired to take her life. He walked to a table in the food court and sat down, trying to collect his thoughts, trying to reason his feelings. The more he thought about it, the more he wanted to go through with it. *But where would I put her body? What if somebody saw me?* Under his breath, he said, "I need to kill her."

He was frustrated by working at the mall, but on this day, he wanted to slaughter a customer. A couple minutes went by.

He was visited by Freddie. He was a custodian there, friendly for the most part, and tall with an innocent look.

He knew the ins and outs of the mall and had worked there for almost fifteen years. "I heard that bitch giving you a handful. Forget her. She's a cow. If you had the chocolate ice cream, she would put you out of business."

That joke made Perry smile, but he still had the feeling of killing. "Thanks. That makes me feel better. It's just been a bad day."

"Oh, I had my shares of bad days in this mall. Fights with customers, fights with security, questioning what the fuck I'm doing with my life working here."

"So how do you keep going? Why do you keep coming back here?"

"I need money, but most importantly, it doesn't matter that you have bad days here. What matters is how you relieve the stress from this bullshit. That customer giving you a hard time? I have seen that hundreds of times, been around it countless times. I know the feeling you have. You want to kill her but not jokingly, honestly wanting to kill her. The key is to relieve some of that stress, and pretty soon, I'll show you what I am talking about, because I had the same look you do now a couple years ago. Until then, have a good one." Freddie walked away.

He'll show me what he's talking about? What the hell does that mean? Did he hear me when I said I need to kill her? Perry was more confused than ever. With Freddie, it was like speaking to The Riddler.

He got up to go home and eat dinner with his family. On his way out, one of the older women custodians said to him, "Hi. How are you doing today?"

"I'm having a ball."

He walked into the parking lot and to his car. It didn't matter that Julia agreed to go out for a cup of coffee. His outlook on his day revolved around that customer.

2.

GEORGE

Perry got to his van, clenching his fists. When he got home, he was going to have dinner with his family, and later that night, he would hang out with his friend, George. Perry hated to drive his old family van. It was paid off and had been running since he began driving it at eighteen, which he believed to be a miracle. He pulled out of his spot and was playing some music when he saw the owner of the mall yelling at some security guard. "What an asshole," Perry said, but he would never say this within hearing distance of the owner. He texted his mother that he was coming home.

While he was driving, he said out loud, "What am I doing? What am I doing?" These questions were about his life; he had no plan, no execution, and just getting by was not enough for him. Driving was the usual aggravation at its best. The car in front of him wasn't moving, while the car behind him was right on his bumper. "Of course the Lexus gets to ride me. Douchebag thinks they can do anything on the road because of their bullshit car. If I had a gun, I, I guess I would shoot them, but then how would I get rid of the body?"

The Lexus driver was a woman in her forties. He noticed the silver SUV was too big for one person and reasoned that she must have a family. The car in front was barely going the speed limit. He could tell the driver was a kid, a boy who barely looked like he had graduated middle school, too scared to go anything over the limit. *This fucking Lexus won't give anything up. Jesus Christ, and she has those big stupid sunglasses like she's Jackie Kennedy. Maybe I should pull over and let her pass, but then the kid in front won't know how to handle this. I want to see what this bitch is going to do. Yeah, that's right. If I had a gun, I would kill you.*

He was thinking these thoughts and saying this blasphemous statement, but what alarmed him was that he was not sure if he was serious. At each turn, the Lexus was getting closer. He saw the driver texting or doing something on their phone.

What a big surprise. She's on her phone, probably telling her followers that the van in front of her is not moving fast enough.

He was trying to tell the boy in front of him sorry and that this was not his fault but to no avail. The Lexus was getting closer. He could not see the bumper, just the hood of the SUV. She could have easily passed him and the boy, but she wanted to make their days even worse. She was tailing them and being relentless about it. He and the boy were heading to the next traffic light, which was next to a church. There was not a single car in the large, abandoned parking lot. Signs in front of the church said, "Peace Be With You" and "Don't Text and Drive." He wanted to slam that sign on the SUV behind him.

At the red light, he began to scream and scream and scream. The woman behind him paid no attention, in her own universe behind him. The light turned green, but he was not moving. The car in front was long gone, and the Lexus behind was beeping its horn. He stopped screaming but was still not moving. He needed a break. He wanted to aggravate the Lexus as much as possible. The boy was probably in great spirits because this mess was all over for him. Now he could read the woman's lips: "What the fuck? Move, you asshole."

There were no other cars in sight. The "Peace Be With You" sign was still in his head. He was just trying to drive home, not going crazy with speed or anything. He wanted to get home in one piece, but this woman had other plans. She almost tapped him a couple times. He did not know what to do next. A bit of him wanted to throw his van in reverse and start backing into her. He pictured the car ablaze and a large explosion at the end of the scene, but before he could imagine anything else, he heard the woman's voice clear as crystal.

Perry was at an intersection with only one lane on either side. He knew that if the Lexus was going to drive through the intersection, that she would have to pass him on the left. The right side had a curb and grass, and he figured she was not going to harm her precious vehicle. He left her no choice because he was not going to move, but before she was going to do anything, he saw the pickup truck driving toward them doing well over the limit. She was not going to see the truck because the height of his van. So, without thinking, he motioned for her to pass him.

"What the fuck are you do…"

The Lexus was swerving to pass Perry, because at the last second, he opened his door so she could go on the wrong side of the road in an even more dangerous manner. The pickup truck tried relentlessly to brake but could not slow in time and had nowhere to go. There was only one lane. The collision pushed the Lexus seventy feet behind him. Completely totaled. Perry was not sure if the drivers in either car were alive, but instead of looking, he continued home. He did not care that he was the reason behind the accident. *Sure, I wasn't moving, but the Lexus was staying up my ass the entire time. Oh well. Sucks for her.*

The rest of the drive was a cakewalk with no car of any notice on the road. The signs sketched in his head were "Don't Text and Drive" and "Peace Be With You." Now he had peace, and so did the woman.

He pulled into his driveway, shut off his music, and opened his door. The only thing he could hear was the music blasting from his neighbor's car across the street. *The car is parked, and all I hear is fuckin' bass, idiots.* He was walking up to his door when he heard loud sirens and saw two ambulances drive through his development. *I wonder what that must be for.* He opened his door and walked in.

"Hi, Perry. How was your day? How much tip money did you make," said his mother.

His childhood was great. He had two loving parents, two younger sisters, and a medium-size house, but he wanted to move out, because he wanted to be on his own. His parents were hard workers. His father was an excellent cook, and his mother was usually the volunteer for class parties, even while working, but they were always there for him. Sometimes he was not there for them. His mother sometimes got on his case about his future. She realized his potential but never gave him the benefit of the doubt about reaching it.

His younger sisters, Laura and Leah, were identical twins, and he had a great relationship with both of them. They finished high school and were going to the same college in September. They both received excellent scholarships and were going to live on campus. Perry did not live on campus when he attended college; he commuted. He did not receive scholarships, although he was smart.

     John P. Burdi

He didn't care about schoolwork, though he loved learning about history and psychology. He went on vacation with his family, went to baseball games, and had a lot of fun, but lately he was short tempered with his family. He was losing patience with them, with himself, and with the life he was making.

"It was fine. I didn't make much. What's for dinner?" He seldom told her the truth or any details about his life. He kept his family in the dark.

"I ordered Chinese. I got you pork lo mein. Isn't that your favorite?"

"It is. Thank you," he said quietly.

"Your father should be home in about ten minutes. You guys left work the same time. I have to get Laura and Leah. They're outside in the pool."

"Okay. I'm going to take a quick shower." He was walking upstairs and looked at his phone. He received a text from George: *My house at 10 tonight. We can watch some Twilight Zones.* He texted back, *Sounds like a plan.*

Perry went on the computer. The only news he wanted to check was about the accident he was involved in about twenty minutes ago. He was scrolling through *Brine County News* but saw nothing yet. He did not feel relief. He wanted someone to feel the consequences of that accident: the Lexus driver. He went to the shower, turned the water on as hot as it could get, and let the water hit his head.

He got out of the shower, threw on an old T-shirt, and hurried downstairs. He was extremely hungry. Everybody was at the table, waiting for him.

"Hi. How was your day?" said his father.

"Better now. I'm starving." Perry ripped open his take-out container and began eating. "It's very good," he said with a mouthful of pork lo mein.

"You girls know what you're going to major in yet? Don't be like your brother," said his mother.

"What the hell is that supposed to mean?" This got his attention. His major was always an argumentative issue with his mother. He loved psychology and history but could not find work with those degrees. His mother wanted him to major in business. She felt that would lead to a job faster. She wanted what was best for him, even if he was not happy.

"It means I hope they put more thought into their major and pick something that leads to a job."

"You don't just pick something, you pick something that you want to do. I'm sorry that I love psychology," he said sarcastically. Perry felt that his mother always had to start this argument. He always felt that she was ashamed of him. "I chose to study psychology because I wanted to do something with my life that I love doing, not like you guys, who have shitty jobs." He never wondered if he crossed the line with his parents. They treated him like an adult, so he spoke to them as adults, not parents. This time, the line was crossed.

"All right, I just want to eat. I had a busy day at work," said his father. His father rarely raised his voice. His wife did the yelling for him.

"Okay, but Mom, I have my degree. I can't change my major. Get over it, or you can pay for my student loans." This was a sensitive topic with his parents, because although they lived in a medium-size house, his student loans were his responsibility. His parents would pay them if they had the money, but they did not, and he never truly understood that.

"Perry, enough!" yelled his father.

The table was silent. Perry wanted to throw his plate against the wall, and he felt like his mother was attacking him.

     John P. Burdi

"I haven't decided yet. Maybe I want to major in biology or chemistry. I know there is a need for teachers for those subjects," Laura said.

"I thought about the same thing. Maybe even teacher special education," said Leah.

"Of course, they pick the political answers with you guys. You think they really want to do that bullshit? They only said that so you won't be on their backs, Ma. For Christ sakes, can't you see that?"

"The only thing I see is a young man who is not applied to anything except complaining about everything," his father said.

"Fine. I'll stop."

"Just eat your dinner. We might have to go to the mall after we eat," said his mother.

"Are you out of your freaking mind? I am not going back there."

"I was talking to Laura and Leah. We have to get supplies for their dorm rooms," his mother said calmly.

"Did you guys hear about the car accident on Church Road?" said Leah. "Some car got slammed by a pickup truck. Both drivers are dead." This was no doubt the accident that Perry caused, but all of the sudden, he had a small smile.

"You're laughing about this?" said Laura.

"No, of course not. This is some good Chinese food."

Perry was not smiling about the Chinese food even though he enjoyed it. He was smiling because he had wanted to kill the driver of the Lexus, and the driver was dead. He was thinking how involved he really was in the accident, but that did not bother him. What bothered him was if there were any witnesses. His van was not moving, causing the Lexus to try and pass him, and after the accident, he drove away, not caring if they were hurt or alive. His van was easily recognizable; it was burnt orange. "Were there any witnesses?" said Perry.

"It doesn't say," said Laura, who was reading an article on her phone. "One of the drivers was only twenty-seven years old."

"What a shame. That's why you guys need to be off your phones when you are driving and pay attention," said Perry.

"Who said anybody was on their phone? The article doesn't mention that," said Leah.

Perry realized he might have said too much. "One of them had to be on their phone. That's what causes most accidents nowadays." He knew his father was going to love that answer.

"Perry, you are right. People are always driving while on their phones. I see it every day, so you girls promise me that you will be more careful about that." His father drank his soda, waiting for a response.

"We will," Laura and Leah said in unison.

"And don't try passing anybody to go onto oncoming traffic," said Perry.

Nobody answered. At that point, nobody knew the cause of the accident; both drivers were dead with no witnesses, and it looked like Perry was in the clear.

After dinner, his mother, Laura, and Leah went to the mall. Perry drank a cup of coffee and was talking to his father.

"You need to have more patience and be easier with your mother."

"Well, what about her? She doesn't have to throw in my face how I don't have a real job and how she hated my major. This is getting ridiculous. It's over, and I graduated."

"I agree with you, and I'll talk to your mother about

that, but you need to be more relaxed with her and help Laura and Leah with going to college.”

“I know, but she aggravates me so much and…”

“What doesn’t aggravate you anymore, Perry? You get mad about everything and let everything bother you. You need to let things go.”

“I know. I don’t know why I get infuriated so easily.”

“You need to learn how to relieve stress.”

Perry realized this was what Freddie had said to him earlier in the day; he knew how to relieve the stress from the mall but did not tell Perry how. That part was a mystery. When would he learn how to release the stress?

“Anyway, what are you doing tonight? Do you have any plans?” his father said.

“I’m going to George’s later and maybe watching *The Twilight Zone*.”

“Great show. Be sure to watch Monsters on Maple Street or the episode where the boy wishes people into the cornfield.”

“Definitely Monsters on Maple Street. I’m going upstairs to take a nap.”

“Okay. I’ll be down here if you need me.”

Before taking his nap, Perry wanted to check his online dating account. As much as he liked Julia, and even though she had agreed to get a cup of coffee, online dating was his backup plan. He had had the profile for a couple weeks but did not meet anybody. He observed the mailbox. He sent four messages out the night before, hoping for a response, but had none. He thought it was harder for a man to be successful at online dating than a woman.

Lying in his bed, Perry thought about the customer who gave him such a hard time. This prevented him sleeping, so he began to think about Julia and taking her out to dinner. He closed his eyes and, before he knew it, was sleeping. Forty minutes later, he woke up and watched some television. His mother and sisters came home.

"Mom, I'm going to George's house. I won't be home until like midnight," he said to his mom as he was coming downstairs.

"Okay. Have fun. Don't make too much noise coming in."

Perry opened his car door and remembered his drive home from the mall and that he was the reason for two people dying. Still, he did not hear any word about whether there was a witness. He did not care if there was one. *The Lexus was the driver breaking the law.*

George lived about five minutes away in his new home. Perry could only dream about having his own home. Perry met George in elementary school almost twenty years ago, and they had been best friends ever since. They used to be on the same baseball team and had hundreds of sleepovers when they were younger. George's parents had a great basement for sleepovers, but with George's new job, they hung out less. George was the one person who Perry never lost his temper with. He didn't need to, and they were both there for each other whenever one needed help. On this night, Perry clearly needed George's help, but he did not know if he was going to tell him everything. Not only what happened on the drive home, but those feelings he had in the mall. It was as if Perry was about to have a breakdown.

On the way, he noticed a text from George. *Hey, you can stop and get some snacks if you want? I don't have that much food in my house.*

Perry made a sharp left turn into a convenience store. *Sure. I'll be over in a couple.*

Inside the store, Perry was looking at some nacho chips and salsa when a voice called, "Yo, Perry, how are you?" The voice sounded happy and belonged to another guy who worked at the mall, Chris, who was a custodian like Freddie. Perry and Chris did not know each other at all. Perry and Freddie were acquaintances, but Perry and Chris hardly spoke to each other. Chris was short with longer black hair, was a couple years younger than Perry, and seemed more of a mystery than Freddie.

"Not bad. How are you doing, Chris?"

"It's a great night. Just heard from our mutual partner about what happened today."

"What the hell are you talking about?" Questions came to his head. *Is he talking about the car accident? Did he see it? Were there any witnesses? Who was the mutual partner?* Perry became nervous. What would happen if Chris saw the accident? He did not trust him and was not close enough to Chris that Chris would lie for him. He did not have any money to keep Chris from telling the truth. The comment from Chris was like a detour in the middle of the road.

"You know what I'm talking about, partner."

"No, I don't, and why are you calling me partner? We barely talked before. I wasn't even sure if you knew my name."

"Oh, I know more than your name. He said you had an incident with a person today," Chris whispered, "and you wanted somebody dead."

"Look, I have no idea what the fuck you are talking about. I really don't have the time for this. Just leave me alone." Perry was panicky. *It is one thing if Chris saw the car accident, but how does he know that I wanted the driver dead?*

"I knew you weren't ready for this. You seem like a little bitch."

"Ready for what? And you don't know shit about me. I'll show you how much of a bitch I am. I'll end you in the parking lot. I don't care anymore!"

People began looking at him. One person seemed to be recording him. Perry tried calming himself, not wanting to create a scene where people were watching. He just wanted to leave and hang out with George. This day was extremely bizarre for him. "I'm going to pay for these. I am done talking to you, and do not talk to me when you see me at work."

"I take that back. You are ready for this. Next time I see you at work, you will want to talk to me. Until then, peace, brother."

"Yeah, whatever."

Perry walked to the register, handed the cashier a ten dollar bill, and left. He looked at his phone, saw that he was running late, and drove to George's. He began to imagine the conversation between him and Chris did not occur. He was unsure what Chris was talking about or what he knew. He tried putting that conversation in the rearview mirror and looked forward to seeing George. Perry arrived a couple minutes later and rang the doorbell.

George answered. "Hey, don't mind the mess."

George had moved in a couple weeks ago. There were still boxes and the sense of the rooms being unfinished with the lack of furniture. "The new TV was delivered today. It's smart, so we can basically watch anything."

George was good looking and single by choice. Girls were interested, but he wanted to concentrate on his career before a relationship. He was a little taller than Perry, slender, and had a short haircut.

"Cool. I just want to relax a little tonight. Weird day." *Weird day. I had a big fight at work with an asshole, Freddie telling me he's going to help relieve some stress, I caused two people to die, I had another fight with my mother, and I have no idea what happened at that convenience store.* Perry wanted to tell George everything. He felt the pressure of saying what

     John P. Burdi

happened, and for the first time, he felt guilty. He never hid anything from George. "I brought nacho chips and salsa."

"Good. I have some cheese. We can make a poor man's nachos."

Perry was thinking about telling George that Julia had agreed to have a cup of coffee with him, but right now, he was still thinking about the bad experiences of the day. *Jesus, I basically killed two people today. I need to tell the police. That's what George would say if I was to tell him, but I don't want to. I don't want to get in trouble over this. That driver was an asshole, a bigger asshole than the customer. I'll tell him about the customer first, see how I feel next.* While George was making nachos, Perry was arguing with himself, zoning out, turning away from George. Perry began to sweat, his legs were shaking, he was losing balance, and he was about to confess about the car accident. "George, I…"

"What's wrong? Sit down. I'll get you some water."

George handed him a cup, and Perry drank the water in a couple seconds, wiping the sweat from his forehead.

"I, I, uh, I could use another cup of water." *I can't say it. I know what he's going to say.*

"Sure. Geez, you're thirsty. What, were you exercising before coming here?"

"I haven't exercised in years. Nah, I just had a long day." George put the nachos in the oven and handed Perry his second glass of water.

"They'll be done in like five minutes. What happened?"

"I had another fight with a customer. This was a big one."

"Oh yeah. You need to watch yourself over there. Watch for Mr. Thompson, don't be on his bad side. I hear he can be vicious."

"I don't have to watch out for him. He's an asshole. The customer was some fat ass woman who wanted chocolate ice cream. Our machine was broken, but she wouldn't leave. She kept asking about the machine being fixed and the corporate number. Then I was yelling back at her and kept saying why do you care so much? I found her after my shift and asked her, but she only said because I do."

"Wait a minute. You approached her after your shift?"

"Yeah. She really got to me, this one. I just wanted her to answer my question. It's not like I was going to hurt her or anything like that."

"Perry, come on. That's not worth wasting your time about, and she sounded like an asshole. Some people are like that because they just want to be. Now I'm preaching what you preach, Mr. Crane." George sometimes called Perry "Mr. Crane" because of the TV character Frasier Crane, who was a psychologist.

"You know I don't like it when you call me that. Call me Mr. Freud." Perry laughed and began to relax.

"In all seriousness, you just need to relax. Don't you know like any methods for relaxing? Maybe get a massage."

"Yeah, but afterward, I know I'll ask for a happy ending."

"That's the spirit. I'll get the nachos. Sit on the couch. Ha ha, happy ending, huh."

Perry knew that George was right. If he was more relaxed and did not let anything get to him, he would not have caused the car accident, and two people wouldn't have died. *I still can't talk about that. I'll bring up Julia after a couple episodes.* "So what's with you, George? How's the job?"

"It's not bad. Not the kind of work I would like to do, but it could be stepping stool for my future, you know." George worked for a pharmaceutical company that he interned with when he was in college. "The internship led to a job. I'm sure this job will lead to a better one. That's the plan."

Perry said, "Plan? I don't even have a plan. I don't even have a goal to make a plan."

"What about graduate school? Don't you want to become a psychologist?

"Yeah, obviously I'll need to go to graduate school, and I don't want to take out more student loans."

"You know what? I know you will figure it out. Just try and enjoy yourself some *Twilight Zone*. Which one do you want to watch?"

"Definitely Monsters on Maple Street."

"Of course. That's a classic."

After watching a couple episodes of *The Twilight Zone*, Perry was relaxed. George always made him less stressed. He was comic relief for Perry and his best friend. Perry wanted to tell George about what happened with Julia today, but the car accident was still on his mind. He needed to tell somebody, but George would report it to the authorities. *Forget about the car accident, forget about the car accident, forget about the car accident…*He could not forget about the accident. *Maybe I should bring up the accident and see what he knows.* "Did you hear about this car accident earlier today, not too far away from here? A couple people died."

"Yeah, I saw something online. No witnesses, nobody knows what happened. I'm sure some truth will be brought to light sooner or later."

Christ, I can never tell him. I know he will tell the police, and he should. I'm basically a murderer. It's either tell him and go to jail, or I can just keep my mouth shut. I need to bring up Julia. Maybe that will make me feel better. Perry said, "I asked a girl out today."

"Oh yeah? Good job. Who is she? Do I know her?"

"No, you don't know her. She works at the mall with me, and her name is Julia Breckenridge. She's a sweet girl, she has this zest for energy, it's very positive, kind of what I need, and she is cute."

"Sounds like you have liked her for some time. So how did you ask her? What are you guys going to be doing?"

"I have liked her for about seven months. I've been talking to her at work, and she works across from me. I finally just asked her to go out for a cup of coffee. You know, keep it simple. Hopefully we can go on real dates after." As he was talking about Julia, he realized that he really liked her. He had a feeling deep down in his stomach and was breathing heavier.

"Real dates after a cup of coffee. Geez, you really like this girl. Are you sure her intentions were of an actual date and not friends getting coffee?"

"Yeah, I do like her, I really like her. No, this is an actual date. I thought I made it clear to her when I asked. She has to know that I like her more than a friend. She's the only girl I talk to in that store. A cup of coffee is obviously an introductory date." Perry was getting nervous. He knew that George might have a valid point. What if this was just a get together for friends?

"Well, is she seeing or talking to anybody?"

"Yeah, she's talking to me." Perry knew his joke was not very funny, just a statement by someone who was nervous. "No, I'm pretty sure that she isn't seeing anybody. I barely see her on her phone, and no guy ever comes up to the store to visit her."

"I don't mean to make you nervous, but I want you to make sure that you know what you're getting yourself into if she's seeing anybody or if she wants to just be friends."

"Friends. I hate that fucking word when it comes to a girl."

"Who knows? Maybe a friend can lead to a relationship, but let's see how the coffee is going to be first."

     John P. Burdi

"You'll be the first one to know. What do you think, want to call it a night?"

"Yeah. I have a nine o'clock meeting tomorrow, but at least I don't have to leave my house for it."

"Okay. I'll see you later. Sorry if I was acting a little weird tonight. It's been a long day to say the least."

"No worries, my friend. Hopefully we can hang during the weekend."

"Sounds good, man."

"Bye."

As George closed the door, Perry looked up at the sky; it looked like a storm was coming. He saw lightning in the distance followed by boisterous thunder. He ran to his car, started it, and took out his phone to see if there were any texts. He saw none but figured no text was a good text. He was becoming alarmed about what would take place with Julia and if it was an actual date and a start of a relationship that he desperately wanted or something he did not want: being friends with a girl. When he got home, he checked his phone again, but still there was no message. He ran out of the van and to the door and slammed it shut to avoid the storm. Nobody was downstairs; everybody was upstairs asleep. It was about ten minutes until midnight. Perry took a water bottle from the refrigerator and went upstairs to his room.

He took off his clothes, threw on an old shirt and shorts, and looked at his phone. Still no messages. He wanted to go to sleep, but before that, he wanted to text Julia. Not a message to make plans for coffee but just a hello. It was just an excuse to talk to her. He sent a simple *Hello*. He looked at his phone thirty seconds later, but there were no messages on his screen. He went to the bathroom to brush his teeth and get ready for bed.

When he returned to his room, he looked at his phone. Still there were no messages. He was getting worried about her not answering him, but 11:51 was a little late to send a text, so he figured there was about a 40 percent chance that she was going to answer him. *Maybe she's with some friends or some guy.* He began pacing his room, wanting an answer from her but not getting any.

He shut off his light from his fan and laid on the bed, pulling the covers near his face but leaving enough room to see if his phone lit up, indicating a text. He thought about the fight with the customer. Still no text. He thought about the car accident and the driver behind who was yelling at him. Still no text. He thought about Julia and if she was with somebody else. Still no text.

He grabbed his phone off his nightstand and shut it off. He knew he could never sleep if he kept looking and thinking about it and saw no text. He closed his eyes and would not open them until morning. His last thought was of the conversation with Freddie.

3.

MICHAEL THOMPSON

THE NEXT MORNING, PERRY WOKE UP AND QUICKLY turned on his phone, yearning for an answer from Julia but seeing nothing.

He had to work the opening shift, which was 11:00 a.m. to 5:00 p.m.—an easy shift looking at the time but tough when dealing with what he dealt with at the mall. Considering the kiosk only sold ice cream, 11:00 seemed a little later for Perry, especially since the rest of the mall opened at 9:00. Every time he was ready to open, he had a line of waiting customers. He tried to reason with them that it would take at least a half hour to have everything ready, but they did not want to hear reason. They only wanted to get their product and to be on their merry way, not caring who was insulted or embarrassed on the way.

He headed downstairs to have breakfast. It was 9:30, which gave him plenty of time to eat and get ready to go to the mall twenty minutes away. He hoped the drive would be less dramatic than the one coming home yesterday. He looked at the kitchen table and noticed a note from his mother: *Good morning. I had to run to work earlier, won't be back until 6ish. Have a good day. Love Mom.* His mother worked at a grocery store as the produce manager. He opened the pantry, took out the box of Honey Nut Cheerios, and heard Leah say, "Hey, having a better morning than last night?"

He did not want to talk to anybody, especially since he had no message from Julia, and he especially did not want to take life lessons from his younger saint of a sister. He answered in a groggy voice, "Yeah, I suppose. Not bad starting your day with Honey Nut Cheerios."

"I have a few questions to ask you about college."

"Shoot away, little sis." *Oh, this should be interesting. Did Mom put her up to this, talking about college and embarrassing me about my major? I'm going to be as astute as possible in case she goes running back to Mom.*

"Well, I know this is a sensitive topic with you, but I have a question about your major. When did you know that psychology was going to be your major? I feel that Mom would love me to purse teaching special education, but I'm not sure if my heart is in it. I really love English, especially Shakespeare."

"It sounds to me that you already made up your mind. I knew I wanted to pursue psychology because in my intro class, I loved writing research papers. I thought it was fun, and I felt like that only for psychology class."

"I understand that aspect, but Mom really wants me to be a teacher and…"

"Who gives a shit what Mom wants you to major in? Look at her job. It's not exactly like she's lighting the world on fire."

"Perry, things were different back then. College is a necessity these days."

"Fine. You know what, since you sound like a philosopher with your college thinking, stop asking me for advice about college since you know all the answers." He was agitated as he ate his cereal. He felt like this was not an

 John P. Burdi

argument with Leah but with his mother, and he had the same argument in his head hundreds of times. This was an argument he did not want to let go of or lose.

"Okay. Sorry, Perry. I have another question. Do you still talk to Samantha?"

"Well, that came out of fucking left field. Why do you want to know?"

"I'm sorry, but I really liked her. You guys were so close before you had a relationship. I always thought you would end up with her." It was true. Perry and his ex-girlfriend, Samantha, were very close before they decided to take their relationship to the next level. Samantha was one of his best friends, and he was one of hers, but they wanted different lives.

"No, I do not talk to her, and I don't intend to. She's an asshole, and she'll always be an asshole. Do you know how many times she lied to me?"

"She was young back then. She might have matured."

"Who the fuck do you think you are, Leah? Seriously, you're defending that piece of shit? Want to know something? She never liked you or Laura or Mom or Dad. She never liked our house or me for that matter. Yes, I was in love with her. When were still together, I would have thought about marriage, but that time is over. I want nothing to do with her. I don't want to know anything about her. I could care less what she's doing. In fact, I hope she is miserable for the rest of her life. She embarrassed me too many times for me to care about her." He was not as mad as he was last night, but if he had had this conversation a year ago, his reaction might have been different. He still did not like to use her name when he did talk about her, which was a finite number of times. He usually referred to Samantha as "her," and people knew what he was talking about.

"She didn't even like me or Laura?" said Leah.

Perry was laughing. "You know, I told you a lot, and the only thing you take from my soliloquy is that she didn't like you or Laura. Jesus, you're just like her, you know that? Now go upstairs, and let me eat in peace. I can still salvage a little of my breakfast."

"Well, you enjoy your day. Hopefully I'll see you later tonight, and maybe we can go see a movie."

"Yeah, I don't think so, not unless I have a great day at work, and I doubt that will happen."

"Why are you so negative all the time, Perry? You never used to be like that."

"How about we look at this from my perspective, shall we? I am single, had a terrible breakup, and the girl I think I asked out is not answering me. I graduated but have no job in sight, nothing on the horizon, nothing even on the same planet. I work at a place I cannot stand, and the only alternative is there is no alternative. It doesn't matter what job I have, because everything in this fucking town is retail. I still live with my parents, and it seems like this entire town, with the exception of George, is against me. Oh yeah, and we live in a town that is run by two brothers who make up a political machine that nobody talks about. Now let me ask you—would you have a positive outlook on life if you were in my situation?"

"Well, I would try and make the best of things and…"

"That was a rhetorical question, Leah. Now go upstairs without asking me another question, and leave me the fuck alone. Understand?"

Leah turned around with tears in her eyes and ran upstairs.

Perry was close with both of his sisters but especially Leah because she made more of an effort to be close to him than Laura. At this moment, he was not close with anybody in his family. He sat down and ate his breakfast in peace. The truth of the matter was that he felt a sense of loneliness but was happy when he was by himself. He finished his breakfast and watched some television. The time was 9:56.

He still had plenty of time to get ready, and so he took out his phone and tried the online dating. He messaged a lot of women, hoping some would answer him. He was attracted to older women, so he messaged them more than girls his own age. He opened his profile and saw one message from Virginia. She lived in the same town and was very attractive, but she was forty-seven. He did not care. He was going to find out if she cared about age. He only messaged older women for one reason, and he did not want to have a relationship with any of them. A couple days ago, he had messaged Virginia, *Hi. I think you are so incredibly beautiful. What's your idea of a perfect day?*

He really thought she was incredibly beautiful, but he could care less about her perfect day. He just wanted her to answer so he could try to talk to her more, to ask someone out. He had not been with any women since Samantha. With Virginia, he was trying to change that. He only wanted to be with Virginia for one night, but he wanted to be with Julia for a long time. With Julia still not answering him, he was skeptical of her.

Virginia's response was *Thank you so much :)*

Perry was flattered but disappointed, because she said nothing about him and did not answer the second part of his message. He looked again and saw another message.

Ooohh, that's a good question. I guess my perfect day would be relaxing, going to the beach, a nice dinner, and maybe a bonfire at night. What's your perfect day?

Perry was excited that she answered him, especially with a question indicating that she wanted to know his response. He replied, *Pretty much the same thing except maybe add the driving range and visiting a museum.* He purposely answered her without a question to see if she would continue the conversation. He knew he had to start getting ready for work soon, so he headed upstairs and then saw Virginia had messaged him again.

You are very handsome by the way and very nice, but you might be too young for me.

He looked at the message and threw his phone down. He did not want to talk anymore. He figured he would answer her later in the day with something about how age did not matter. He got dressed, threw on his ice cream shirt, and left for work early. He was trying to have a better day, and being early to work might help.

He wanted to message George. He felt George was acting peculiar last night and wanted to clear the air with him. He still was not going to tell him about the car accident. He was not going to tell a soul about that. He was going to use an excuse about not feeling well. He was sweating a lot. He figured he could use being sick as an excuse. He grabbed his phone, still had not received a message from Julia, still did not care about Virginia, and messaged George. *Hey, sorry about last night. I didn't feel that well. I could use a vacation.*

He knew that George would respond quick, not worrying about his answer. Perry wanted to apologize to Leah when he had the chance. She and Laura had a busier schedule than most. They were popular at school, and he was accustomed to them bringing home different boys to have dinner. They could easily not be at home when he came home from work, even if Leah did ask him to hang out later in the day.

   John P. Burdi

He went for Leah's door. She and Laura had separate rooms. He knocked to the tune of "We Will Rock You." He heard that she was still crying and upset from their argument. A faint voice said, "You can come in."

He pushed his glasses against the top of his nose and entered. He saw that she was really distraught, and he knew he had to make her feel better before he left for the mall. He knew he had to make an uninterrupted speech. "Leah, I need you to listen, okay? I'm very regretful for what happened today. I want you to know that just because I said it doesn't make it the truth or that I mean a word of it. You know that I love you, even more than Laura," his attempt at a joke did not make her laugh, "but I've been going through a lot recently. It's from the end of my relationship with Samantha, but there's a lot more bothering me."

"Why can't you ever talk about it with us? We feel like we don't know you anymore."

"Leah, please, let me continue." He realized his family did not know him anymore, because he blocked them from knowing anything about himself. He kept everything secret. "I hope that you and Laura never feel like I feel after you graduate college. I feel like I've been falling down a hole for the last couple months. I have no direction, no guidance, and no idea how to stop myself from falling. I have this strong feeling that I am useless in this world and have no purpose. It's like I've been living like a robot, and there is no end in sight. I know there is nobody who can help me. Nobody will get me a job, nobody will give me money. I know I am the only person who can do that, but I have this strong sense that I will fail, that I am useless, and the scariest part is that there is not one person outside of you guys that will care when I fail. The world will keep spinning. It doesn't matter what I do. I feel like I have no place in this world, and that terrifies me. I hope that you and Laura never feel like this." He comprehended that Leah was the only person he could say this to. Not even George. Everything he said to Leah was the honest truth. He felt so lost, and there was no point to getting found.

Leah sat like she was listening to the speech. She wiped her tears from her eyes and blew her nose with a crumpled tissue.

He took a deep sigh and began to walk away. He had his hand on the doorknob when he heard her say, "Perry, you know that we will do anything to make you feel you are not useless. You're my big brother. You know Laura and I look up to you, and we love you." She leaped from her bed and hugged him. He hugged her back but did not show much affection. "Bye, Perry. Tell me about your good day when you get back."

"Sure. Will do. Bye, Leah."

Perry knew his family loved him, but that was not enough for him. He knew other people did not have a family. Some people were abused by their family, but he felt like the most he could get was a loving family. Some people would do anything for that. He would do anything to have more, although it seemed he was about to quit at anything.

He made his way downstairs and looked at his phone. There was a message from George. *Hey, no need for an apology. I didn't think there was anything wrong with you, and feel better, man.*

Perry was glad that he didn't have to further explain himself to George. He responded, *Thanks, I'll talk to you later. Have to go to work.*

He opened the front door and walked to his car. His neighbors had one car running in the driveway and were blasting their music. He could not hear any words, just an incredibly loud bass. He wanted to run across the street and destroy the car, burn it, and throw the neighbors into it while it was on fire, but he knew he was not going to do anything. The threat alone frightened him, and he was unsure what exactly he was capable of.

He started his car and mumbled under his breath, "Fucking neighbors take twenty minutes to leave their house. It takes me twenty seconds." He did not know any of the neighbors in the house across the street from him. They moved in nearly a year ago, and they had not had one conversation. Every time they were outside and he was outside, Perry put his head down and did not look at them. He did not care about their names or where they came from. After hearing their music, he wanted nothing to do with them except to try and get them to be homeless. He thought about planting drugs in one of their cars and calling the cops with a drug tip, but it was too tough to pull off. He needed another person to help him, but he did not want the other person to think he was too extreme. All they were doing was playing loud music in their cars.

On the drive, he kept looking in his rearview mirror, but nothing was there except himself staring back. He was driving on the same road as the accident was the night before and stopped at the intersection. About sixteen hours ago, he had caused two deaths, and now he had returned to the crime scene. He noticed that the glass from the accident was still in the street, and the blood was washed away. Aside from the glass, it was impossible to tell what had happened the day before. There were no cameras on the traffic lights, but he realized there were cameras in the church to help catch people who vandalized the property. Doubt materialized in him. How was he going to get the camera footage from the church? Were investigators already looking at the footage? He knew they could identify his van, but it was possible that the security cameras did not even get the accident. Uncertainty was in control of his life in more ways than one.

The red light took forever to turn green. He was staring at the glass for the longest time, his conscience sunk into the abyss. Deep down, he knew he should have called the police. Not only was it the right thing to do, it was the humane thing to do, but he did not speak up. He took a deep breath, pushed his glasses to the top of his nose, and waited anxiously for the light to turn green. It was too late to call the police. If he had called last night, he would probably have been in the clear, but he wanted the driver to suffer just like he was suffering, except in this case, the driver lost her life. It was not suffering.

He wanted to cry. He knew he was not the person who would not call the police. He knew he was not the person who would cause the demise of two people, and he knew that he never had these strong feelings of vehemence toward the customer and neighbors and Samantha. He knew that a change must be made. He could not continue to live like this. The boy who graduated and wanted to become a psychologist desperately needed a psychologist. The anger built, the thoughts becoming more ferocious, and he was becoming terrified of what he might do to a person.

The light turned green. Perry stepped on it. He wanted to get away from the scene of the crime as fast as possible. He was doing well over the speed limit, and with no cars in front or behind him, the coast was clear. He stopped at the light leading to the entrance of the mall's behemoth parking lot. He pulled out his phone and texted his mother. *I'm there.* He pulled into his usual spot and was almost fifteen

     John P. Burdi

minutes early, so he decided to wait for about five minutes. Even though he arrived early and wanted a fresh start to his day, he needed five minutes to relax and not worry about anything. Not think about the events from yesterday.

He pushed his seat back slightly and heard a hammering noise. The dumpsters were to the left of his car and were shared by the food court. The employee parking lot was on this side of the mall where Perry parked. He turned his head to the left and saw the most chilling figure: a large brute wearing a blue, button-down shirt tucked into khaki pants, a large belt button, and a hygienic shaven beard. It was Michael Thompson, the younger brother of the mall owner. He was the unquestioned, no-nonsense figurehead of the mall. There was not one worker who would question him and not one customer who would interfere with him. The only person who had any influence over him was his older brother, Bruce.

The reason for the hammering noise was a poor mall worker.

Perry did not know who he was, but he was wearing a uniform with a lanyard around his neck. Michael slammed him on the side of the dumpster. Michael's three security guards watched, not saying a word, not helping the poor, defenseless employee. Perry wanted to take out his phone and record what was happening, but he was too worried. There were cameras all around the parking lot. Him film-ing crimes against the mall was worse than actual crimes committed by the mall. He wanted to go out there and help the employee. After getting slammed on the side of the dumpster, the employee fell, wincing in pain. Perry guessed his age at thirty. Michael picked him up by the back of his shirt, stood him against the dumpster, and used him like a punching bag. Blood was going everywhere, mostly on Michael.

Perry was witnessing a beating. He never really saw one, only heard about it. It was never done outside. The employee must have did something terribly wrong.

"Please, please stop! Why are you doing this?"

After hitting the employee in the ribs and stomach countless times, Michael grabbed him by the throat and banged him against the dumpster. It looked like a miracle was going to happen; one of his security guards tried to stop him and pulled on Michael's arm. Michael let go of the employee, and he fell, catching his breath, wiping blood, begging that the beating would stop. Michael punched the security guard and shattered his nose, and he fell on the pavement. Michael grabbed the employee once more, stood him up, and punched him beneath his eye. He slammed his head hit against the dumpster, and he fell. Michael had blood all over his knuckles, shirt, and face.

Perry could not believe what he saw. What Michael Thompson did to the employee was what Perry wanted to do to the customer and neighbors. He was scared that he was not scared of what happened. He still wanted to help the employee, and he despised mall management, but he almost respected what Michael Thompson did. He wanted to be that intimidating. He heard one of the security guards say, "Mr. Thompson, that van over there? Somebody is watching. He might have seen everything."

Michael turned his head, made eye contact with Perry, and started toward him. He was not moving fast, most likely catching his breath from the beatings. Perry was not worried, because if he was in serious trouble, Michael would send the security guards to get him. He was getting closer.

Perry rolled down the driver side window. "Yes, Mr. Thompson?" He saw Michael's "come" hand sign to the two security guards.

   John P. Burdi

"What is your name?" Michael spoke in an intimidating voice without a stutter. He spoke like he rehearsed what he was going to say.

"Perry Miller, sir."

"Mr. Miller, what exactly did you see?"

Perry thought how loaded this question was. If he said he saw anything, he was pretty much dead. If he said he saw nothing, Michael would know he was lying. He needed to think of a smart answer. "I didn't see anything that shouldn't have happened."

"Excellent choice of words, Mr. Miller. May I ask where you work in the mall? You are parked in the employee's lot."

"I work at Dom's Ice Cream, sir."

"Excellent. I love the ice cream, and Dom is a good employee." He made another motion to his security guards, and they wrote down Perry's license plate number. "Now Mr. Miller, I would like you to listen to me. What you saw was an employee pushing his luck and not following my rules, so I ask you: will you follow my rules?"

Perry knew the mall rules, but he did not know exactly what the employee had done. He did not believe anything Michael or his brother said. "Of course I will follow the rules, sir. I would be a terrible mall employee if I did not."

"Another excellent answer, Mr. Miller. We have your license plate number, and I know where you work, so if I find out you say anything, you will not make it outside to the dumpsters, understand?"

"Yes sir. Nothing will be said."

"Carry on with your day, Mr. Miller."

Michael walked away with his guards and made a third hand motion. The two guards savagely beat the guard that Michael had punched. After they worked on him, they left him there. Two men were stationary on the pavement on the side of the dumpsters. In broad daylight, Michael and security might have murdered two people, and the customers of the mall were going about their day like nothing happened, Perry felt that he was the only employee who saw any wrongdoings by the Thompsons.

Perry opened his car door, biting his lip and pushing his glasses against the top of his nose. He grabbed his phone out of his pocket and noticed there was still not a message from Julia. He walked past the two people on the ground, not helping them even if he wanted to. He was about to open the side door to get into the mall when a calming, tranquil voice called out to him, "Help, please help." It was the employee who needed to be rushed to a hospital. The plea was so quiet that it reminded Perry of being in a dream state. He contemplated what to do. *Walk away, just leave him there? It is not worth it, and you will be next if you help, but it's the right thing to do.*

"Do you have your cell phone on you?"

"No. I need help, please," the employee begged.

"You know I can't help you. I'll be next in line for a beating, but this is what you need to do. Time is of the essence, because I need to get to my shift. Can you crawl?"

"I think so."

"Crawl to a member of the Defense and take out his phone to call 911. That way, if you do make it, the evidence is on his phone. The EMTs will come and save you."

"But what about the Thompsons?"

"They will be furious when they find out a member of the Defense called 911, but they will make an excuse. Just do what I said. Good luck."

Perry walked into the mall. In a couple of minutes, he heard sirens.

   John P. Burdi

4.

THE DEFENSE

THE MALL WHERE PERRY WORKED WAS CALLED THE Brine County Mall after Brine County where he lived. The county was small. There was not much tourism or industry except retail, mostly from the mall. Flourished with 150 stores, each more impractical than the next, the stores never sold anything that people truly need, and that upset Perry. He saw how people spent their money on ice cream. How much was spent in actual stores was worse. He hated the fact that each day it seemed like more people were shopping, one after another, shopping, one after another, shopping. He said, "Why do they keep coming back? They shop like a herd of animals, just walking and shopping, not looking at anything. They complain about the price after they buy it, never before it."

The mall was shaped as a hexagon with a department store at each point, and at the middle was the painting of the Brine Mall owner.

There was no uncertainty that Perry hated the Brine Mall and the customers, but there was another demographic he hated associated with the Brine Mall: the Defense. The security team called itself the Defense, but they were more like a gang of retail vigilantes. The Defense didn't have legal power to arrest wrongdoers, but when the crime was done inside the walls of the mall, the jurisdiction was theirs. The Defense was larger than the police force of Brine County. If anything happened in the Brine Mall, the Defense took care of it. They didn't have guns, but that didn't stop them from using excessive force. The police could do nothing, because one of the political leaders of Brine County, Bruce Thompson, was also the co-owner of the mall.

Bruce Thompson's picture was on display at the center of the mall, almost in celebration. He was of average height and skinny, with a hooked nose and had his hair slicked back with the sides shaved, but most importantly he looked like a villain in Perry's eyes. Bruce ran Brine County as a political machine. He made the money, he made the political decisions, and nobody questioned him. He knew how to make the people of Brine County shop at his mall and how to influence votes so that the people he wanted elected won. Astuteness was one of his strongest attributes, but what he was missing in brutality, his little brother made up for. Bruce was the brains at the Brine Mall, but his little brother, Michael, was the girth and the leader of the Defense. Michael Thompson was terrifying, but Perry and the rest of the mall workers were more petrified of Bruce. If Michael disagreed with a worker or the worker broke one of their rules, he would beat them, but Bruce was different. Bruce would use somebody to the best of his advantage, embarrass them in the process, and do what was necessary to get rid of them. Another Thompson brother, a younger one, was mysteriously murdered a while back. Bruce and Michael killed in his honor. The Thompson brothers wanted the mall to be run one way: their way.

Brine County Mall had three rules for employees, and they were given to every person who worked there: We are right (meaning the Defense and the Thompsons), customers are always right (except when conflicting with the first rule), and very often you are wrong. The mall only employed younger workers. If an employee got on Bruce's good side, he would help the person tremendously. It was a risk many young people in Brine County wanted to take, but Perry was not one of them. When he started working at the mall, the plan was to get on Bruce's good side, but it never came to fruition.

The Defense was run like any other mob: a couple people at the top followed by a few captains but mainly composed of pledges. The captains were the ones going around the mall, walking with their hands on their belt buckles and causing havoc for the workers, but Perry was friendly with one person of the Defense, Steve. Steve was an older member. His best years were behind him, the brutality was behind him, and he stopped walking around with an intimidating air but rather with sincere emotion. He often talked to Perry, especially during closing time. He did not flirt with younger workers with an immoral stare in his eyes.

Another reason why Perry hated the Defense was that they talked with the female workers and customers—some obviously not the legal age, but that did not stop them. Julia was on their list of prey, but she never fell into their trap of promising better treatment. She ignored their advances. It was another reason why Perry was infatuated with her. She did not care about their power, and in the walls of the mall, they did have power. Julia was similar to Perry in that regard; she did not care to get on Bruce's good side, but with her attractiveness, she never became his enemy.

Perry was going to apply for full-time jobs and ultimately leave Brine County Mall. Two days ago, he saw the most savage beating of his life, and he could not tell anyone, because they would not believe him, and he knew what would happen to him. He applied to jobs every day in every profession from marketing to car dealerships and banks. He had a couple interviews but to no avail. He was in a sour mood because Julia had not answered him. He wanted to talk to her, to vent to her about his life.

The first thing Perry did after waking up on this particular day was to see if the car accident was in the news and, more important, if there were witnesses. With both drivers dead, nobody else in the cars, and no other witnesses, Perry would be in the clear, but he needed to pay a visit to the church to see what the cameras had recorded. He thought that if they did record the accident, the police would have already gotten to him.

Every report had the same explanation: there were no other cars on the road at the same time, and the conclusion was that the Lexus driver was on their phone, went to the wrong side of the road, and caused the deaths. The news made Perry happy about not facing punishment for his actions, but he did not care that two people died because of what he did. He showed no remorse. He did not want to change anything, as he thought he was in the right. Three days after the accident, he was definitely in the clear.

So far, the online search did nothing to appease him. Every entry-level job required experience, and even if he did apply, he knew he would not be considered, especially because he did not know anybody in the business. He still applied to the jobs, hoping for a miracle, but knew he would not get one.

Perry walked around his neighborhood, listening to music to relax. He had his phone in his pocket, felt a vibration, and took it out, wishing that it was a text from Julia.

Instead it was a text from Dom, the owner of the ice cream kiosk. *Hey, do you think you can come in to work tonight? Lenny called out, and you would be doing me a huge favor.*

On his day off, he did not want to work. He never called out. He was very responsible when it came to showing up to work, but he needed the money. *Sure, I can come in at 5.*

Dom thanked him. Now he had to work at five, but he thought, *Maybe Julia is working tonight.* There was still no answer from her, but he was anticipating that he would see her in person.

He arrived to work ten minutes early, relieving the opener, and took his place in the kiosk. He stood there with an angry look in his face and his arms crossed, looking at the horizon in the mall, people walking toward him on one side and past him on the other. "This is going to be a long night."

He looked across to see if Julia was working but felt a tap on his shoulder. He turned around, and it was Julia. "Sorry to not get back to you, but I would like to talk to you about our cup of coffee."

He was extremely pleased to see her. This could make his night, and he was now going to make plans with her. She looked so beautiful in his eyes, the curly black hair that he was in love with. "Okay, what about it? What night can you do?"

"Well, I just wanted to know when you asked me, you meant grab a cup of coffee as friends, right?"

The statement hit him like dropping bricks. It was obvious he wanted more, and he wanted to be in a relationship with her. He stared at her with a look of bewilderment, and he needed to say something to show some dignity. "Well, I was kind of looking to see what would happen." *What the hell does that mean?*

"Okay, because I'm talking to somebody, but we can grab lunch sometime as friends."

Lunch? The classic hang out with only a friend.

He closed his eyes for a second, but it felt like an eternity. He felt like he was in a free fall, not being able to land on his feet, not being able to recover. He had no idea what he was going to say or do next. The only thing he was thinking about was that he cared deeply for Julia, he wanted to be with her. Alternative situations did not cross his mind, but he knew he must wait until the person Julia was talking to nosedived. His body felt like he had just run a marathon, extremely tired with perspiration on every inch. He opened his eyes and the only response he could manage was, "Okay, sounds good."

"Sounds like a plan. Have a good night, Perry. I'll see you later." She walked away from the kiosk into her store.

He said softly, "Please come back…Okay sounds good, okay sounds good, okay sounds fucking good, that's the best I came up with." He turned around and faced the back of the wall so nobody could see him talking to himself. "I couldn't say I really care for you, or we would have been talking for a while, probably longer than you talking to this asshole guy. She would say well that's rude, we were only talking like friends do." He went back and forth in this conversation, playing himself and playing Julia. He was unaware whether customers were coming to the counter. He was in his own world, not caring if people were staring at him or if Julia was staring at him from across the way.

After arguing with himself for ten minutes, he began to cry. Not because Julia had rejected him, but he had no idea what he was going to do next. It had taken him seven months to find the courage to ask Julia out, and it was too late. He did not want to find another girl and wait another seven months. Everything felt like a gigantic waste of time. He wanted to go in the garbage dumpsters outside and make that his new home. He wanted to give up.

Trying to hold back the tears, he took off his glasses and was wiping his eyes when he saw Bruce Thompson walking toward him with three members of the Defense. It was a rare occasion that Bruce talked to Perry, but when he did, members of the Defense were not following him. *Great. He brought his puppies with him.* Perry was not nervous about whether the Defense were going to keep him in order on their terms. He did not care anymore, so when they approached, he did not back away but crept closer to the counter.

"Hello, Mr. Miller. I hear good things about you from Dom. You're like his right-hand man."

"Nice to see you, Mr. Thompson. I've known Dom for a while. I guess he can trust me," Perry said. What exactly did Bruce want with him? If he was in trouble, he would have already been taken away from the kiosk.

"Oh, that Dom is some kind of character. It seems he failed to notice it being the fifteenth, which happens to be my favorite day of the month, so I will never forget when it is the fifteenth because the rent is due. It seems that your absent-minded manager did forget, but lucky for him, this is the first time."

"Well, I can give you Dom's number if you need it. Whatever is the most help to you, Mr. Thompson."

"No need for that. I have Dom's number. What kind of manager do you think I would be if I didn't have a subordinate's number?" Bruce laughed. "I mean, I'm sure Dom has your number, right?"

"Yes, sir, he does."

"And Dom is not a better manager than me, is that right?"

"No, sir, you're the best manager in Brine County." Perry was getting edgy. He hated working at the mall, but he did like Dom. He respected him, because he knew that Dom would help him if he needed anything or an advance on his pay.

"So that means I obviously have his number, but I want you to do something for me. This is going to teach you a lesson, something you can take with you for your future. You understand so far?"

Perry was not sure if this message was for Dom or was really a message for himself. Bruce outsmarted every subordinate and knew exactly how to get a rise out of everybody. He was the top of Brine County for a reason.

"Uh, yes, sir, whatever you need,"

"Don't get nervous, Mr. Miller. You're not in trouble unless you did something you're hiding, because I know what happens inside these walls, and if you did, I would have sent my brother to see you instead. Your manager is the one who is in trouble. He forgot today is the fifteenth, but since this is his first offense, I'll give him a warning through you."

"Why through me, sir? I know for a fact he will give you the rent if you asked him. Something must be going on today that he forgot." Perry was not meaning to be rude to Bruce, just trying to defend Dom.

The look on Bruce's face was aggravation; Perry was the one asking questions and trying to lecture him. "I don't need you to tell me what to do, so I'm going to give you the message and tell you why, because your question took stones to ask, and I respect you a little more now. If I asked Dom myself to give me the rent, he will for sure, but he might forget in the foreseeable future, and I like my money the first thing in the morning on the fifteenth. I made rent day the fifteenth every month because of the ides, but that's neither here nor there. If I give you a message to give to him. He will pay me tonight, and he will never forget to pay me again. It all depends on the message, and this one is a boulder of a message. Tell him his wife, Elizabeth, lovely woman, is in my office, and if he ever wants to see her again, he pays me the rent in the next hour. I do not care how he gets it to me, in person or he wires it to me, but if the money is not in my bank account in the next hour, he will not get his wife back."

Perry did not know what to say. He wanted to call the police, but it was his word or Bruce's, and they would not believe him. "Of course. I'll give him the message, but why me, sir? And what if I can't get in contact with him?"

Bruce had a sinister look on his face. "I'm giving you the burden of this message because I want Elizabeth's death on your conscience if you fail."

Perry could barely get the words out. "Why, sir?"

"You don't know why, Perry? All right, I'll enlighten you. That woman you yelled at a couple days ago is a dear old friend of mine, and this is your first strike. The retribution is delivering the message, but the real punishment is if you don't deliver it. If you see my dear friend again, you will treat her with respect, but I will leave you with this. If you bad mouth my mall again, I will beat the shit out of you myself. Until next time, have a good night." Bruce walked away his Defense following him, his threats delivered as if taking a breath.

Perry stood in the middle of the kiosk with his hands on his head, not knowing what to do. One thought that crossed his mind, other than the wife of his boss could die, was that Bruce threatened him more when it came to his mall being under attack than his friend. "Christ sake, he is fucked up. He would kill a woman because he did not get his rent. A woman's life is worth one month's rent," Perry whispered so nobody could hear him.

Any conversation in the mall came back to Bruce Thompson one way or another, so Perry was extremely careful. Frantic was an understatement of how he felt, and he had only fifty-five minutes to save Elizabeth. He put a "Be back in five minutes" sign in front of the cash register. He needed to do this without distractions from the customers.

He ran to the stockroom, took out his phone, and tried calling Dom. A text would take too long, and time was of the essence. Dom did not answer, so Perry had to leave a voicemail. In the most relaxed voice that he could do, he said, "Hey, Dom, this is Perry, and this is an emergency. Bruce Thompson came up to the kiosk and demanded you pay his rent, or you will not see Elizabeth again. She is in his office, and you have less than an hour. This is not a joke!"

After he hung up, he realized how crazy his voicemail sounded. How could Dom believe him? He had forty-eight minutes left, and he could never live with himself if Elizabeth died because he could not deliver the message. He tried again, his hands shaking, sweat pouring down the sides of his face. He could care less that the sign at the kiosk was going to expire. The second time, Dom did not answer. Perry tried a third time. *Come on, the third time's the charm. Come on, and please answer!*

The third attempt was the same as the first two.

Perry sat in the corner of the stockroom and began to cry. His life was going nowhere, he was miserable working at the mall, Julia only wanted to be friends, and Elizabeth could die if he could not get in contact with Dom. He knew Dom would wire Bruce the money if he received the message, but he could not deliver the message. Perry ran back to the kiosk to call there. He needed to take the sign away, because if Bruce saw the kiosk unattended, he would be in trouble. As he turned the corner, he saw Dom standing at the kiosk.

"Dom, Dom, check your voicemail, I left you a message!"

Dom looked at him with a relaxed face and calmly said, "Everything is taken care of. I just gave Bruce the rent, but what were you talking about with Elizabeth? She has been with me the entire afternoon."

Perry's shirt was drenched, and he wiped tears and sweat from his face. The last ten minutes were torture. "Bruce Thompson said that if you did not pay the rent in an hour you would never see Elizabeth again."

Dom came into the kiosk to talk quietly. "Perry, listen to me. Bruce Thompson is an asshole. He only did that to you because of what you said to the customer yesterday. I told him a couple weeks ago that I might be a little late with the rent, and he didn't have a problem, so he was just trying to fuck with you. Ignore him for now, but you need to do a better job with the customers. I know they're assholes just as much as Bruce, but be patient with them. I would like to thank you on how you handled the situation that you thought was true. Thanks for trying to get in contact with me that urgently."

Perry was pleased with Dom. He had his back with Bruce, and he felt he was loyal to him. "Of course. I would do anything so Elizabeth isn't in trouble like that, especially with him."

"Thank you. You have no idea how he runs this place. I've known Bruce for almost twenty years. He manipulates everybody until we have no choice but to work for him. Just be careful with him. You are already on his list, and it is almost impossible to get off of it." Dom said goodbye and left.

Perry needed to sit down and take deep breaths. Bruce did not like him and wanted to mess with his head. Perry knew it was not because he was rude to the customer but because he talked negatively about the mall. The only question was who told Bruce about Perry's negative comments. He had a lot to think about. He still had an hour left on his shift, but a surprise visit would change his life forever.

"Oh, hello there. Perry. How are you doing tonight?" Freddie was wearing regular clothes. He was not working at the mall tonight, just paying a visit.

"Hey, Freddie. I'm doing all right. You know, same old shit, different day in this place, right?" This was obviously a lie. This night was an unmitigated disaster, but Perry did not want to tell anybody what Bruce did to him, because he did not trust anybody.

"I heard you had a run in with one of my acquaintances, soon to be one of our acquaintances. You know, good old Chris."

"That makes sense. Yeah, I saw him a couple nights ago. He said something about us being mutual partners, but I still have no idea what you guys are talking about." He did not care anymore that Freddie and Chris were not making sense. Emotionally, he was gone.

"Well, Chris and I would like to know if you can get a drink after your shift, and we will tell you all about being partners and everything. I promise."

Perry did not believe a word of this, but he could use a drink and hoped this meeting would bring clarity to the weird situation. "Okay, sure, sounds good. Do you guys just want to meet at Applebee's at ten?" Applebee's was in Brine County Mall. Perry did not feel like driving too far just for a drink and with Freddie and Chris of all people, the latter he did not care for much.

"Yeah, sounds like a plan. See you then, and remember, treat the customers with respect. Bruce Thompson is walking around this place tonight."

"Oh, definitely. Yeah, somebody mentioned that they saw Bruce. See you at ten."

Freddie disappeared into the crowd of people, being a complete enigma in Perry's life.

Perry began his closing routine. He had to make sure the custard machine was filled. The toppings had to be filled: crushed Reese's Peanut Butter Cups, Reese's Pieces, M&Ms, crushed vanilla wafers, crushed cone, Heath Bars, Nerds, peanuts, wet walnuts, gummy bears, Snickers, and chocolate and rainbow sprinkles. He changed the container of cones for good measure. Next came the garbage bags, which he changed and put on a cart. He hoped one of the custodians would pick it up for him as a favor or a free custard. He wiped down the counters and mopped the floors. The routine was embedded in him, and he was tired of the same mundane tasks every shift. He wanted some excitement in his life. This closing routine took about fifteen minutes, and he was the fastest at it. He shut off the lights at the kiosk one minute after closing time and began to count the register. A customer came up, asking for ice cream. "Sorry, closing time is at 9:30, and I locked the cases."

"But it's 9:31."

"Sorry, those are the rules." Perry was sure what the customer was going to say next. He had this type of customer come up way too often. After closing time, they still wanted more.

"Can't you just give me something? Don't you have any extra ice cream?" The customer asked in a sincere but lying voice.

Perry answered in a sincere, lying voice. "No, I am very, very sorry, but I'm working tomorrow, and if you come during store hours, I will give you an item of your choice free of charge." He did not work tomorrow, and if he did, he would not give the customer anything for free, especially since he did not know him.

The customer turned and walked away, probably realizing that Perry was not telling the truth.

He pushed the cart with scoopers of ice cream and the register drawer and went to the back stockroom to lock up and leave. After washing the scoopers and other dishes, he was skeptical of going out for a drink with Freddie and Chris. He did not know them well, and he had extreme doubt about Chris because of the encounter the night before. He trusted Freddie slightly more because they were acquaintances, but he would never consider him a friend. The mystery of the two intrigued him.

As Perry was about to leave, he texted his mother. *Hey, I'm prob going to be late coming home. I'm going out with a couple friends from work.* He was not going to tell his mother about Freddie and Chris, so he gave the least amount of information as possible. His mother replied, *Okay, have fun.* He shut the lights off of the stockroom, locked up the register, and locked the door. He returned the key to one of the mall offices and walked to his car.

He drove to Applebee's, which took thirty seconds, and walked to the front door. Freddie and Chris were waiting for him, which was a surprise. "Hey guys, what's up?"

Freddie said, "Hey, Perry, come on, we have a table in

the back. We were too excited to sit down, so we waited for you in the doorway."

Why were they too excited to wait at a table? Perry followed them toward the back of the restaurant and the last table in front of the kitchen. He had no choice but to stay with them now. As they sat, Perry noticed what looked like blood on one of Chris's shoes. Chris did not say anything and barely looked at Perry, but Perry was keeping his eyes on Chris.

The waitress gave them menus and told them the drink specials. They ordered and had a moment of silence before Freddie said, "Do you know why we asked you to meet us here?"

Perry knew the answer, but he was not sure how to answer, because he did not want to offend them. Even though he did not care for them that much, he was not sure how they would handle sarcasm.

"I'm not sure. A couple nights ago, Chris mentioned that we are partners or something like that, but I have no idea what that means." Perry nervously waited for the response from Freddie, because Chris was not saying anything.

The waitress came back to take their order, but Freddie said, "We aren't getting any food, just the drinks for now." The waitress walked away aggravated, because she knew the tip was not going to be high for just a drink order.

Freddie took the role of leader and presented Perry with a mission statement. "I do not want you to answer my rhetorical questions. I want you to feel what I am talking about, so here it goes. Remember yesterday, after that fat ass asshole dipshit customer walked away from you, the feelings you had afterward? Remember how angry you were when she left, hell, how angry you were when you were talking to her? The feelings you had, the heavy legs, sweat pouring from your forehead, you holding in every ounce of rage you wanted to use, wanted to beat her with, wanted to kill her with? I had those same feelings before, but I can show you how to get rid of them. Think about those feelings, and think about how she treated you like a little piece of shit with no rights. Hell, you couldn't even talk to her. Anything you said to her she ignored or downplayed anything and exaggerated everything she believed. It was like you didn't exist in that conversation. It was like she was having an argument with herself. In that conversation, she had all the power. Hell, she was God in that conversation, and you were like one of the unlucky souls God gets to humiliate, but what if I was to tell you that when talking to customers, I have a way in which you have all the power, a conversation that only you exist in? Hell, a conversation that makes you God?"

Perry remembered every feeling Freddie was talking about. He remembered how angry he felt, how demeaned he was after talking to the customer. He took a big drink of his beer. He needed some alcohol in him when he was talking to Freddie, especially since he had no idea where this conversation was going.

The waitress was coming back to see if they needed anything, but Freddie brushed her off and continued preaching. "Yesterday, I told you it doesn't matter if you are stressed out about the customers, but what matters is how you relieve that stress. I don't want to tell you any more, but when you leave here after we have our drinks, I want to bring you to the place where you relieve the stress from the customers, the place where all that bullshit goes away, and the place where you are God. Chris goes there too. He has the same feelings you do, the same feelings I do, but after we go to this place, all those feelings go away until we talk to the next asshole customer. So enjoy your drink, but if you follow us there, will you become our new partner?"

Perry was shocked. He figured Freddie made the same speech to Chris however long ago. He observed that when Freddie was making that speech, Chris was almost like a follower, nodding his head in agreement, especially at the mention of God. He had to make a decision. Was he to follow Freddie and Chris down the rabbit hole, and was he to be their new partner? He finished his beer, wiping his lips, noticing he was getting warmer. Looking across the booth into their eyes, he did not trust these two, but he decided what he would do. He took a deep breath and said, "So how far away is this place?"

5

THE SHED

THE THREE PARTNERS PAID THEIR PORTIONS OF THE check, looked at the waitress again, and headed out. Perry walked to his car and contemplated if he was going to go to the so-called place where all their feelings went away until he talked to the next asshole customer. *Well, I went and had a drink with them. Maybe I should go to the place, and if I don't like what I see, I'll leave.* He started his van.

Freddie rolled down his car window, Chris in the passenger seat, and yelled, "Just keep behind us the entire time. If you think anybody is following you, do not follow us. The place is at my house, and it's only like four miles away." Freddie rolled up his window and drove away, giving Perry no time to think but only to follow. He put the van in reverse, pulled out of the spot, put the van in drive, and was on his way to Freddie's house. He checked the rearview mirror to see if anyone left the Brine County Mall to follow him, but the coast was clear.

The drive to Freddie's house did not worry Perry, but he was trying to answer two questions. *Why am I following these two psychopaths? Maybe that makes me the biggest psychopath, because these two can't be trusted, and why can't anybody follow me to Freddie's house?* He could not find the answers to the questions but was still not worried. He drove three miles with only one left and still nobody following him. Freddie was not driving fast. He did not want to bring attention, but there were not many police officers in the proximity of the Brine County Mall. Bruce Thompson only wanted the Defense in the proximity. "More police, less power," he often said. Freddie put his left blinker on and began to brake. Perry tightened his grip on the steering wheel.

"Okay, this is it. Hopefully some questions will be answered tonight, and hopefully this is the last time I will hang out with them." Hanging out with Freddie and Chris bothered Perry, because he knew George would not want to hang out with them. George had a good sense of judgment, much better than Perry. Sometimes Perry considered his moral character to be less than George's, so hanging out with other people with less moral character appeased him. He had other friends but none like George. George always stood by him, even if he was in the wrong. George would have his back, and he was like a cushion for him. He would always have George's back too, but George never did anything like this. He knew Freddie and Chris would never have his back, and he was sure he would not have theirs either.

He followed Freddie into the driveway and parked his car. He looked down at his phone and noticed there were no texts. He was not expecting any, but a nice surprise would have been pleasant. He sent out two texts: one to George and one to Julia. Both were the same: *Hey, do you have any plans tomorrow?*" He figured at least one of them would answer, and he presumed it would be George.

Perry looked at Freddie's house. It was a small ranch, nice and cozy, but he didn't know how Freddie could afford a house for himself. He saw another car parked parallel to the curb and guessed it belonged to Chris. He stepped out of his van and saw that Freddie and Chris were waiting for him in front of the garage door. He walked up and hoped that they would do the talking. At least Freddie, because Chris did not say anything all night.

Freddie welcomed Perry. "Hey, partner, I can't believe you followed us here. You must really want the answer to how we lose those bad feelings. Did anybody follow you here?"

Perry nervously said, "Not that I could see." He wanted to ask *why are you so secretive about your house?* He realized that he would not get an answer. He had a feeling this entire night was a sham, and they were going to drink more or maybe smoke a little. Maybe marijuana got rid of the feelings.

Freddie said, "Good. Well, just follow us. We are going to go through my garage and walk past my backyard, but I must tell you, because I know what you're thinking. How can I afford this house all by myself? Well, the answer is this house used to be my parents, but they died a couple years ago. My mom died of cancer, and my father killed himself when she died. Guess he didn't want to live with the problem child, so the place is all mine. My mother put me in the will. I don't think my asshole father would have. Now I'm going off course, so without further ado, follow us."

Perry followed them through the garage, which was very clean with almost nothing in it, and through a door that opened to the backyard. The backyard was fenced in, and thirty feet beyond the fence in the back were woods. Freddie opened the back gate that led into the woods and followed the trail. He looked around to see if any neighbors were looking through their windows, but there was nobody there, just the three of them. Perry took his phone out of his pocket and looked at his messages. There was one from George.

     John P. Burdi

Freddie turned around. "Oh yeah. Before we find the place, shut your phone off. We don't want any ass dialing in there or anything."

Perry shut his phone off but was concerned. No phone? What were these two planning on doing with him?

The walk felt like an eternity. Perry had zero idea where he was or this place where they were taking him. Freddie stopped and turned around, and Perry noticed this little shed. They were in the middle of nowhere, in the middle of the woods, which was in proximity of the Defense and the place they took him. The place where they would lose the feelings of hate was this little shed.

Chris said, "Now, when we open that door, you can't say fucking anything to fucking anybody, understand? What goes on in here is just between the three of us now. You are in too deep, and there is no turning back. You may participate, whatever you feel like doing, but you are one of us, and if you do not want that, then our night just got a whole lot longer."

Perry stood there stunned. The first words to come out of Chris the entire night were threatening to his life, and he had no choice now other than the option not to participate, whatever that meant. "Sure, let's open the door, but who owns this shed?"

Freddie said, "My parents, and now it's mine. I have a lot of property. I put up the fence to avoid suspicion that I own this little shack of heaven." The shed was no bigger than a small room in a house—it was large for a shed but small for a place to hang out. Freddie took a few more steps, and turned the doorknob. There was a creak when the door opened, but it was surprisingly noiseless in these woods. Nothing could be heard, and nothing could be seen.

Freddie and Chris walked in. Freddie said, "Can you do me a favor and shut that door after you come in? Thanks."

Perry had no choice. He shut the door before he could look around the shed. After he closed the door and locked it for good measure, he looked around and almost pissed his pants. There was a person tied to a chair with a bag over his head. He was unsure if the person was alive. He wanted to scream, but that would bring attention to a place where he did not want to be anymore. He was now involved in this crime if it was kidnapping or hiding a murder victim. He wanted to wake up and find that this was all a dream, but the reality was far worse.

Trying to put together a sentence, he said, "I, I…is that person a-a-alive?"

Freddie laughed, which made everything more uncomfortable for Perry. Chris stood there with his arms crossed and a hint of a grin.

Freddie said, "Yes, he's alive. This little piece of shit caused me a lot of trouble at the mall. He put in many complaints about me that I was not cleaning the bathrooms fast enough. He put complaints in to Mr. Bruce Thompson, that other piece of shit, so this is what I and Chris do to get rid of these feelings of hate. We kidnap any customer who wrongs us at the mall and bring them to our level. We let our aggravation and frustration out at them inside these four walls. Nobody can hear the screams. Nobody leaves this shed to tell what we do."

Perry wanted to throw up. He wanted everything about this night to end. He wanted to go home and not leave his room for a week. After all of those feelings about how much he hated this night came to fruition, a surprising thought came to his head. *Maybe they're right.* The thought terrified him. Maybe this was the best way to work at this mall. "Who is he?"

"His name is Calvin. I don't know much more about him. He complained to Bruce a couple times about me, different occurrences, and each time I was embarrassed and threatened by Bruce, so now I'm doing the threatening. This asshole couldn't wait two fucking minutes for me to clean the bathroom, so he had to continue to shop. That's all they do, shop, shop, shop. They could care less about us, and they don't care what our shifts are, what the holiday hours are. Sometimes we have to work on holidays to appease these animals. Every fucking Thanksgiving when my mother was alive, I had to cut the dinner short. Every year, I would have to leave my home at four o'clock and get ready to work at the mall. They complain about us because they think they have the right to. Well, they have no rights in this shed. Hell, let me ask you a question, Perry. Do you like any customers you get at that kiosk? I have another one. Do they make your life any easier?"

Perry needed some time to take this all in. If there was anybody who would agree with Freddie about customers, it would be him, but was this going too far? Was Freddie right in this moment? To question George on this was out the window. He would have called the police the moment he saw what was in the shed. Perry said, "No, I don't like any customers, and they make my life harder."

Freddie said, "That's why I recruited you. I've watched you over the years, especially lately, and without a doubt, when you had the fat ass bitch the other day, I knew exactly how you were feeling. I have been there. Hell, a couple years ago, I did something about it, and last year Chris decided to do something about it. We are all from the same mold, and now you need to do something about it.

We kidnap them with chloroform. It knocks them out, and we drag them into my van, bring them here, and give them their punishment. We never kidnap them at the mall—we follow them home and do it there. We might have a lucky contestant every month or every couple weeks if we are super pissed. Nobody suspects a thing, not out here."

Chris took a turn. "After we are done, we bring them out in the woods and throw them in the hole. We dig it before we kidnap to save time. We know exactly what we are doing. We already have a spot for this guy."

Perry's adrenaline was pumping to new extremes. They were talking about kidnapping and murder, and the worst part was, he wasn't scared, he was sincerely interested. He knew those feelings the other day were not normal, but this went to a new extreme. The best part was they had this all figured out. No crime was taking place at Brine County Mall, so the Thompson brothers would not suspect anything. Nobody knew this place existed, and nobody could hear anything. They had a place to get rid of the bodies, but nobody suspected anything, so these woods would not be checked for bodies.

Perry was genuinely excited; his life was going nowhere with zero direction and ambition. A couple minutes ago, Perry wanted to throw up from what he saw, but now he agreed with it because of the speeches from two people who were not his friends and who he did not trust. What if this was all a setup and they called the police on him? "What if the point of this night is to get me in trouble?"

Freddie said, "Why would we get you in trouble? You never did anything wrong to us, and you never gave us a hard time at work. Remember, you don't have to participate if you don't want to. Just watch and try and have some fun."

     John P. Burdi

Calvin was in his mid-forties, married without children, and for the most part, not many employees complained about him, but he had the unfortunate luck to run into Freddie. Freddie had revealed that he complained to Bruce Thompson about not cleaning up the bathroom fast enough, but for a few complaints, he was going to lose his life. Perry wanted to question that. He wanted to hear Freddie out, and he wanted him to get a chance to explain the situation, so he said nervously, "Because he gave a few complaints, you guys are going to kill him?"

"You are correct, Perry." Freddie walked over to Calvin and was about to take the bag off his head but was interrupted.

"But why?"

Irritated, Freddie said, "Okay, Perry, we only have time for one more talk, and after that, if you still have questions or doubt, you will be joining our friend Calvin. What Chris and I have been doing, and hopefully you will be joining us in, is that we create a salvation for the assholes in that mall. You see, Perry, in the walls of this shed, there are no laws that we follow, and without laws, people are not people. We do unholy acts. Now tell me, is this any different than the Defense or Michael Thompson or Bruce Thompson? Instead of having a mall with no laws, we have a shed with no laws, so in here, we are Bruce and Michael Thompson. We are no different, and the people we bring here are like us out there. If they slip up, if they do anything that makes our life worse, we end it. Right, Perry? I mean, this must stop somewhere, and in here, we are right, the customer is always wrong, and very often the Defense is wrong. We put our feet down in here. We stick up for ourselves, because we cannot in the mall. We can never defend ourselves there. We are the victims, so we reverse the course, and we are very good at it. We torture in here, because they torture out there, but we do one better. We kill them and lead them to salvation, away from being tortured. Hell, they torture themselves out in the real world, but they don't know it. Instead of spending money and making our lives a living hell, they should correct their wrongs, but they don't. Well, in here, we correct the wrongs, but let's get one thing straight. We do not under any circumstance kill people we do not run into the mall. We correct people's wrongs in the mall, but we are not animals. Perry, let us do what we do best, and join in if you like. First, we tell them why they're here, so without further ado."

Freddie walked over to the Calvin took off the bag. He looked out of it, not entirely there. Freddie lightly slapped him to wake up and said the most disturbing statement, "Rise and shine. Time to meet God."

Calvin had incisions and bruises all over his face. One eye was completely closed, and it was clear that Freddie and Chris beat him before they went to Applebee's with Perry, giving the answer to why Chris had blood on one of his shoes. Calvin had no idea where he was, and he looked like he was not going to be living for much longer without more torture. Perry looked into his eyes, sensing that he wanted to die. Perry had no idea how long they had kept him—it could have been a couple of hours or days—but it was clear they were making their mark on him.

Calvin tried to speak. "Are you going to just kill me?" It looked like it took all his energy to produce that one statement.

Freddie pulled up a chair and placed it in front of Calvin. The shed had a couple chairs in it: some chains, knives, pipes, a baseball bat, and not much else. Freddie and Chris were not that creative with the murders. They wanted to get the job done. Freddie laughed. "No, not right now, silly. We want you to meet one more person. Perry, you're up."

"I thought you said I didn't have to join, I could just watch." Perry was not scared anymore, especially after witnessing what Michael Thompson did to a couple employees. He wanted to see what was going to happen to Calvin, but he was unsure if he was going to physically participate.

"Well, we lied. Especially after asking me a second time. This is your punishment. I'm God here, and I make the rules, so I want you to start beating Calvin."

"He didn't do anything to me. I would rather begin with customers who had arguments with me." Perry was unsure if he was lying. Did he really want to start torturing people? He was exceptionally disordered. He was using his feelings to make decisions rather than rationality and logic.

"No, Perry, he did nothing to you, but he represents people who did harm to you. He represents the mall, he represents every customer, the Defense, the Thompsons. Remember how angry you were a couple days ago? Get those feelings back. I'll do one better. I know about Julia."

"How the fuck do you know about Julia?" Perry wondered if Freddie was the guy she was talking to.

"I am a custodian at Brine County Mall. I am one step away from being a pledge of the Defense, and I bet you didn't know that."

"What are you talking about?"

"Some pledges are not part of the Defense, and some do not wear the uniform. It's Bruce Thompson's way of controlling everything. If you are a part of the Defense and do what they say, your life is peachy, but who wants to join those assholes anyway? We are the Defense here, and by the way, you like black girls, huh?"

"That doesn't matter. Tell me what you know about Julia. Now, Freddie, no more speeches."

"Wow, you really do like her, and look at you, becoming one of us with your persistency. Well, I know she's talking to some employee at one of the department stores making his way up."

"Are you serious?"

"Yes, I am, but what I want you to do is pretend Calvin is that guy. Pretend he is every person you hate at that mall and take out your frustration, relieve the stress." Freddie turned to Calvin. "Oh, and you, your complaint to Mr. Bruce Thompson got me a warning by him, and you know what happens after a warning? You get a beating from his brother, so it looks like I beat you to the punch. I'm doing the fucking beating around here, you little piece of shit." Freddie was screaming at Calvin. "That's your last time complaining to anybody!"

Perry walked toward Calvin, moved the chair away, and looked around. Calvin was tied up, and there were blocks behind his chair to keep it upright. He looked at his hands and looked at Calvin. Not thinking, he closed his hand and punched Calvin beneath the nose. That was the first time Perry had punched another person. Calvin made no movements, and more blood was added to the sea of blood present. He looked back at his hand, and it was covered with blood, but his feeling of stress was lowering. The punch felt good. For the first time in his life, he was in control, so he punched again. He was thinking about his neighbors, not getting a better job, Bruce and Michael Thompson, the guy Julia was talking to, and that customer.

     John P. Burdi

Freddie and Chris looked in amazement at Perry. Chris broke the silence, ignoring the screams from Calvin. "You look like a professional, Perry. How does it feel?"

Perry was punching and hitting when he finally heard the question from Chris. To Perry, this ordeal felt like an eternity of happiness, but it was only thirty seconds. "I feel amazing, better than I have felt in a while." He realized that he felt amazing from beating a person he had never met before. He comprehended that he was not different than Michael Thompson. He was attacking Calvin's body when Freddie dragged him off, both of them almost falling down in the process. Freddie looked at Perry and said, "Good, but now I want you to finish him and send him to salvation. We have to put him in the hole and start covering him with dirt. We never do this when there is sunlight. We don't want this night to be too long."

"Okay, how am I supposed to finish this?" Perry was gone, abandoning all reason and human affection. He was a minute away from murdering some person who did not say a word to him. He was not thinking about anything except how to kill Calvin, not thinking about his family, Julia, or George.

"Pick one of the knives, and good luck."

Perry looked over at the knives. He wanted to pick the dullest one. He did not care about consequences anymore, and his feelings were in control of the situation. He took a knife and looked Calvin in the eye. He saw a man who was no more, a man who just wanted this night to end, to be put out of his misery. He pointed the tip of the knife toward Calvin's chest and stabbed. It went through with one quick, powerful motion, and he pulled it out with a quick, powerful motion. More blood, more pain at the hands of Perry, who was trying to ignore the screams from

Calvin. Perry stabbed again, this time a little lower in his stomach. Now the only thing he heard were cheers and ovations from two psychopaths.

Perry took the knife out and stabbed for a third time in the heart. Calvin's eyes closed before the blade even punctured him. Calvin was dead.

Freddie said, "Way to go kid. Now you are one of us. You lost your virginity."

He was out of breath, blood soaked, and happier than ever, without a care in the world. He said, "Holy shit, that was awesome, but now what do we do?"

Freddie and Chris were looking at Perry as if he was a sculpture of theirs. They were admiring him as if he was a creation. They never would have figured that Perry was the one to kill Calvin and with such brutality and with no remorse. Chris stepped forward and reached out his hand for Perry to shake. "Even I didn't finish the task on my first night. Jesus, what else can you do?"

Perry was stumped from the question, immediately thinking of Samantha, his neighbors, the customers, the Thompsons, or anybody who wronged him or made him feel inferior. Still catching his breath while wiping blood and sweat, he said, "I'm not sure what I'm capable of, but I want to get rid of this body. What time is it? I can't stay out all night."

Freddie said, "Well, it is 12:08, and if it takes all night, then it takes all night, but if you can't stay out all night, Chris and I can get this one, but you have to get the next, understand?"

"Yeah, sure, but I want to see where you take him so I know for next time. You already dug the hole?"

"Of course we did. This ain't our first rodeo. I forgot to mention that after we dispose of the body, we usually go to a twenty-four-hour diner. It's kind of our tradition, and we have a recap of the night, sharing our favorite memories. So come with us, and we will show you where we dump the waste. Meet us at Mobile Diner at eight tomorrow morning. We can grab breakfast."

Not thinking of the sinister sickness of killing a person and discussing his favorite memory of it afterward during a meal, Perry agreed with no hesitation. He was in control for the first time. He followed Freddie and Chris to the field of trees beyond the shed. The three murderers were walking in a straight line, Freddie pushing Calvin on a hand truck and wrapped in tarp. Calvin was his prey, so he had the distinction of pushing him to his salvation, as Freddie believed. Chris was behind Perry, carrying a shovel, and Perry was carrying a shovel.

Freddie began singing, "Hi ho, hi ho, it's off to salvation this asshole goes." The two others laughed and repeated the psychotic verse and whistled the tune. After the singalong, they reached the destination.

Freddie started another speech, which Perry was getting tired of, though they were effective. "So when we put the body in the hole, we drop it in. We might bring him to his salvation, but hell, we aren't fucking priests." The joke got a chuckle, and Perry saw there was no evidence of other holes. They did an excellent job of hiding the evidence.

Perry was nervous because he had one more question, and if he asked it, he might be joining Calvin, but he could not figure it out by himself. Freddie and Chris helped him relieve stress in the most monstrous way, but he still did not trust them. Quietly and almost sincerely, he said, "Freddie, I have one more question."

Freddie looked at him almost in admiration. "You know what, I will answer it, because you took a big step tonight, and I'm kind of proud of you like in a teacher and student kind of way. What's your question?"

"I'm confused by what you mean by sending them to salvation."

"I thought you might. When they live their lives, we believe they are suffering and living in a type of hell. They care about nothing except buying useless shit, but we are different. We could care less about shopping, and when they complain to the Thompsons about employees, they know that the employees will get a warning or a beating, so in a way, they are responsible for that. They don't like getting their hands dirty, but we do. Besides, the only people who deserve complaints are the Defense, but the customers have their backs, and the Defense has their backs, so the people getting fucked are the employees. Not in here, and definitely not us."

Perry understood what they were doing and agreed with it. "Thank you for showing me the way."

Freddie said, "You're welcome."

Chris stood there feeling left out. On his first night, he did not commit murder, and he did not ask as many questions. He felt like Perry was becoming the second in command and tried getting him to leave so he could be the second in command. "Okay, man, if you have to go, we can take it from here. We'll see you tomorrow at Mobile."

Perry realized he should be getting home. He looked at his partners. "Until tomorrow morning. Have fun tonight."

Freddie said, "Not as much fun as you had tonight. See you, kid."

Perry walked back to the shed, looked in and saw all the blood but felt not one ounce of remorse. He felt nothing. He closed the door, walked back to Freddie's house and through the garage, and got into his van. He looked at his face in the mirror. There was some blood on his forehead, but it was not his. He had a water bottle in his car, so he stepped out and poured the bottle on his head, cleaning the blood. He got back into his van, looked at himself in the mirror, and said, "Good as new."

He drove home and went to bed without a care in the world. He set his alarm for 7:30 and went to sleep faster than ever and without any stress.

PERRY WOKE TO THE "BLUE DANUBE WALTZ" FROM HIS alarm, and images from the night before came to mind. He woke with the most pleasant of reminiscences. He woke up with a proposal for Freddie and Chris, an idea that he believed could be a true transformation. He got dressed, ran downstairs, grabbed his keys, and said, "Bye, Mom. I'm meeting friends for breakfast." He was out the door before his mother could answer.

Mobile Diner, a good twenty minutes away, was on the outskirts of town. It was a classic diner, recollecting to the golden past, a diner used by truck drivers because of their twenty-four-hour schedule.

Perry opened the doors and heard, "Hey, Perry, over here, buddy."

The voice was Freddie's. He and Chris were at a booth, both spotless. They obviously took a shower before coming. No worker or customer at the diner could tell that the three of them had murdered the night before.

"Hey, guys, how was everything?" Perry was nervous asking this question. He was unsure if they talked in a secret code or did not talk about anything and just ate because they were up all night.

Chris said, "Excellent. The cleanup was excellent. We do not talk in code or anything. We don't use names for obvious reasons, no weapons either, but don't be scared. Nobody notices anything when it's right in front of them."

Freddie said, "Sit down at least. Aren't you going to join us?"

Perry sat down and noticed a third cup of coffee on the table. "We took the liberty of ordering you a coffee. I assume you drink coffee for breakfast?"

"Thank you. Yeah, I love coffee. I like it with milk."

"Oh, that's no problem." Freddie raised his hand, and the waitress ran over. "My friend would like milk with his coffee." The waitress smiled and turned around to get the milk. "We are regulars here. The staff love us, and so we'll be taken care of here. We treat workers with respect, and in return, they give us respect. It's a shame nobody else does that. Anyway, how are you feeling the morning after?"

Perry was not expecting that question. He figured these two would talk about last night without asking how he felt the following day. He was confused about whether they were his friends. "I feel fine. I went to bed with no stress, not a care in the world, and woke up very relaxed."

"That's awesome, good to hear. Here, take a menu. I already ordered steak and eggs, and Chris ordered French toast."

Perry looked through the menu. The waitress came back, "Know what you want, sweetie?"

"I will have the corned beef hash with eggs over easy, and no toast, please."

"The corned beef hash is homemade. It's our breakfast specialty. Everything will be out together. Shouldn't take long."

Freddie answered for everybody. "We are in no rush, cutie." He looked at Perry, "I really want to get in that one's pants. She's kind of like my version of your Julia except this one is white."

Perry took offense but said nothing. He did not want to get on Freddie's bad side. "So when is the next project?"

"Oh, probably a couple weeks. We don't do too much at once. I mean, we aren't serial killers, Perry. We are difference makers."

Chris said, "We have nobody on the radar yet unless you have someone in mind."

Perry did, but he was not sure if they did outside jobs or only people they met at Brine County Mall, so he brought up the customer, which set his feelings in motion. Freddie saw the interaction, so he knew the customer and what she looked like. "I know that fat ass. She doesn't come to the mall too often, but when she does, a lot of people know. Next time you see her, text one of us, and we will follow her home."

All their meals came at the same time, and the boys dug in. They were eating for a couple minutes, and Perry made a proposal. "You guys should give yourself a name so we can get more partners and really make a difference, like counter against the Defense."

Freddie and Chris put down their silverware and looked at him. Freddie said, "What do you mean? Like start an underground movement?"

"Yeah. I mean, I can't be the only other person working at the mall with feelings for the Defense like this. We can continue with customers and work our way up to the Defense, and I don't mean an underground movement but an underground revolution."

Chris said, "Who fucking made this guy boss?"

Freddie interjected. "Shut up. He might have a point. We can bring the Defense down with enough people, but we must select the other partners carefully. We can make our own Defense, and to truly kill then, we must kill the Thompsons."

Perry said, "Exactly. We can start something here that will end the tyranny of the Defense and the Thompsons. We three can be the holy trinity of the revolution. We are bringing people to their salvation after all."

Chris loved the idea, especially because he was a big part of it now. "What should we name ourselves? How about the Fury Fighters or Unholy Trinity?"

Freddie said, "No, Fury Fighters is too over the top, and Trinity can't be in the name, because there has to be more than us three. You have a name, don't you Perry?"

The waitress came back. "How is everything? Anybody need a refill?"

They answered in unison, "I'll have another coffee, please."

"Yes, I have the name. It sounds lame, but I'll explain the meaning. Ready? How about the Myrmidons?"

Freddie said, "What the fuck is the Myrmidons?"

"You guys ever read the *Iliad* or hear of the character, Achilles?"

Freddie and Chris nodded.

"Well, the Myrmidons is what Achilles' personal army was called. They were the toughest and best warriors. Achilles called them lions."

Chris said, "So I assume you want to be the Achilles of this revolution?"

"No, that's Freddie. You are second, and I'm third." Perry considered himself higher than Chris but smartly knew that he should tell Chris he was second in command.

The waitress came back, refilled their coffee, and went back to get them the check.

     John P. Burdi

"I love the name. Achilles was such a badass," said Freddie.

"Yeah, and when we do the kidnappings, we should wear lion masks. That will be our calling card."

Freddie said, "I don't know about the masks, but I love everything else. How did you think of this?"

"Honestly, I woke up with it. We will make a difference here. The Thompsons are going to lose their power, I promise that." The waitress dropped the check off, Perry grabbed it, put in more than enough for himself, and said, "Until next time."

He left the diner and got into his car. Not one person in Mobile Diner heard anything they were saying. Nobody was paying attention.

6.

VIRGINIA

After returning home from Mobile Diner, Perry did nothing for the rest of the day except think what would happen with his revolution. He did not keep in contact with anyone in his family or even George. He was scheming to finally bring justice to anybody who had victimized him.

The first people to come to mind were Samantha, Bruce and Michael Thompson, and his neighbors. Freddie and Chris were aware of the customer. Perry knew he needed to find her name, but he did not mind referring to her as "the customer." Freddie and Chris were going to be the ones to follow her, because Perry had never kidnapped a person. The Thompsons were an obvious choice to plan for, but they were the end game in the revolution. Freddie and Chris did not know about the neighbors. Perry would have to enlighten them the next time the Myrmidons were together.

For the rest of the day, Perry was trying to figure out who Julia was talking to. Freddie told him that he worked at one of the department stores at the mall but could have been lying to make Perry angrier. He wanted to send a message to Julia and ask, but he knew that was not going to happen. Why would she tell him? Another option was that she was not talking to anybody, and she was lying to

Perry to not hurt his feelings, but the lie would upset him even more. He knew he would have to ask Freddie about the guy, but that might lead to more smoke in mirrors. He wanted to text Julia and try to pry the truth out of her without being obvious.

Hey, how are you doing on this beautiful day? He figured that if they were going to have an actual conversation, maybe she would bring the guy up.

While waiting for her to respond, which he knew would not be a strong possibility, he applied to more jobs. He was searching, but none were standing out. All the best jobs available were entry-level positions with experience needed, and he had no experience except in retail.

He decided to answer Virginia. He wanted to persuade her that age had nothing to do with them meeting for a drink. He messaged her, *I'm not too young to buy you a drink, which is what I really want to do. You are more attractive than girls my age anyway. You think I'm handsome, so what's the big deal of getting a drink?*

He logged out and waited ten minutes to see if she answered him. To his amazement, she did. *Yes, you are very handsome, but you are my son's age, and that is too weird for me. Good luck with dating.*

She had made up her mind, but he wanted to show her how persistent he was. *She's attracted to me, and that's half the battle.* He responded, *You think I'm attractive, and I'm so attracted to you. This isn't rocket science. Let me buy you a drink.*

Virginia countered, *Kid, take the hint. I'm not interested. Maybe if you lost 100 pounds then I would talk to you.*

He saw the message on his screen and started to shake. He knew he was overweight, but a hundred pounds? He was insulted. "Fuck you, you old cunt!!!"

Perry knew that his profile would be deleted. All Virginia had to do was report him for profanity, and his profile would be gone, so he blocked her. He supposed if they saw that he blocked her before she reported him, they might not take it seriously. He did not care. He used the online profile for hookups, not relationships, and he was only successful once.

He was starting to have the same feelings as those with the customer. He was getting stressed out and knew he needed to relieve some of that stress. He knew that the Myrmidons' next victim was going to be Virginia.

He started to think of ways for this to be done. He had no idea where she lived and no idea if Freddie or Chris had ever seen her. The mall was not the cause of the problem in this instance. He wanted to talk to her more online, but she would never message him again. *What if I got an older picture and made up a new profile? She would have no problem if my age was the same as hers. The picture would have to be of a skinny guy, and she seemed desperate.*

He wanted to talk to Virginia as a forty-two-year-old. He would have to create another email to use on the site and another profile. He needed a picture of an older man who was slender and realized he could use his father. Even though his father was pushing fifty-five, he was slender, and Perry could improve the picture by using his phone. When his father came home from work that day, Perry would have to take a picture of him that he would use to kill a person.

He knew he was going to have to talk to Virginia more but in disguise, so he created another profile. Thomas Hill was his new alias. His new job was a college professor, aged forty-two, with no children, divorced. He felt he could lie his way about being a professor and being divorced, but he also felt that if she saw that age on his profile, she would not question anything. He did not want to start talking to her without a profile picture. She would not believe that profile was real.

He knew he was eventually going to tell Freddie and Chris about Virginia. He did not know if they wanted to bring a person to salvation who they had not meet at the mall. In fact, it was clear that Freddie did not want to do that, so some persuasion would be necessary to make this happen. Work was in a couple hours, and he was not sure if they were working tonight. He was hoping he would catch his father to take a picture before he left for work. Talking to Virginia was going to be his new assignment at work.

His mother called from downstairs. "Perry, Dad is going to be home early today. Do you want him to pick up a pie?"

Perry said, "Yeah, of course. That's great news." Getting a picture of his father was going to be awkward considering that Perry did not take many pictures with his phone, especially of his family. While waiting for his father, he searched the online dating site for Virginia. He found a few of attractive older women and sent them messages, but without a picture, there was a finite chance they would answer. He came across Virginia's profile. The woman who had embarrassed and insulted him must be eliminated in the mind of Perry.

His father opened the door, shouted, "Pizza," and dinner was ready.

Perry ran downstairs, took his phone out, and took a picture of his father's face.

Surprised, his father said, "Perry, what the hell are you doing?"

"I want to make a family album, so I'm starting now and taking pictures of insignificant events to make it seem spontaneous."

"Oh, okay. A little heads up next time."

"Then it wouldn't be spontaneous." Perry was already upstairs when he responded to his father. Perry was not making any kind of family album, but this kind of lie was one his parents would accept, because he did not lie to his family, and this seemed like the truth. The family huddled around the table taking pizza, sausage, and meatballs. There were some garlic knots and rice balls, but Perry was not eating yet. He was uploading the picture to his new online dating profile. Thomas Hill was complete, and he sent Virginia the same message he sent as Perry Miller. *Hi. I think you are so incredibly beautiful. What's your idea of a perfect day?*" He figured she would not recognize the message, because it was sent by a man instead of a boy. It worked. Virginia was messaging him back and forth without making the connection that she had talked to him before.

He went downstairs, ate three pieces of pizza, four garlic knots, and two rice balls, and went back upstairs, barely saying a word to anybody when he was at the table.

He and Virginia messaged back and forth for almost an hour as he was by himself in his bedroom. They were developing a connection—a woman and a boy who could be her son. He started to get ready for work, hoping they would talk for his entire shift. His plan was already working better than he had imagined. Next he had to let Freddie and Chris know to have the plan come to fruition.

Perry saw a message on his phone from George. *Hey, you working tonight?*

Perry answered, *Yes. Come and visit*. Although it was Saturday and the mall was going to be busy, he was going to work with another person, Tara. If George was to visit him, he could enjoy his fifteen-minute break. He messaged Virginia, *Okay, my nieces and nephews are coming over for dinner. I'll message you later, sweetie.*

He got a return message: *Can't wait. Talk to you later.*

He smiled as he logged off, because he knew he had his hooks in Virginia. He had to bring home the plan later at work. He arrived at work a little early and noticed Bruce Thompson talking to Steve, the older member of the Defense, the only one Perry liked. It looked like they were having an argument. He walked past the food court, got to the kiosk, barely said hello to Tara, and took out his phone. He messaged Virginia, *Would you like to grab a drink sometime?* He waited for the answer, but the response was taking longer than the other messages he had sent her.

He noticed that Tara was upset. There were no customers in sight, so he said, "Hey, are you all right?" He was hoping this was not high school drama. She was only seventeen and going to be a senior in high school. She was very sweet, but he did not know much about her. They barely talked and had worked together only a handful of times. She was acquaintances with Laura and Leah.

"My boyfriend, well, my ex-boyfriend now, cheated on me." Tara was holding back the tears. She clearly did not want to cry in front of Perry. There was an eight-year age difference, and conversations about their personal lives were awkward.

He did not want to answer. He wished that he had not asked her anything. "Well, I'm sorry to hear that. How did you find out?"

"My best friend told me. She was at a party and saw him with another girl. She took a picture and sent it to me. Now we are done, and I am a loser."

"You are not a loser. Your boyfriend is crazy to cheat on you." He was telling the truth. Even though she was younger, he was very attracted to her.

"You really think so?"

"Yeah, are you kidding me? You are so pretty, guys must be hitting on you all the time." After he said that, he realized that he was one of them, but he did not regret it. He did not care that she was younger. The law did not matter in his eyes anymore.

"Aw, that's so sweet. You're very cute and extremely smart."

He was getting worried. What was happening between the two of them? He did not mind telling her she was pretty, but this was crossing the line. They were attracted to each other, and both kind of desperate, a dangerous combination.

"Hey, if you ever want to talk about anything like this, just text me. You have my number, right?"

"Of course I do. Thanks, Perry." Tara leaned over and kissed him on the cheek, there at the kiosk in the middle of the Brine County Mall. Just two minutes ago, they had barely said a word, and now she had kissed him on the cheek. He wanted to return the favor and do a lot more, but he was nervous about anybody seeing him with an underage girl. The only person he wanted to see was Julia to make her envious.

Perry said, "Hopefully it doesn't get too busy tonight."

He checked his online dating profile on his phone and saw that Virginia had messaged him. *Yeah, sure :) Can you go on Monday night?* He laughed and did a fist pump. Tara was busy with a customer and did not notice.

He replied, *Excellent. How's the Applebee's at the Brine County Mall, 10:00?*

That sounds like a date.

Now his plan was closer to completion. He just had to tell the rest of the Myrmidons. *What a day. A plan is getting closer to accomplishment. Tara is interested in me. I think she just wants to get her ex jealous, but who cares, I'll take what I can get. When it rains, it pours.*

Customers were not that dire that day. There were a lot of them, but for the most part, none were rude. Tara and Perry were looking at each other and smiling every chance they had. This was an enjoyable work shift. George was making his way down to the kiosk and gave a big wave. He went up to the counter and ordered a vanilla milkshake.

Perry asked Tara, "Hey, is it all right if I take a break now?"

"No problem, Perry."

He motioned for George to meet him around the kiosk, and they started walking to the food court. They were talking about George's work. George had been trying to get Perry a job with his company but to no avail.

"Hey, anything is better than this place, so keep trying. I don't care how long it takes as long as it happens."

They saw Bruce Thompson approach but with nobody from the Defense behind him.

"Hello, Mr. Thompson."

Bruce gave an ominous smile. "You enjoy that kiss? How about a little more vigilant next time?" He followed his statement with a wink and walked away briskly.

Perry leaned toward George. "Did you see that?"

"Yeah, I saw that he winked at you, but what the hell was he talking about enjoying that kiss?"

"I have no clue, but I don't think it's a good thing. He's up to something, and he has some idea for me."

"You are so overdramatic with this place. What can he possibly do to you?"

Perry wanted to tell George what Michael Thompson did to those workers and what Bruce did to him with Dom's wife, but he was too afraid. The less George knew, the better, and now Perry had a new fear: Bruce Thompson knew he was kissed by an underage girl, and that meant he was as good as dead. Only the Defense did such things and got away with it. He was hoping he would be put out of his misery.

"You're right. It's just that I've been here for too long." Out of the corner of his eye, Perry saw Julia walking from the food court to her store. "Hey, want to meet Julia?"

"Yeah. Did you guys go for your coffee yet?"

"No, not yet, just setting up the date." Perry yelled, "Julia!!!"

She turned and looked startled. She saw Perry and smiled at him as she walked to them.

"Hey, how are you, Perry? Sorry I was busy and could not get back to you."

"Oh you know, I'm having a ball at this place. No problem. This guy is George. He's my good friend."

"Hi, Julia. Perry has told me a lot about you. Good things only."

"Nice to meet you, George. Well, there are no bad things."

The two of them shared a laugh, but Perry was not amused. He wanted to tell George that she was talking to another guy and had not been answering him when she had said yes to having a cup of coffee or lunch as friends. The three of them were talking and having a nice conversation. It was the longest conversation Perry had had with Julia since asking her out, and he was loving every minute of it.

George put a stake through it. "Hey Perry, it looks like your store has a big line now, and that girl is by herself."

Irritated with George for breaking this up, he said, "You're right. I should be getting back." He pushed his glasses against his nose, and the three of them began to walk back. "I'll see you later, Julia."

"Okay. Nice to meet you, George."

"Nice to meet you." Turning to Perry, George whispered, "She's gorgeous, man. Good for you."

"Yeah, good for me. I deserve it. We should get dinner sometime."

"Okay. I'll talk to you later. See ya."

Perry got back into the kiosk and saw George walk away. He looked into Julia's store and waved at her. She waved back, and a feeling of revulsion went into Perry.

Was he the guy? Customers were coming much faster than before. Perry and Tara had to work hard for the first time all night. More people were coming, but surprisingly, none acted as animals. The Defense did not have a strong presence in the mall except for a few talking to Julia and Tara, but that was normal. Perry heard somebody emptying out the garbage and recycle cans behind the kiosk and saw that it was Chris. He went to the back of the kiosk and whispered, "Hey, is Freddie working tonight? I need to talk to the two of you."

Chris said, "Yeah, he's on the other side. We have to make it quick. What's it about?"

"The Myrmidons' next attack."

"Man, this is going way too quick. We do it like twice a month, not twice a week."

"Just tell him that you guys should meet me by the dumpsters in the employee parking lot."

"Are you fucking crazy? The Defense is always there at night."

"Stop being a pussy, and do it. I expect you guys to be there after work."

"As you wish, Achilles, the asshole."

Perry knew he was being a jerk to Chris, but he did not care. These two guys were murderers, but in Perry's eyes, they could be easily manipulated. Where Freddie and Chris saw a sick hobby, Perry saw a revolution.

The rest of the night went by fast. It was a quiet night, which was his favorite. He and Tara went into the back and were washing the equipment. Perry had to wait a little for Freddie and Chris. The dumpsters were only a few hundred feet from the stockroom. Tara punched out her card and said to him, "So expect a message from me." She kissed him on the cheek again. This time, Perry returned the favor and kissed her on the cheek. They looked at each other, and there was a knock on the stockroom door.

Perry yelled, "Come in."

Freddie and Chris opened the door and noticed Tara.

She looked confused about why they would come into the stockroom. "I'm going to leave. See you later, Perry."

"Okay. Have a good night."

As she left, Freddie and Chris did not make eye contact with her or check her out, but Perry knew they were uncomfortable with something. Freddie said, "Look, Perry, we love the ambition, but you might need to relax with this."

"No, no. Our next victim will start the revolution."

"And who is our next victim?"

"Some woman who insulted me online, and she must pay for what she did. Before knowing about the shed, I wouldn't have done anything, but now we have a place with no rules."

"You see, Freddie, this is why I don't trust him. He's so fucked up. We don't kill people who we didn't run into here."

"Hold on. Give him a chance to say his peace."

"I figured the revolution will start with her because we are going to kidnap her at the Brine County Mall. Trust me. I figured everything out. If we have a victim and embarrass the mall in the process, say a kidnapping taking place there underneath the nose of the Defense, we can cripple their power and stronghold."

They gasped. Freddie said, "Perry, are you out of your fucking mind? The Defense will be swarming the parking lot. They will find out with the cameras."

"You two need to trust me. We will kidnap this woman, and the mall will get embarrassed by doing so."

Freddie and Chris were silent for the first time.

"Just get the chloroform ready."

7.

LUNCH

Perry came home from work with a sense of happiness for the first time despite receiving a threat from Bruce Thompson. He knew he was going to embarrass the Brine County Mall, and in his mind, that was as good as going out with Julia, which seemed impossible. His self-image was even more disturbing. In the last few days, he had killed a person, had a plan for killing a second person, and had an interesting relationship, to say the least, with an underage girl. He went up to his room to change out of his work clothes and threw his shirt in the hamper. He wanted to burn his lanyard but instead threw it next to his garbage can and laid down on his bed.

He had no messages from Virginia, but he did not care. The time and place were already established. The date was the day after tomorrow. He needed to contact one more person with his plan but noticed an unread message on his phone. It was from Tara.

Hey, wanna come over tonight? My parents aren't home.

Perry was more than excited to answer her but thought about the situation. He still had strong feelings for Julia. He needed more work on his plan so he would not get caught. He had no idea what time her parents were coming home, and Tara was underage.

After thinking for a couple minutes, he answered. *Sure. Where do you live?*

With that message, he knew that George and he were going to have a falling out. He would never approve of this fling that was going to happen, but at this point, Perry could care less what anybody thought. Besides, what he did the night before was much worse. He wanted to have relations with Tara. He was very attracted to her and jaded. Tara sent him her address.

He left his house without telling his parents where he was going with such gusto at a late hour. He would probably arrive at Tara's house around eleven. He stopped at the twenty-four-hour grocery store and picked up a few flowers to give her. He was trying to seal the deal that night.

He parked in the street across from her house. Nobody was in the driveway. He walked up to her door, was about to knock, and felt a vibration from his phone. Maybe it was Tara telling him where to go. He saw that it was from Julia. *Holy shit, holy shit, She finally answered me. I forgot why I texted her in the first place though.* His hands were sweating. He was getting nervous but the good kind of nervous. He ran back to his van to answer her. He knew he should never have gone to Tara's house. Julia was the girl for him.

Her text read, *Hey, sorry about taking a long time to answer, but would you want to go to lunch with me, Rose, and Duane tomorrow?*

"Who the fuck is Duane?" Perry yelled. "He must be that asshole she's talking to, and fucking Rose, she's an idiot. Does she want to set us up or something?" Perry had known Rose as long as he had known Julia. She worked with Julia, and they were close friends, but he did not like her as he liked Julia. He did not like her even as a friend. He was nice to her only because he knew Julia was friends with her. He did not want to go out with her, but if going out to lunch with Rose would get him to go out to lunch with Julia, he would do it. There was one more aspect of this lunch. He was going to meet Duane, and he was going to try and learn as much about him as possible. *Yeah, that sounds great. Is Duane the guy you are talking to?*

Duane is my boyfriend.

That answer destroyed Perry. He stared at it for a couple minutes, ignoring the calls from Tara, and punched his steering wheel, making a soft whimper. He answered Tara's call.

"Hey, are you coming in? Is everything all right? My parents aren't supposed to come home until tomorrow morning."

"Yeah, I'm fine. I'll come in in a minute." He hung up the phone, left it in his van, and walked to Tara's front door. He knocked twice, and she answered wearing tight yoga pants and a small T-shirt.

"These are for you, and you look beautiful."

"Awe, thanks, Perry. Come in."

He walked in the house and looked around. He noticed some family pictures and realized her family did not look familiar.

"Where are your parents? And they're not coming home until tomorrow morning?"

"Yeah, it's their anniversary. They went to a bed and breakfast upstate, so they have no idea you are here. You are better than me throwing a party with fifty people."

Perry was thinking about Julia. He wanted to be with her. He wanted to go to her house, not Tara's. He knew this was a mistake, and it was probably going to lead to

 John P. Burdi

a bigger mistake. "Cool, cool, well, happy anniversary to them. Why exactly did you invite me here?"

"You got me thinking when you said that I could talk to you about my breakup. You are more experienced and smarter than me, so I wanted to talk to you about everything."

"Shoot, fire away. Ask me anything, cutie." He realized he had said cutie. It was too late to take it back. This was leading to a place he had no business to be in. The two of them talked for twenty minutes. She gave him a glass of water and some chips, and as she was getting them, he could not stop looking at her. He wanted her, knew how wrong it was, knew how he should not have been there, knew how much he cared for Julia, and still made his move with Tara. In what seemed like the next moment, they were making out, his hands caressing her breasts, slowly moving down her body to her legs. He stopped kissing her and began massaging her inner thighs and began kissing her down under. Joys of pleasure were coming out of her mouth. Her inexperience was the best thing for Perry, and she had no idea if he was really good or really bad. They began moving from room to room to get closer to her room. He had brought protection in case he needed it. He was not mindful of the law, but he was not an idiot.

They were taking each other's shirts off. It seemed like they were in a race. The more he was kissing her, the more he was thinking about Julia. He was not proud of what he did, but he took out all his anger on Tara, a little aggression, all his anger at everything, like he did with Calvin, except he did not harm Tara. They were under the covers when he resurfaced to look at her clock. The time was 1:32. He knew he had to get back home. Tara did not want Perry to leave but held little resistance. They both got what they both wanted. He got dressed in front of Tara. They kissed goodnight, and Tara whispered in his ear, "Until next time."

Perry got into his van and drove home.

He answered Julia. *Okay, when and where?* He knew she was not going to answer him until after he woke up. He wanted to see her, but he wanted to meet Duane, and he knew that after lunch, he must talk to that one person for his kidnapping to work. He parked in his driveway and hurried upstairs to get some sleep. A lot of change had happened in the last forty-eight hours, change that he wanted but would not understand how to handle.

PERRY AWOKE FROM THE MUSIC BLASTING FROM HIS neighbors across the street. He knew they were next on the list following Virginia, and hopefully Freddie would do more with that customer. He was hoping to see an answer from Julia, and to his amazement, he did.

Hi, do you like Mobile Diner?

He thought, *Great. They are really going to know me over there. Maybe Freddie and Chris will be there.*

Yeah, I love it there. What time?

How does 1:30 work for you?

See you guys there.

He realized how fast Julia was replying to him and wished she did that every time he messaged her. He had plenty of time to get ready and to rehearse how to act. He knew he needed to put on the performance of a lifetime. He had to impress Rose, which would mean that Julia would have more respect for him, and he needed to be friendly to Duane, even if it meant laughing at his jokes or caring about anything he was going to say. One thing he wanted to do was to collaborate more with Freddie and

Chris, so he sent a group message to them.

"*Yo can you guys do Applebee's today?*

He went downstairs to grab some breakfast, and the only person there was Laura. He felt like he had not talked to her in a week. As he was pouring a cup of coffee, she looked at him with a grin.

"What's up?"

"My friend Tara posted a picture of flowers from a Miller man, and I realized you were not home last night, and you and Tara work at the same place."

"What exactly are you getting at? You think I gave your friend those flowers?"

"Well, it would be a pretty big coincidence if you didn't."

"Laura, I was out with a couple friends from work last night. I don't talk to Tara outside of work, and it must be another Miller or something." He knew he was going to have to talk to Tara now. This would not look good for him if people found out.

"Oh, thank god, because she is only seventeen. You would get in trouble."

"You think I'm that stupid?"

"No, no. Anyway, who were these friends you were hanging out with?"

"Their names are Freddie and Chris. Do you want a picture of them too, fucking detective?"

"That is not necessary. I'm going to the mall. Wanna go?"

"Not a chance in hell. See you later."

As soon as Laura left the room, he took out his phone and messaged Tara. *You need to listen. Do not under any circumstances post a picture with my name on it. Do not even mention my name, nobody and I mean not one person could know about this.*

But why?

Is that a serious question? Does this really need further explaining?

He tried asking these questions as humanely as possible, but his frustration was increasing to the boiling point. It was clear that the events of the previous night were not the construction of a serious relationship, at least in his mind. He realized he might have been harsh with Tara, but he could not be kind anymore. He wanted one thing from her and her with him, unless she wanted more, which was a possibility he did not foresee.

But why did you get me flowers then? I'm not in a good place right now.

It was a kind gesture. Perry thought it was a type of payment but would never say that to her. *Look, are you home right now? We should talk about this and be on the same wavelength.*

My parents are home. We could meet somewhere if you would like.

Sure. The Coffee Shop in 20?

Sounds good. See you there, hon.

Perry knew this must be stopped. He also realized that this had to be a quick breakup, or whatever he wanted to call it, because he had more important plans with Freddie and Chris, and they needed to understand the plan, or their lives could be over if they implemented it wrong. He threw on his prescription sunglasses and a hat so nobody would notice him in public. He ran out of his house and was on his way to have an awkward conversation.

The Coffee Shop was the name of the place. It was normally crowded, and more people could mean more people would recognize him with Tara. Upon arriving, Perry chose the table in the back, ordered two hot chocolates—he was not sure if she drank coffee—and waited.

     John P. Burdi

He messaged her where he was sitting, hoping not a soul would see him.

When the door opened, a bell let everybody know, and as the rings amplified, so did his unwillingness to stay. He had to meet the Myrmidons in thirty minutes. This had to be quick, and she was running late. He messaged them saying he might be a little late. He had to take care of business at The Coffee Shop. He was also thinking about this lunch, but the aspect he was thinking about the most was seeing Julia. He was going to eat a meal with her. Unfortunately, her boyfriend was going to be there too, but in his mind, that was better than no Julia. The bell rang, he looked up and gasped at who had entered: Michael Thompson.

What the fuck? Why would he come here? Nobody else was with him, and he was wearing a sweatshirt and jeans, not his usual blue button-down with khaki pants. *Is he really going to sit down and drink a cup of coffee, one of the most feared men in Brine County?*

Perry tried to avoid him, took a newspaper, and buried his face in it. He had the pleasure of talking to Bruce Thompson, but he was unsure if Michael knew him. He would not pass the message that Bruce warned Michael to keep his eyes open about Perry. He was thinking this was all from the kiss that Tara gave him in the kiosk. Bruce saw it and told his brother, but how would they know that he was at The Coffee Shop? Tara was the one who kissed Perry, and as far as he knew, she received no threats or peculiar winks. He was more paranoid than ever. At least the Thompsons had no idea about the shed or Calvin.

The bell rang, and Perry looked up because he had a feeling that it might be Bruce, and it would be the end for him. It was Tara, and when Perry saw her, he smiled and got excited. He was attracted to her but knew this could not go on. This could not happen again. Once was enough. It looked like she had just worked out. She had on a bright-color sweatshirt and yoga pants that were tight, which he didn't mind, and she had her hair up, which he liked better. It made her look older.

Tara walked in and went to somebody else. "Hi, Uncle Mike. It's been too long."

Perry dropped his hot chocolate. He knew he could not break things off harshly, but he also could not continue. He was in a corrupt situation.

Tara hugged Michael Thompson and kissed him on the cheek but with the kiss of seeing a family member. "I didn't expect to see you here, Uncle Mike."

"I love the coffee here, and it's relaxing. What are you doing here?"

"I'm meeting a friend for a cup. Excuse me, but my friend and I have a lot to talk about."

"Okay, enjoy. Tell your parents I say hello."

Tara walked over to him. Perry called for a barista to help the spill, and they gave him another hot chocolate. She sat down, and they looked at each other.

"I ordered you a hot chocolate. I was not sure if you drank coffee, and oh yeah, how do you know Michael Thompson?"

"Uncle Mike? He's a family friend. He used to go to school with my father. I don't really know Bruce though. Michael comes over sometimes."

"Do you know how much of an asshole he is? His brother is much worse." Perry did not care about ending it with Tara anymore. He was more concerned about her connection to the Thompsons.

"He is not an asshole. They are both misunderstood. Sure, they can be mean sometimes, but they are running a business, of which is like one of the best in the county."

"You sound like a bullshit advertisement for them." What he wanted to say was that they committed murder, made death threats, probably did money laundering, sexual harassment, and a bunch of other activities, but he did not, because he did not trust Tara. Whatever he told her, she might tell Michael right now.

"We have more important things to talk about than the Thompsons. What about our situation?" She was right, but he had one more question he wanted to ask about Michael Thompson. He could ask it later.

"Tara, I think you are gorgeous and nice, but I do not see a future in this relationship. Last night was great, but I think that can be the only time and the only kind of relationship we can have. I know I sound like a douchebag, but I know you just had a messy breakup, so I want to be as honest as possible. I do not want to give you false hope or anything like that." He knew he said a lot and laid a lot on the table for her. He waited for her answer while drinking his hot chocolate.

"Would you want to do it again?"

He was not expecting this. He thought she would either leave out of anger or push for a relationship, not friends with benefits. With Michael Thompson there, he figured the best case for him would be to leave without having her cry or be upset, even if he was lying, but he was not sure what to say. He did want to do it again even though he knew it was wrong.

"Honestly, yes, I do, but we should not rush for next time. Let's wait a little, but I want to make myself clear, there will be no future relationship from this. I hate to cut our time short, but I have to get going. I have a prior commitment, but it's good we had this talk. Until next time." He had his hand out for Tara to shake as if they had made a business transaction, and in his observance, they might have. He needed to make her somewhat happy in the presence of Michael Thompson. "One more thing. Did you tell Michael Thompson to be at The Coffee Shop at this time and come in before you did?"

Tara drank from her hot chocolate. "No, but it was a pretty big coincidence."

Perry waved goodbye and left, not believing one word she said. He knew she told him to be in there. Because of Michael being there, the entire conversation changed. He was more worried about him than anything else and knew he could not tell Tara anything about his life anymore. She was a direct link to the Thompsons, and she was technically his enemy. He left without looking at Michael and did not turn around to see Tara. He had to get to Applebee's to meet with Freddie and Chris, and he was running late.

Perry drove a few miles over the limit to get there on time. He turned into the parking lot, almost on two wheels, which made it worse in his van, and parked next to Freddie and Chris. They were not in their cars, so they must already be inside. He was not going to tell them about Tara and seeing Michael Thompson. It would only make them nervous for Monday night. He walked in, and they were in the same booth as before. There were three drinks on the table, but the two did not drink from them yet. Perry knew they were concerned.

"Hey, guys, sorry I'm late. I had to take care of something." He sat down, took a big gulp from his beer, and wiped his lip. He knew they were not going to say anything until he laid out this plan. He talked, and the more he talked, the more Freddie and Chris were getting interested. They were believing they could really do this. He told them what time to be at Applebee's and what they had to do. It was not as crazy as they thought it was going to be. He told them about the other person he was going to have a conversation with. After he told them everything, they said in unison, "We got this."

Freddie said, "You are talking to this person you are not telling us about tonight for the mission tomorrow?"

"Yeah. I'm going to have lunch with Julia and some friends, and then I will talk."

"Lunch with Julia. Good for you."

Chris interrupted. "Are you sure this person will do what you say they can do?"

"Absolutely. They hate the Thompsons as much as I do and will do anything to embarrass them."

Freddie said, "You want us to pick up lion masks? Isn't this a bit too much?"

"To beat the Thompsons, we must put up a show as much as they do in the mall. Trust me, this is going to work."

The rest of the short time was filled with laughs from corny and sexual jokes. Perry did not like spending time with these two. He liked spending time with George and Julia, but he needed these two for his revolution. They said their goodbyes and drove their separate ways to mentally prepare themselves for Monday. This was their first murder that was not going to be a customer. This had nothing to do with letting out frustrations from their jobs, just a dream of desperate young men.

Perry left Applebee's with a big smile. He had to end a fake relationship, tell his partners about their next mission, and have lunch with Julia, all in the same day. He had been thinking about this moment for a while, but it was going to be only the two of them. No Rose or Duane.

Perry had to rush around town to make the lunch on time, speeding. He was blasting "Paint it Black," one of his favorite songs. He was swerving in and out of lanes, realizing that Julia was going to be with another guy. He knew that Duane was going to be at lunch, but they were officially a couple, and Perry was a sorry excuse to be with Rose. He was wondering if Duane and Julia were going to be all over each other, kissing, touching, and leg groping. He did not want to see any part of it. He knew he was going to have to ignore their behavior if he wanted to try this friend thing, but he was not going to ignore them. Those two kissing was going to make him sick to his stomach, especially because she was going to be happy about it.

Miraculously, he got to the Mobile Diner early. He messaged George. Perry ignored his last couple messages because he was busy with Tara, the Myrmidons, planning a revolution, and this lunch date. He ignored the one friend who never ignored him. He was not confident that George was going to respond quickly. He took out a book that was in his back seat and started reading. It was an Edgar Allan Poe collection. He was reading "The Pit and the Pendulum" when George answered fifteen minutes later, which was a record for him. *Hey, we still doing lunch?*

"Oh fuck!!! Shit, I forgot I made plans with George." It did not matter that he forgot about making plans. He knew he was not going to cancel lunch with Julia, no matter if Duane was there, and he was not going to cancel if the Thompson Brothers were the other two people at lunch. He texted George, *That's why I texted you. I feel like shit today, I don't think I can make lunch.* Perry did not feel as bad as he thought he was going to. He knew George would understand.

K, get better.

He knew George was upset, but he still wished him to get better. It was a step up from just *K*, but he knew he was going to have to hang out with George eventually. He was not going to respond to make it seem like he was too sick to talk. The next time he saw him, he'd make up another excuse.

One crisis averted, he thought about lunch. He knew what he was going to order: a corned beef sandwich on rye, replace the fries with red cabbage. He thought that replacing the fries might impress Julia or surprise her. For the next couple minutes, he read and listened to music. He looked at some jobs online, but nothing caught his eye.

He messaged Julia, *Hey, I just got to the diner. I'll get a booth for us.* The hostess sat Perry in a booth that looked smaller than the rest. *Oh no, Julia and the asshole are going to be closer than I want them to be.*

A couple minutes later, they arrived. Perry was waving them over, but he was only looking at one of them, and she looked more beautiful than ever. Her hair was straight and not in tight curls, and she was wearing jeans with a black leather jacket. He wished for the two others to disappear, but it did not happen.

Julia spoke. "Hey buddy, you know who Rose is? This is Duane."

Duane looked like a real piece of filth. He was tall, seemed to be in great shape, and was wearing a white polo shirt with shredded jeans and a pair of boating shoes. *What a fucking joke.* Perry could not stop staring at Julia. He had never seen her in jeans, only in her work uniform, but he realized he was going to have to stop admiring her; he could not make it that obvious. He had Rose, who was a pretty girl, but Perry was not interested, but he needed to play the part.

"Hey, Rose, you look very pretty."

"Aww, thank you. You look very nice." Rose hugged him. He returned the hug but wanted to go no further with her.

Duane had his hand out, waiting for Perry to shake it. Perry extended his hand, wanting to kill him but instead saying, "Nice to meet you, Duane. Julia has told me a lot about you. Only good things, of course." The handshake seemed a lot longer than usual. Perry had the upper hand and had a firm grip. Duane let go first. That was victory number one for Perry. Duane seemed a lot stronger than he really was. They all sat down, and there were four glasses of water and a pitcher of soda for the table. "I took the liberty of ordering the drinks for the table. I was not sure who wanted what, so I had them bring the water and soda," Perry said.

"That's very nice. Duane and I will drink the water."

"And I'll have the soda," said Rose.

Perry did not miss anything. He was aware that Julia said she and Duane would drink the water as if they had been married for twenty years. That comment was not going to deter Perry. Not today.

The waiter came to the table. "Everyone ready to order?"

Perry spoke up as the leader. "Everyone good?" The others nodded, and he spoke first. "I'll have the corned beef sandwich on rye. Is it possible to replace the fries with a vegetable?"

"Yes, I believe we have glazed carrots and red cabbage."

"The red cabbage sounds perfect. Thank you."

Duane was next. "I'll have the Caesar salad, no croutons please, and I'll have bacon instead. She will have the chef salad."

Rose was last. "Can I have a chicken salad wrap, please, on a tomato basil wrap?"

"Certainly. Everything will be out soon." The waiter went away almost at a jog. Perry noticed that was unusual, but so was this lunch, especially because Julia and Duane ordered for each other now.

Perry asked the question that he was going to regret asking. "So how did you two meet?"

They looked at each other. Duane said, "You want to tell it, or should I?"

"I'll tell it. Let me know if I tell it was well as you do."

Oh, for fuck sake, I don't give a shit how you two met, and I want to stab you like twenty times, you Caesar salad-ordering asshole.

Julia began to tell the story. Rose listened intently, clearly interested in the tale, even though he knew she had heard it before. Perry made it seem like he was, nodding at times and saying, "That's very interesting."

Julia was saying, "Well, so it was my first day at the gym, brand new member, and part of the deal of signing up is that you get a free thirty-minute session with a trainer. You don't have to do it right away. You can save it as long as you want to as long as you're a member, but something told me to try working out with a trainer. I had never worked out with a trainer before, so this was the first time for me."

Great, a fucking trainer. I can't compete with that, and look at him with that stupid, condescending grin. He knows I like her. She probably told him, but she didn't need to. I'm making this way too obvious. I can't stop looking at her. Christ, she is so beautiful, and she's with this behemoth of a man, all brawn but no brain, not like me. I have to figure out a way to end this, but she seems cheerful.

"Wait, wait, wait," Duane interrupted. "Before you tell them how we met, you forgot to mention who was supposed to train you instead and what happened to him."

"I was just about to." Julia rested her hand on top of Duane's, and they looked deep into each other's eyes. Rose was looking at Perry, but Perry could care less. She was boring to him. "The manager at the front desk told me to go to Calvin's office, he's the head trainer at the gym and…"

"Fucking who?" Perry interrupted, not caring about the volume of his voice. When he heard that name, everything stopped. It felt like he was back at the shed, and the only person he saw was the bloody mess that Calvin became because of him. This was the first time since it happened that he thought about Calvin. Visual pictures were coming back like flipping through a photo album. The punches, the laughter from Freddie and Chris, the old knife, the stabbing, the crying, the pain from Calvin, and for the first time, the pain Perry felt. He felt like his world was coming to an end, much worse than getting rejected or broken up with, much worse than getting yelled at by a customer. The only sound he heard were the screams. "I'm sorry, pardon my French, but what was the trainer's name?"

Julia, Duane, and Rose looked at each other, thinking that Perry had lost it and made the lunch very awkward. Julia helped him out and began to laugh, giggling as she answered. "He's the head trainer. His name is Calvin, but it's nice to feel that my story is that interesting to you. Maybe I should sell the copyrights."

Perry didn't know what to say. He wasn't interested in the story at all—the only thing he was hoping for was that it would end and that the head trainer Calvin was not the same person as the customer he murdered, even though the customer had not been in particularly great shape, but anything could surprise him at that point. *Thanks for saving*

 John P. Burdi

my ass, Julia, but please stop telling this story. "You should definitely sell the rights. It's like *The Notebook* all over again."

"Aww, I love that movie," said Rose.

Yeah, but nobody gives a shit. I would rather listen to this story than to hear about your favorite movies.

"Me too!" said Julia. She turned to Duane. "We should watch that tonight."

"Yeah, of course. I like Nicholas Sparks." Duane winked at Rose.

Of course you like Sparks. What else do you do, save homeless animals, volunteer at the fucking hospital? I bet Julia thinks he is an alpha male. I can outsmart any alpha male, so what would that make me? I swear if he gets in Julia's pants, I might go on a killing spree, and I would save you for last, Duane. I just want to rip your head off, I don't care what I have to do to end this, and fucking cannibalism might be an option. "Please, continue with the story," he said.

The waiter came with the food. It was almost record time but seemed like an eternity for Perry. "Does anybody need anything else?" she said.

"No, everything is accounted for and looks great," Duane said.

Perry picked up his sandwich and took a big bite, noticed that the rest of the table was not eating, and put it down, embarrassed.

Julia continued. "Well, I headed over to Calvin's office and noticed that the lights were off, and nobody was in there. He seemed to be missing."

Another stab into Perry's side. It seemed like this Calvin was the Calvin he had murdered, and as he heard the name being spoken, it hurt more.

"So I left his office and went to the office next to Calvin's, knocked on the door and answered..."

Let me guess, Duane.

"...this woman named Anna, but Duane was also in the office. You see, it was Duane's first day there. He was just hired, and Anna said that he should train me, both of us being newbies."

"Aww, that's so nice. If Calvin was not there, you two might have never met," said Rose.

Perry said, "I doubt that. This sounds like a small gym. I'm sure they would have bumped into each other eventually." He didn't care if he was rude to Rose. He didn't like her, and he hated this story. He wanted to leave despite Julia being there. He couldn't hear Calvin's name anymore. He was thinking about that night, thinking that joining Freddie and Chris was a mistake and forming the Myrmidons was a mistake. He did not want to kidnap and murder Virginia anymore.

Duane said, "It is a small gym, but I have to adjust from working in a big place to working in a small place."

Well put, you fucking moron. What big place could you have possibly have worked at? Freddie did say that you worked at a department store at Brine. He could have just been bullshitting me, though, but first. "Sorry if that was rude, Rose. That came off all wrong. How's your lunch?"

"Oh, don't worry about it. It's really good. I can tell you really like your lunch too." The two others laughed at his expense.

You little bitch.

Julia said, "We had a training session, and at the end of it, we asked if we had any plans for the rest of the day. We didn't, so we decided to grab a cup of coffee, and we decided to go for more cups of coffee, with a couple dinners, and movies and such."

"Well told, sweetie." Duane leaned in and kissed Julia—a little peck on the lips, but it was more than Perry could take.

"Excuse me, but I must use the bathroom."

Rose got up so Perry could leave the booth. He almost jogged to the bathroom, thinking they were talking about him and his unusual behavior. He wanted to leave. He was trying to think of an excuse. He was thinking about that kiss and a way to leave being partners with Freddie and Chris, but he knew they would let him leave only by killing him. Going to the shed was the biggest mistake of his life. Freddie and Chris caught Perry at his worst and most vulnerable, and being mad at his own life had nothing to do with Calvin. He was terrified at his own impulses. He was unsure if he wanted to do all the things to Duane he was thinking about at lunch. He had no idea if the real Perry was the one committing murder or the one who was regretful about Calvin.

Perry walked back to the booth, and Rose moved in so it would be easier to sit down. He began eating, not caring what the others thought. He wanted to get out of there and noticed that Rose was putting her hand on his leg, starting at his knee and working up to his crotch. He wanted none of that, gently took her hand off, and placed it on her leg in a way that Julia and Duane could not see.

Julia and Duane kissed again.

You know what? Fuck it. They're going to be kissing in front of me, and I'm going to be doing stuff too. Perry placed his hand on Rose's leg and began massaging it. She obviously liked it and did not move his hand to stop. After a couple seconds, he stopped and realized how ridiculous he was. Rose took his phone and put her number in it, but he was not going to call or message her. He still had one more question to ask Duane.

"Where did you work before this gym, Mr. Cupid?"

All three laughed. For the first time, Perry looked interested in what Duane was going to say.

"I worked at the Brine County Mall."

"Oh yeah. Well, you probably know that the three of us work at the mall."

"Of course I do, but you guys never saw me at the mall. I worked the overnight shift. It was a pain in the ass sometimes, so I left and became a trainer. I was certified and figured what the hell. Even though I loved working at the mall, I didn't like the hours."

I loved working at the mall was not a sentence that Perry knew existed, but he needed to know if Duane was telling the truth.

"Where did you work? Did you stock at a department store?"

"No, I was on the Defense. You know, the security at Brine."

His eyes closed. Freddie lied to him. The guy Julia was talking to never worked at a department store, he was a member of the Defense. A member of the Defense going out with Julia. He was disappointed in her as much as he hated Duane. "Yeah, we all know the Defense. You loved being a member?'

"Oh man, Michael Thompson is like a hero of mine. I didn't know Bruce that much. I worked with Michael a lot. He was like a second father to some members of the Defense."

Perry began laughing, almost howling. *Oh yeah, a second father, a second father who kills his children. This guy needs to die!*

Duane continued. "Anyway, I still keep in contact with Michael. He says things are good at the mall."

Perry realized he worked the overnight shift of the Defense. He thought they were mostly used to beat people, the ones they caught during the day who broke one of their golden rules. Julia had no idea what kind of a guy he was.

"That's good to hear. It seems you love every job you have, and the newest one helped you meet Julia."

"I am grateful every day." Julia and Rose seemed like they were going to eat out of Duane's hands. Everything he said was golden, and they thought he was the best guy in the world, but Perry knew better. Perry knew what kind of monster he was. He realized that being partners with Freddie and Chris was the best thing to happen and that they must stop people like Duane, other members of the Defense, and customers at the mall. They needed to be put in their place, and the Myrmidons were the ones to do it. He knew what he had to do. The next night was going to be huge in his revolution.

The four left the booth, and Duane overtipped the waiter, putting in five dollars more than Perry. The only decent thing Perry did was to pay for Rose, even though he ignored her ninety percent of the time, and the rest of the time he massaged her leg to make Julia jealous, but that did not work.

They said their goodbyes and left in Duane's pickup truck. Perry waved goodbye and walked toward his van, took a couple deep breaths, let out a sigh of relief, and opened his door. He took out his phone and sent a message to Freddie and Chris. *Get plenty of sleep tonight. We might not get any tomorrow night.*

Perry went home to call the guy who was going to bring this plan to fruition. They spoke about twenty minutes, and it was as if they had been friends for twenty years. All the logistics were figured out for the following day. This might be the most important day of his life, and he thought they might have a fourth member in the Myrmidons if Freddie and Chris approved it.

Perry was in his room and was listening to music when he messaged Julia. *Hi. I had a good time at lunch today.* He figured she would get back to him tomorrow, but she messaged him immediately.

So did I. Rose really likes you, you know.

Yeah, I kind of got that feeling, but I might only like her as a friend.

Please don't hurt her. Anyway, have a good night.

Yeah, you too.

Hurt her how? The same way you hurt me. Do you have any idea how much of an asshole Duane is? Do you have any idea what I'm like, what I want to do, what is planned for tomorrow? He wanted to open up to her, but he suspected she wouldn't listen. The last person he thought about before he went to bed was Tara, not Julia, for the first time in a long time.

8.

THE KIDNAPPING

Perry awoke, and the big day was there. It was almost like an athlete with the most important game or match of their life. Only twelve hours ago, he had placed the call to a man who helped set up the ins and outs of his revolution. Although it would not start until ten that night, it was difficult to feel cold feet in this experience. He knew that after completing the plan, there was no going back. They would become outlaws, and he fantasized about Robin Hood and Bonnie and Clyde and wondered if Freddie, Chris, and he would turn into those legends.

He walked downstairs, and to his amazement, nobody was home. He did not know how long or why, but he made the most of it, sat on his couch, and did nothing but think for a couple hours. He thought in the peace and quiet of his home, contemplating if everything was figured out. He kept imagining during the middle of the job that Bruce and Michael Thompson would jump out and kill all three of them. The fourth member would be in a place all by himself. He messaged George to reach out to the one friend who was always there for him. *Hey, I'm sorry about yesterday. We need to hang out soon.*

Perry wanted to tell him everything, but he knew that George would not give him advice. George would call the police, and the only advice George would give him would be to see a psychologist, the very thing he wanted to become. In the rearview mirror of his life, he had not thought about the next steps such as graduate school and counseling in a long time. Freddie and Chris were replacing George, murder was becoming a normality, and all this change was happening in a couple weeks. Perry was never a big fan of change, but he welcomed this new lifestyle with open arms.

He heard a buzz from his phone and saw that George had answered him, even though he was working in his office building. Although Perry was moving from George, George was trying to hold on to their friendship. The text read, *No problem. Can you hang out tonight at Applebee's?*

Perry knew he could not. Maybe this was the universe telling him not to do the revolution, but he did not pay attention or care. He knew what he wanted to do. He responded, *I can't tonight. How's tomorrow, maybe for dinner?* Before he could put his phone down, there was a new message.

Sure, that works. Maybe we can get some seafood?

Cool. I'll let you know the time tomorrow.

Sounds good.

That's good. He doesn't seem to be mad at me, nor should he, just because I have been hanging out with other people for once. People change, George.

He made a large lunch, a wrap that he could barely close, of bologna, mustard, cheese, and lettuce. He took out some pretzels and a power bar and messaged Freddie. *Are you ready for tonight?*

He had finished his lunch when Freddie got back to him. *I guess so, and we picked up the masks. Only the three?*

Perry laughed out loud. In the entire scheme of the plan, the one question that Freddie had was a wardrobe

     John P. Burdi

one. *Yeah, just the three. The fourth person will not be allowed to wear the mask where they are stationed.* He was proud of himself at the moment. He felt like he had real power. He was the general making all the calls with all the information, and some people on the team did not know the other people.

"Okay. Chris is pumped up for tonight. I'm just nervous that we might get caught. Hell, this whole plan is insane."

Perry was disappointed in Freddie for being worried, but he was saying too much in the messages. *Fucking idiot. I bet the Thompsons will read these texts in a couple days when this town is going to be a complete shit show.*

Just relax. Everything is going to work out. This town is going to be crazy in the next couple days.

Okay man. Everything is ready on our part.

All right, man. Perry tried to say as little as possible, for as smart as Freddie was with hiding evidence, he did a poor job in conversation. He had to make sure of one thing: He had to drive to the church across the street from where the two drivers crashed and died. He had to make sure there was no camera evidence. He was wearing a bright-green shirt to go inside the church. He was driving with a sense of tranquility, which would not be the case later in the night.

He parked his van across from the scene of the crime and walked outside to investigate. He walked around the entire church to look for cameras but saw none. He was not sure if there were going to be any hidden. He did not know what to look for, security measures not being his strong suit.

He did the unthinkable and walked into the church even though he had murdered a person, had sexual relations with a minor, and caused the deaths of two motorists in a short period of time. Walking in, he assumed the stereotype of being struck by lightning at the hands of God, but nothing occurred. The church seemed deserted. He began going through every room. He wanted to make sure there were no cameras, and he knew he needed to speak to somebody who knew the answer.

He walked past the worship space and forgot how large a room it was. His family used to go when he had Bible studies but had not gone since. There was nobody in sight, and the lights were on, but nobody was in the pews, not even a person cleaning or dusting. He walked through a hallway, trying to see if a priest lived in the church. To his amazement, the priest was kneeling before a portrait of two people. To the sides of the portrait were flowers, so many that they covered the wall. He did not know what to do. He did not want to interrupt the priest, but he walked closer. He could not tell who the people were and needed to get a closer look.

His mouth dropped open when he saw the car accident victims. His victims. He wanted to turn and run out of the church, but the priest would definitely notice, and that would cause suspicion. *Okay, relax. He has no idea who you are. Nobody does, and there are still no witnesses. I need to be sure that there will never be evidence or a witness.* He cleared his throat, figuring that was the best way to get the priest's attention.

The priest turned around and said quietly, "My son, come and pray with me." The priest was in his seventies, thick glasses, and had a thick head of white hair. Even in the quiet whisper, Perry knew he had the commanding voice to give an effective mass.

The last thing Perry wanted to do was pray with a priest. He belonged in prison, but he thought of the possibilities.

If I tell a priest of all the illegal and crazy shit that I've done, would he still call the police? Maybe he can absolve me of all my sins, but I don't give a rat's ass. Besides, what the Thompsons do is much worse. Maybe I should mention Tara. No, he would tell somebody. I need to keep my mouth shut. I have to pretend I am somebody of significance. I need to know about the evidence, and it's the only reason why I'm here.

Perry went down on both knees besides the priest and said, "Father, I'm not sure what to say."

The priest smiled in a way that made Perry comfortable. It was similar to when a student asked a teacher for advice, especially when the teacher had a passion for their craft. "My son, I will say a prayer for them. Just listen. It is said when there is sorrow and loss, and I did not personally know these people, but their deaths were on my doorstep, so I feel responsible that they reach salvation."

He continued. "May you see God's light on the path ahead when the road you walk is dark. May you always hear, even in your hour of sorrow, the gentle singing of the lark. When times are hard may hardness, never turn your heart to stone. May you always remember when the shadows fall, you do not walk alone. May love and laughter light your days and warm your heart and home. May good and faithful friends be yours wherever you may roam. May peace and plenty bless your world with joy that long endures. May all life's passing seasons bring the best to you and yours. May God give you for every storm, a rainbow, for every tear, a smile, for every care, a promise, and a blessing in each trial. For every problem life sends, a faithful friend to share, for every sigh, a sweet song, and an answer for each prayer."

Perry listened intently to the words and wanted to make his confession to the priest then and there. He felt embarrassed and ashamed to even be in a church and did not ponder what was going to be done later that night. *What the fuck am I supposed to do? It was like he was speaking directly to me, not to the two people who died. I caused their deaths, and let's say that one of them was a complete shithole. Am I supposed to confess everything to him and everything that I want to do, but what will that bring me? An enlightened soul and jail time. You do not walk alone? Well, I do. Nobody in this world ever helped me with anything, and I don't walk alone, not anymore. Freddie and Chris, we walk the same path. God hasn't given me an answer once. What God, the same one who protected that employee from the hands of Michael Thompson? The only person who can protect you is yourself. My heart is stone, but the mall and others have done that to me. Nobody there ever showed me kindness. What am I supposed to say to him?*

"That was a very emotional prayer, Father. I think it is most fitting for these two souls. May I add, may they rest in peace."

"Thank you, my son." The priest crossed himself and put down the rosary he was holding tight while saying the words to the fallen.

Perry came to the church for one reason, and it was not to confess to a priest. It was not to apologize or seek forgiveness from God or Buddha or any other higher entity. It was to cover his tracks. He said, "Father, the reason why I am here is to find out some truths. I work for the *Brine County Times,* and I would like to know if there is any surveillance of the accident."

The priest looked at Perry in a disappointed manner and answered solemnly, "That was the first thing the authorities asked, not the media, but alas, we do not have any security cameras outside. Now we are going to have some. We are not letting this accident happen again. God is our security."

You sure about that.

"Thanks so much, Father. I hope some light is uncovered in all this darkness. Hopefully justice prevails."

"It could have been divine intervention. It might not have been an accident, just a warning to future motorists. Why do you look so pleased with everything?"

Perry needed to wipe the smirk off his face. Of course he was going to be happy. There was no evidence against him, and with his planning, there was not going to be any in the future. "I'm sorry. I guess I am happy because the church is in such good hands," Perry said quickly. There was no smirk on his face as he was holding his emotions inside.

"Thank you. Is there anything else I can help you with?" The priest did not want Perry to stay at the church. There was something suspicious about his character, but he could not place his finger on it.

"I believe you covered everything, and thank you for letting me be a part of the prayer for the two lost." *Thank God, literally, for no evidence. I want to get the fuck out of here and not come back again.*

"Have a good day, my son."

"You also, Father." Perry turned and walked out the same way he came in. He still felt uncomfortable, but the good news made his day. He was exonerated. He walked past the statue of Joseph of Arimathea and saluted him. Luckily, the priest was not looking.

When Perry got home, he took a nap. He needed rest to do what he needed to do that night. If a mistake was made because he was tired, it could mean his life. He awoke from his slumber and heated some Hot Pockets. Nobody was home. *Did they go to the beach or somewhere without me? I'll text Mom.*

Where are you guys?

Perry threw his phone on the couch and lay down with the plate of Hot Pockets on his stomach. He surfed through the channels but nothing satisfied him, so he shut the television off, waiting for an answer. His mother was extremely punctual at texting him. She usually answered him within a minute, but today, he was by himself. After he devoured his Hot Pockets, he did what any other twenty-something would do. He began to satisfy himself. Not to anything in particular. He took his laptop and tried having a good time. A couple minutes later, his mother messaged him, and when he saw "Mom 1 Message" on his phone, everything was ruined. He said out loud in the empty house, "Jesus Christ, she even ruins it when I try to jerk off. Does she know I was doing that?"

We are on our way home from the beach. You were sleeping, so we decided not to wake you up. See you soon.

Can't finish now.

He went upstairs and jumped in the shower, and it was a cold shower indeed. By the time he got out of the shower, his family was home, including his father, who had taken the day off, and he never took days off from work.

"You took off from work?"

"Perry, I need to have a word with you real quick."

What the fuck? This never happened before.

His father and Perry walked outside to sit at the patio furniture. He barely let Perry grasp what was going on. He began talking and wanted Perry to listen, not answer. "Son, I feel like you have been drifting away from this family, and that is understandable for someone of your age. I know you want to go out on your own, but when you are under this roof, you need to respect me and your mother as much as possible. That is a tough pill to swallow, because you have lived with us for so long. With your sisters living on campus very soon, I am trying to spend as much time as possible, you know watch some movies, maybe go to a museum, and you damn well knew we were going to the beach today. I was there when you agreed and chose the day because you were not working at the mall today. For you to not wake up and spend time with your family is unacceptable without an apology. You have the balls to ask us where we are. Shape up, and get over whatever is going on. You have become a ghost to us."

Perry was stunned. He wanted to cry and say sorry. He wanted to hug his parents and sisters, but he did not say one word. He looked down and, for the second time that day, felt ashamed. *Holy shit, I forgot I was supposed to go to the beach with them today. What do they want from me? I have a revolution to plan. They wouldn't understand. Besides, I wouldn't have had a good time today. He has never spoken to me like that before. What's the big deal about this?* He was gently kicking the table outside, thinking of something to say, hoping a diversion would happen to end this awkwardness. His father was looking for the apology, but Perry did not listen.

His mother came outside, and his diversion was present. "You want anything to eat, Perry?" She looked upset but was not as mad as his father. His sisters were upstairs. If they had been there, he would have felt like this was his intervention.

"No, thank you. I made some Hot Pockets. They were good. Buy the same ones again, please."

"Sure thing, will do." She walked back inside.

His father was not budging.

"You're right. Sorry, Dad. It won't happen again." He apologized, but whether he meant it was another story.

"It better not." His father walked away and left Perry outside by himself, back to square one. His world was changing around him; he was losing his best friend and essentially traded him for two people who should be in jail. His family had begun to isolate him because of his actions, and his revolution was the prime result of these changes, but among all the vicissitudes, there was his sense of conceit. For the first time, he was in control, for better or worse, and that was what he loved most.

For the next couple hours, Perry stayed in his room, reading and watching television, still not talking to anybody in his family. He reached out to Julia. Although they messaged not too long ago about Rose, he still wanted to talk to her, so he shot her a text. *Hey, so when is the next time you are working?*

I want to tell her how much of an asshole Duane is, but in due time, I will do something about him. Sometimes it's better for somebody to crash and burn.

His mother hollered, "Perry, dinner time."

He took his phone with him in case Julia answered, but that thought was covered with doubt. He was flabbergasted that he had heard nothing from Tara, but with her age, he figured she had moved on from him. He walked into the kitchen, and everybody was there. It was like he was looking at a postcard from a bed and breakfast. They looked like a complete family without him.

"So what's for dinner?"

"Won't you like to know," Laura said with the snottiest of attitudes. He knew it was not going to be Leah with the bitterness.

     John P. Burdi

"Yeah, I would, you arrogant child." *What a fucking bitch, seriously. I'm her older brother, and she treats me like she's the older one. Here comes her bullshit act in front of mommy and daddy.*

"Knock it off you two, or you're both going to eat outside, and Perry, we just had a talk. Do you need another one?"

Do I need another talk? I'm twenty-five years old, and they still treat me like I'm sixteen. Christ, I need to get out of this place soon.

"No, you're right. I'm sorry. Sorry, Laura."

"It's fine," Laura said in a cerebral way. She was still upset with him. The Millers were a tight-knit family, but one of them was going their separate ways.

"Anyway, we are having meatloaf and mashed potatoes for dinner." His mother was trying to be the peacekeeper and answering a question that seemed like it was asked an hour ago.

Yeah, I know that now. I can clearly see. Maybe if my younger sisters did not interrogate me like an animal.

The family dug in without saying anything. The girls were not on their phones, but Perry felt a text notification. It was from Julia. *Hey, I'm working tonight, why?*

Can anybody not give me attitude? Why? Because I fucking asked you and want to visit you. Not everything is a detailed mystery, Julia.

I might be stopping by the mall. Just wanted to give you a shout out if I do stop by. He figured she would answer him in about an hour, but she did answer him to let him know that she was working the night of the beginning of his revolution.

"The meatloaf is amazing, Mom," he said, hoping to win back his family, but his mother was the one least upset.

"Thank you."

That was the biggest conversation of dinner. Perry felt that there would be nonstop conversation if he was not at the table, but he was for now. As much as he wanted to move out, he realized that he still needed two or three years to save money and needed a job that could support him.

One by one, people were leaving the table: first his father, then Laura, and then Leah. His mother stood up to clean the dishes and load the dishwasher. Perry was at the table by himself. *Tonight can't come fast enough. At least I'll have some fun.*

He walked upstairs and began preparing for the night. All he needed was to go to Applebee's to meet Virginia. Freddie and Chris were supplying the chloroform and possibly the lion masks, and that was about it. The plan was simple but needed exquisite timing. He wanted to go to the mall early to see Julia, even though she still had not responded, and tonight might not be the best night to see her.

He walked downstairs to tell his mother that he was meeting friends at Applebee's. "Mom, I'm going to Applebee's with George. Maybe I'll go back to his place afterwards."

"Okay, hon. Have a good time. Say hi to George for us."

"Will do. He's been asking to come by our house. Maybe sometime later in the week."

"No drinking and driving," said his father.

"Obviously." *I know not to drink and drive. He thinks I'm a real asshole.*

Perry drove to the mall wearing his button-down green shirt tucked neatly into gray pants, the same outfit he wore to church. He passed the church, did the sign of the cross, and the feeling of exoneration came back to him. A sign for tonight.

He arrived at the mall at 9:01. Closing time was 9:30 sharp, and his date with Virginia was in exactly fifty-nine minutes. He parked as far away from the mall as he could and looked around for Freddie or Chris's car, but he did not see them. There was still plenty of time, and they only needed one vehicle including his van. He marched to Julia's store. He could care less if his kiosk was across the way or if he saw the Thompsons. He heard shouting in the distance. He could not tell who it was, but it sounded like an argument that might blow into larger proportions. What he did see was alarming. Julia and Duane were in the store, and he was yelling at her.

Perry could not understand what they were yelling about, but now was his time to prove to Julia that he cared for her. He walked in and shouted, "Back up, and if you want to yell at somebody, yell at me!" He had his fist clenched and was waiting for a response that involved Duane's hands and not his words.

Duane yelled, "This doesn't concern you. Now get your ass out of this store before I beat the shit out of you!"

Good, yell at me, hit me even, and prove in front of Julia how much of a scumbag you are. He walked up to Duane, a couple inches from his face. "I'm ready, you little prick. I don't care how big you are. I'll fucking knock your teeth in!"

He was nervous about fighting Duane. He needed a weapon of some sort and a little luck, but first he needed to avoid the punch being thrown at his eye. He fell to the ground faster than Duane punched him. He thought that Duane was going to jump on top of him, he would wake up in the hospital, and the revolution would be lost. After Duane knocked Perry to the ground, he continued to yell at Julia. He knocked a display right off the wall, and the pieces were everywhere, but there was a metal arm beside him. The arm was used to hold up the display. To his luck, there was one next to him.

Perry stood up and wiped his eye with the back of his hand to make sure there was no blood. He needed to stop Duane before he harmed Julia. Duane's back was turned. Perry tapped his shoulder and swung the metal arm as hard as he could across his temple. Duane fell to the ground, and Perry fell on top of him and hit him two more times with the arm. Duane's eyes closed, and he did not yell. Most likely he was knocked out from the first hit.

Perry stood up and threw the arm on the ground. "I'm sorry I knocked him out, but I needed to make sure you wouldn't get hurt." That was one hundred percent the truth.

A strong and determined girl, Julia was speechless but extremely appreciative of Perry. She hugged him tightly. "Thank you, Perry. I don't know what happened. He lost control, and it looks like you took the worse of it."

Jesus Christ, she's hugging me. This is so much better than having sex with Tara.

"Quick, call the Defense. They should be doing this stuff. It's their job." Perry never waited to insult the Defense, but in a way, he was right. A couple minutes later, Duane was still on the ground with his eyes closed and blood covering his face.

Bruce Thompson and two members of the Defense walked into the store. Bruce said, "What has happened here? Why are you here, Mr. Miller?"

Perry wanted to fight him on the spot, but Julia said, "You guys didn't hear all the commotion? He was yelling at me and wouldn't stop. I don't know what he was going to do next. Perry saved me, and he has what it looks like a black eye. This man hit him first."

This man hit him first? Wow, she doesn't even use his name when describing him. Their relationship is about to end.

Bruce stood there speechless. He looked at Perry and sensed that he did something wrong or was in the wrong place at the wrong time.

Perry stood there touching his eye and trying to fix his shirt. It had come untucked during the fight. "Do I get some kind of reward for taming this monster?"

"The reward you get is us watching you with both eyes, because I still do not understand how you helped with any of this," Bruce said.

Julia said, "Mr. Thompson, with all due respect, this isn't that hard to understand. This man was going to harm me, and Perry stepped it. He heard the arguing and tried to handle the situation."

Bruce was agitated. He did not like Perry or trust him, and now another employee was choosing his side over the mall. "What is your name, young lady?"

"Julia Breckenridge, sir."

"Ms. Breckenridge, do you know this gentleman on the ground? You said you two were arguing, and I doubt that it was about prices of your products or anything that has to do with my mall."

Perry knew where Bruce was going with this. He knew that Bruce knew Julia had some kind of relationship with Duane, and you could bring your outside problems into the mall. Perry was hoping that Bruce would not realize that Duane used to be a member of the Defense. Bruce could not possibly know every person on the Defense. Besides, technically, Michael Thompson was Duane's boss.

"He is my boyfriend, sir."

"So your boyfriend came to visit you and start yelling about your relationship? Well, you know you are not supposed to have visitors this time before closing. Definitely not."

"Are you serious right now? He came in and started yelling at me. He didn't ask to visit me. He did so on his own accord, and I have no idea what he was planning on doing like I said already. We got into an argument the night before, and he didn't want to let it go."

Perry did not say a word. Not many employees stood up to Bruce Thompson like this, but he was more lenient with female employees. If Perry had said these statements, he would already be getting beat up.

"What is his name?"

Did Julia really stand up to Bruce, and he's not doing anything about it? What, are attractive women his weakness?

"Duane Donovan."

"The name sounds familiar, and if I recall, he looks familiar. I would recognize him better without the blood all over his face, courtesy of the courageous Perry Miller. I am certain he was a member of the Defense at one point in time."

Hold on a second. How am I in the wrong for what doing the job of the Defense, you little cocksucker?

"You know if he was still a member of the Defense, you two would be in serious trouble. It's your lucky day."

Julia said, "Sir, it is not our lucky day. He would have hit me or worse, and Perry has a black eye. If anything, it is my lucky day, not Perry's."

Perry thought he should say something. "Sir, look, I am sorry about everything. I should have called for the Defense when I saw the argument, not take the law into my own hands."

"Now you are learning how the mall works. Maybe you should enlighten Ms. Breckenridge next time. Why are you dressed so nicely? You usually look like a slob. I must say that green shirt is becoming on a man like yourself, one who usually isn't very becoming."

"Thank you, sir. I should dress better in the Brine County Mall. I have plans later tonight. Do you want me to clean the blood up?"

"No, the custodians will do it. Have a good night, Mr. Miller, and remember I'll be watching, because something is not right about this story or what you are up to. I'll be watching the cameras." Bruce whistled for the other two members of the Defense to pick up Duane and take him away.

Julia said, "Is he going to jail?"

"What? Of course not, he was a member of the Defense, and he is vindicated in the Brine County Mall. Now if you can excuse me and stop asking me ridiculous questions, I'll be watching the cameras for the both of you." Bruce walked away and did not look at the members of the Defense. He went to his office. If he was present during the start of the revolution, Perry would need more luck.

"Look, Julia, I was only acting like that in front of Bruce Thompson because I'm on thin ice with him. You know that's not how I feel about him or this place, and he's very dangerous."

Julia looked at Perry in a sincere way. "I'm starting to understand that now. You said you have plans tonight? I feel like I owe you a drink."

Of course, she wants to buy me a drink tonight. Are you fucking serious!

"Um, yeah, I can't get out of tonight's plans. Believe me if I could, I would. Is it possible for us to hang out later in the week? I would love to. You might owe me two drinks, one for getting punched and one for saving your life."

"Ha ha, yeah, that would be nice. You are full of surprises, Perry." She hugged him again, and he did not want to let go. He wondered if he should cancel his plans. *I could do both, have the revolution and Julia.*

"Okay, I'm going to let you close up. See you later, and get a good night's sleep. Are you sure you're alright?"

"Yeah, I'm fine. Thanks to you. See around, buddy."

Perry turned around and walked away, wanting to leave Julia on a high note. *Still has to call me buddy. Oh well. I couldn't have been luckier tonight. Now I have to meet Virginia.*

He walked out of the mall to the parking lot and found Freddie and Chris in Freddie's car. He walked slowly, peeked inside, and found the three lion masks. "So you two ready for this?"

Freddie said, "Yeah, absolutely, just as long as you and your mystery person are on board."

"He is. I will be in contact with him soon. First, I have to message Virginia to find out some things." He took out his phone, uploaded his online dating app, and messaged Virginia. *Hey, so what car do you have so I can find you easier?*

"Okay, I messaged her. Now we have to wait, and we still have thirty minutes. Plenty of time." Perry felt a notification and looked at his phone. "Great, my mystery guy is ready."

"So who is this guy anyway?" said Chris, impatiently, almost childlike.

"It doesn't matter who he is. You guys don't know him. You'll find out in due time."

"Do you trust him?" said Freddie.

"Yeah, I do, and he hates the Thompsons as much as we do, so this will work, and he will be a big reason why."

"I think this is going to work. We could bring down the Thompsons," said Freddie.

"It will, and Virginia just messaged me." Perry read the message. "Okay, she has a Dodge Dart, red." Perry messaged back, *Okay, sweetie, you know what, to make things easier, I'll already be at the bar. I'm wearing a lavender shirt.*

"Red Dart, sounds easy enough," said Chris.

"Okay, guys, I'm going inside Applebee's. Which one of you two will make the drop?"

"I will," said Freddie, almost like an eager player answering a coach.

"Sounds good. She will sit with her back turned to the door, so it will be easy for you to sneak up on her. The chloroform is ready?"

"Ready as it ever will be," said Chris.

"Well, see you guys during the revolution." Perry walked toward Applebee's. Now there was no turning back. He was going to go through with it.

By the time he sat at the bar, there were still twenty-five minutes, but he had work to do. He had to scope out the bar and sit at the most strategic place. The bar was more crowded than usual, but that would work in his advantage. The more people, the less of a distraction everything would be. He ordered a gin and ginger and began to relax. He had the easiest job of the entire Myrmidons. He noticed that Virginia had messaged him. *I'm running early, so I'll be there in a couple minutes. I'm pretty excited.*

Perry answered, *Okay. I'm so sorry, but I'm running late. I'm having car trouble, but I will definitely be there, don't worry.* He was going to have Virginia sit at the bar for about ten minutes by herself and then delete his profile. He took a big gulp of his gin and ginger and wiped his mouth, getting a little on his sleeve. He tipped the bartender about what the total of the drink was and headed for the door.

Virginia was walking through the parking lot, looking at her phone. Perry knew he had to run into the bathroom and hide for a few minutes, but he could not keep his eyes off her. She was much prettier in person, her long, black hair was irresistible, and wearing a short skirt made things even more difficult. She was much skinnier in person. Her profile pictures did not do her justice, but he thought about all the planning for this night and knew what he needed to do.

Jesus Christ, she's fucking hot. She couldn't be uglier? That would make things so much easier. I have to get the fuck out of here. She can't see me. He went into the disgusting bathroom, closed the door of the stall, and locked it. The toilet wasn't the cleanest in the world, but he did see worse. He sat and waited, setting his timer for exactly ten minutes. The waiting was not as challenging as he thought it was going to be. He kept thinking about what he was going to say to Virginia when he saw her, but he did not script the conversation as he should have. He had four messages ready to text and saved them as drafts: two to Freddie and two to his mystery Myrmidon. The timer went off. He logged onto his fake profile, deleted it, and walked out of the bathroom to the bar. She was sitting by herself. He felt bad for what was going to become of her, but knew what had to be done for the better of Brine County. He crept closer to her. Her back was turned to him. He sat at the bar, tapped her on the shoulder, and whispered, "He's not coming, is he?"

Virginia looked confused. She looked into Perry's eyes as someone would when they knew the face of a person but could not put a name to it. "What are you talking about?"

In the meantime, Perry put texts through to Freddie and the mystery representative.

Answering in the most confident way possible, he said, "Your date. He's not coming. You must have looked at your phone and noticed he didn't message you, or worse, he deleted his online profile."

"In what possible way do you know that?"

Freddie ran through the doors, went to the bar, and asked the bartender, "What time do you guys close?"

The bewildered bartender said, "Two AM, like it says on the door when you came in."

"Thanks, my man," said Freddie. He knocked over Virginia's drink and made a mess. He took something out of Virginia's purse, but because of how frantic he was, nobody noticed except him. He needed confirmation of what was taken so he could continue. The other patrons at the bar did not notice anything. They were too swept up in their own worlds.

Perry sent another text to the mystery person and answered Virginia while motioning to the bartender for napkins. "Because you are so incredibly beautiful, much too beautiful to be single, so somebody stood you up, and it's their loss. Now let's get you cleaned up, and maybe I can buy you another drink."

Virginia looked skeptical. Not only was a stranger hitting on her, but the stranger knew too much and said words that had already been said to her. She still could not keep her finger on it. "Thank you. That's very sweet of you, but I should be going."

"You didn't finish your drink. Please, I insist. You are all dressed up. Don't waste the night because some jerk didn't answer you. Let me guess—he said he was wearing a pink or purple shirt. It's supposed to be non-threatening."

"Yes, he said a purple shirt. Do all guys think alike?"

"I think most of us think alike, but some are better than others."

Virginia resisted, but she thought Perry was right, and she was flattered that he was helping to clean her off, even though he was getting a little hands on. She ordered another drink, and now she and Perry were having a drink together as he intended it a long time ago. He made up a couple more texts and saved them as drafts.

They were talking about their days and having a decent time. They still did not discuss their ages. It was obvious there was a big difference, but that did not seem to matter to her or anybody else. They were having such a delicate conversation that she did not notice when Freddie came back in the bar and slipped the item back into her purse. The bartender did not notice either.

Perry sent another message to his mystery person and had to follow up on the revolution. He needed to cut his date short. "So what's your idea of a perfect day?"

She looked at him like she had just figured out where the Holy Grail was, and a look of disdain came across her face. "What did you just ask me?"

"What, you didn't hear? What is your idea of a perfect day?"

"No, I heard you, but a couple other people have asked me recently. Oh my God, you are Perry, you little piece of shit!"

"Yes, I am, and I am the guy who deleted your profile, but I forgot his name, so that doesn't matter."

"You little creep. Why would you do that to me?" Virginia did not raise her voice even though she was insulted. She did not want to make a scene in public and make it worse by him being younger than her.

"Why would I do that? What, are you disrespected? Remember what you said to me that ended our conversation? Well, I do. You said that maybe if I lost a hundred pounds, and I thought that was disrespectful and not cool, so I figured I should return the favor. Now let me ask you this. Were you enjoying yourself before you realized who you were talking to?"

"That's not the point. You lied to me and wasted my time." She did not answer the question even though it was obvious to Perry that she was having a good time, she did seem to enjoy talking to him.

"No, it is the point. You were clearly having a good time with me. It didn't matter about my age or weight, and you were having fun, so you are some creature who cares what society thinks and not what you think. When I was pretending to be the older man, you didn't think twice, so how about you do this for me? Think about your priorities next time, and maybe give me a call. I thought you were different from girls my age. You responded to me and talked about what you like to do, not what is expected of you. You see, girls my age talk about working out or shopping or eating healthy. Not you. You talked about life."

"Don't ever talk to me again, you little prick. You don't know shit about this world, and you could still lose weight. Have a nice life, and if you try and contact me again, I will call the police." She stood up and was aggravated to the point where everything looked like a tunnel. She noticed nothing except the screaming in her head because she did not want to make a scene in public.

"Hey, Virginia."

She turned around and looked like she wanted to throw up on him. "It looks like I bought that drink for you after all, and by the way, you have an amazing ass." He sent another message to Freddie and the mystery person.

She did not give a coherent answer; it was more like a growl. She walked out of Applebee's.

In all seriousness, that might be a better ass than Tara, much better than Julia. What I would do to that for a night, but she's the biggest bitch I ever met. He finished his drink.

Virginia walked to her car, still cursing and growling under her breath and still not noticing anything, just as Perry calculated. She opened the driver's seat door and sat down, but before she knew it, a hand covered her mouth. Her eyes closed.

Perry quickly got out of Applebee's and walked to her car.

Freddie got out of Virginia's car and said, "Holy shit, she's hot."

Perry said, "She is, but we must concentrate on the task at hand. Okay, let's load her up in your car, Freddie." No one saw a thing. The Defense was on the other side of the mall via a tip from the mystery person, and they did not have to worry about the cameras, also handled by the mystery person.

As they were putting her in the back seat, they lay her down and covered her with a comforter. Perry took her keys out of her purse as Freddie did earlier, closed her car door, and locked it. "I will meet you guys at the shed. I have to drive my van, and I will follow close in case you get pulled over. Godspeed."

Freddie said, "We have to thank your mystery person for getting us out of the woods."

Perry said, "We are not out of the woods yet, and you can thank Steve tomorrow."

The drive to the shed was much easier on Perry this time around, which was strange, because this time he knew he was going to murder a woman. The first time, he had no idea what he was going to, but now it became his way of life. His function of putting a Band-Aid on a cut was to murder.

Not many cars were on the road that night. A drizzle formed but not enough that he needed to put on his windshield wipers. He saw no movement from Freddie's car. They knocked Virginia out good, but hopefully she would wake up soon. They still needed to go back to the mall before midnight. That was when the Defense had their highest numbers working the perimeter of the mall, and more of them meant more embarrassment. The time was 10:37.

Freddie pulled into his driveway and pressed the automatic garage door remote. Perry parked his van in the driveway. He walked toward the car when Chris jumped out, wearing the lion mask, and yelled, "Boo!"

"You didn't have to wear that on the drive over here." Perry was annoyed.

"See, I told you, and I'm the psycho of the group," Freddie said.

Chris removed the mask. "I have two more for you guys, but maybe I should just throw them out. Am I getting one for Steve too?"

"I don't think that's necessary, not yet at least. We are wasting time. We have to deliver her to the shed and have her wake up so we can bring her back to the mall," Perry said.

"But why don't we just kill her now?" Chris said.

"Because she must suffer a little, and we bring her to her salvation in the shed. What's the matter with you?" Freddie said.

"Well, now we are on the same page. Let's do this," said Perry, excited for what was going to transpire.

Chris reluctantly gave the two others their masks, and they all put them on. Perry had mixed feelings. He felt fulfilled and determined about what was going to happen. He felt like he was going overboard with everything, but after all, they were Myrmidons, and they were lions in their minds. Freddie and Chris grabbed Virginia, put her on a hand truck, put a sack on her head, tied bungee cords around her and the truck, and began wheeling her through the backyard to the shed. With the sack on her head, even if she woke up, she could not see, but they did not want her to wake up, for she would most certainly scream.

Walking to the shed moved faster. Not only were they wheeling a person who was still alive, this was the first time that Freddie and Chris had to dispose of the body back where it came from: the Brine County Mall.

They reached the door to the shed, and Freddie was fumbling around with the keys when they all noticed Virginia moving. Freddie found the keys and opened the door in record time, and Freddie and Chris pushed her in. He followed, closed the door, and locked it. They all shut off their phones. Perry had remembered to grab her phone and shut it off.

Freddie and Chris removed her from the truck, sat her down, on an old wooden chair with arms and tied her. Perry was relieved to see how routine it was for them. They looked like seasoned veterans. "Okay, you two, outside like we talked about. Give me five minutes after she wakes up, and then we have to let her drain her real quick. The blood will come out like a faucet. Do you guys have the bucket?"

"Yeah, we do. It's already in the shed, but this is my shed, and you can let us watch while you begin your revolution. After all, we did the hard part in the parking lot," said Freddie in a tone that was louder and more callous than Perry would have liked.

God dammit, I know these two are glory hogs, but I can't afford to fight with them. I'm on a strict schedule. We have to bring her back before midnight if it's going to hurt the Thompsons, the earlier the better. Their work was difficult, I should throw them a bone.

"Fine, you two can stay. Place the bucket on her left, close to the chair. It might be impossible to collect all her blood. We just need a good percentage." Virginia was still delirious. Freddie did as Perry told him for the bucket on her left. Freddie and Chris grabbed a couple folding chairs and sat on them in front of the door as a cheering audience for Perry.

Perry walked up to Virginia, ripped the bag off her head, and whispered, "Wake up."

Her eyes were still closed, so they had to wait a few minutes. She woke up and screamed in a way that they would remember for the rest of their lives. She had no idea where she was or what had happened to her. She was staring at three people in lion masks: two were sitting, and one was about five feet in front of her.

"Who are you guys?" She began sobbing. "What are you going to do to me?"

Perry stared at her and decided to take off his mask. "Why, hello, Virginia."

"Perry, what the fuck happened? What are you going to do to me? Who the fuck are those guys?"

"Why, those two are my accomplices, and you should be happy. You are the beginning step in the revolution to bring down the Thompson brothers." Perry wiped tears from her face with his wrist, whispering, "There, there."

"Get the fuck off of me, don't touch me! What are you talking about? What do I have to do with the Thompsons? I didn't complain about you or any other worker at the mall."

Freddie said, "See how fucked up everything is? This woman is in a shed, tied to a chair, and she's pleading to us that she didn't complain to the Thompsons. Nobody in their right mind should know the owners of their mall like that, like they run everything. Fuck the Thompsons."

Perry raised his hand like he wanted Freddie to stop but believed everything he said.

Virginia said, "And how did you kidnap me from Applebee's connected to the mall? The Thompsons have cameras. You'll never get away with this!"

Perry said, "See, that's where you're wrong, and I'll tell you how we did everything. Listen up, Virginia, it's story time. I had the idea when you agreed to get a drink with me. Well, when you agreed to get a drink with the older me. You couldn't wait to get a drink with him, well, me, but that's neither here nor there. Anyway, I decided to get back at the Thompsons. We needed a way to make them seem like they lost their grip on the mall, and what better way than leaving a dead body in their car in the parking lot with no surveillance on their cameras."

"But how did you get me? You didn't walk out with me?"

Freddie said, "Want me to set an example of interrupting her?"

Chris was watching.

"No, that wouldn't be needed. Where are your manners? And you, sweetheart, keep listening. Well, you came into Applebee's, and I was hiding in the bathroom. Waited about ten minutes and deleted my fake profile. Right after that, I joined you at the bar and began conversing with you, which I might add was very pleasurable. While you were distracted by me, I sent out two texts, one to my inside man, who is a member of the Defense, the security of the Brine County Mall, if you did not know. He switched the camera view of the parking lot to the other side of the mall, and in came Freddie, who was not under any surveillance. He received the other text to come running into the bar and make a distraction to steal your keys."

"Are you saying one of those little shits was the guy who spilled my drink?"

Freddie jumped up, but Perry made the same hand motion, and he sat down.

"Yes, that's exactly what I'm saying."

"But how did the guy switch the cameras? Wouldn't they know who did it? He would get in trouble, and so would you guys."

"Well, that's what I thought, but he said that they use ID numbers when working the cameras and logged his out and logged someone else in when it needed to be changed. The lucky fellow he logged in was also working that night, and it would not cause the least bit of suspicion. They constantly rotate. That fellow is an asshole from what I'm told, and my inside man hates the Thompsons as much as I do, so he was willing to help. Where were we? Yes, Freddie used your keys to open your car and ran back to put them in your purse. The car was still unlocked, and he sat in the back with his damp towel. You noticed nothing in your backseat, because you were so furious with me, just as I calculated. The other lion, Chris, helped get you out of your car into another one and brought you here. Your car is still in the parking lot, and you'll be there soon. There's nothing on camera, just a parking lot with your car in it, but no sign of struggle, no sign of anything until they find you in it soon."

Virginia was scared beyond belief and crying, "Why me?"

"Because you insulted me."

"So you're going to kill me? Well, I'm sorry, please, I'm so sorry, I, I, I, didn't mean to do anything bad to you. Please don't do this. PLEASE!" She was sobbing and trembling, drool was coming from her mouth and perspiration from her temples. The only word she kept saying was "stop." Her arms and legs were tied to the arms and legs of the chair, making movement impossible.

Perry wanted to kill her to put her out of her misery. She looked like she was having a seizure. Her only movement was her head. It was the cruelest of tortures even though none of them laid a hand on her: waiting to be murdered all because of a comment through a computer screen. A month ago, none of this would have come into Perry's mind, but that customer and Freddie and Chris and working at that mall took the goodness out of him.

"I'm not negotiating with you." Perry got to the left of Virginia and yelled, "Welcome to your salvation! May God give you for every storm, a rainbow." He stabbed Virginia in the neck. The blood exploded like some kind of a geyser, most of it in his face, some in the bucket, the rest all over Virginia. He stuck the knife in her in a nonviolent motion almost like he was cutting a piece of chicken. The blood was all he could see of her face. Her beauty was replaced; his beastly appearance took over him. He was standing above her like a hunter holding the lifeless body of a rabbit. He took the knife out in one motion and looked at the blood on the blade. He saw his reflection. It looked like he was wearing the lion mask, but he was not.

The screams that were so piercing, the pleas that were so constant and forgiving, were no more. Virginia was dead.

Freddie and Chris looked at each other and then at Perry like he was a deity. Freddie said, "Where the fuck did you learn whatever you just said? Just because we send them to their salvation doesn't mean in a literal sense. It makes them fear us more and gives us a sense of importance."

Perry said, "Well, I talked to a priest today, and he said a prayer for two people who were killed a short while ago. The prayer makes sense, so I figured I'd use it. A little much?"

"Yeah, a little," said Freddie.

"Well, we know what to do next. The blood is dripping pretty effectively in the bucket. We need to take the blood out of the bucket and into some bottles. Any volunteers?" *I'm not fucking doing this. Didn't I do enough this night? I want to stab her again, not just once, I want more, especially for what she said. I want to turn her body inside out.* He took off his glasses and wiped the blood off of them. He left it on his face for now. There was some on his shirt and in his hair. It was much messier than he anticipated.

"Sure, I'll do it. I didn't do much anyway," said Chris.

Freddie and Chris took off their masks. It made the job easier, but there was nobody to scare anymore. He and Freddie watched Chris do the unthinkable of taking blood in a bucket from a dead woman and trying to put it in bottles. "Can't we just cut her foot off for more blood?"

"No, that wouldn't make sense. Why would you stab a woman in her car and then take off her foot?" said Perry. "We have to make this look as real as possible. We need to throw money on her passenger seat and add the drugs. It's a drug deal in the Brine County Mall gone bad, and pedestrians are going to discover the body. Bruce isn't going to know what to do."

"Do we have to put all the pot in her car? Couldn't we smoke some?" said Freddie.

"I don't care what you guys do in your spare time, but we need some on her front seat, understand?"

"Yeah, sure," said Freddie. He didn't care that Perry was taking over the Myrmidons. He was happy about not using all the drugs in this charade of a drug scene they were trying to create.

It was 11:05. They had plenty of time and enough blood. Now they had to transport Virginia back to her car at the Brine County Mall. Freddie and Chris placed her back on the hand truck, tied her up, and put the sack over her head. The masks were left in the shed.

"For the record, we never did this before, bring a dead body into the Brine County Mall. This might be suicide," said Chris in a concerned tone.

"It will work. On the way there, I'm going to text Steve, and he will send a fake tip like he did when you guys stole her keys. The parking lot will be clear of the Defense for a short time. We put her in her car, pour the blood on her, and I will stab her again in the same place and leave the knife. The cash and drugs will be on the passenger seat, and we have a drug deal gone wrong, and none of this will be on camera."

"Music to my ears," said Freddie. "Not on camera."

The boys loaded her in Freddie's car. Perry drove behind them in case they got pulled over, although it was not clear what he was going to do. They got to the mall, and it was 11:21, ahead of schedule, which worked for their benefit. Perry and Freddie pulled up next to the red Dart.

"Be careful," said Freddie.

"I will. We are not on camera. I sent out the message."

"Of the people looking from the bar," said Freddie.

Perry knew he was right, but he was in her seat. It was too late, and he needed to do something. He yelled, "Chris, move my van. Do a donut in front of the bar window so nobody will see. They'll pay attention to you, not me." Perry threw Chris the keys to the van, and Chris made donuts.

Perry parked Virginia's car next to others. Freddie parked next to the Dart and noticed there were no headlights in sight. He rushed to open the door and, with Perry's help, threw her in. He stabbed her in the same spot, and they poured the blood on her. Drugs and money were in the front seat. Mission accomplished. The closed the doors and locked them but opened the driver's side window. Chris picked up Perry and drove out of the parking lot, and Freddie went in the opposite direction. The time was 11:27.

Holy shit, that fucking worked. I can't wait until somebody discovers her dead body, and the shit will hit the fan for the precious Thompsons.

For the first time in his life, he truly felt proud about something. This was better than getting a full-time job or going to graduate school, even better than going out for a drink with Julia. He wanted to control the Brine County Mall.

The revolution began.

9.

TIS THE SEASON

Shortly after Virginia's death and the fake drug deal gone terribly wrong in the Brine County Mall parking lot, the town began to pursue the idea that Bruce Thompson was losing control. The media that seemed to protect Bruce and Michael, to a lesser extent, were not shying away from the story that a murder had taken place in the parking lot, and there was not a single witness. Every time Perry, Freddie, and Chris ran through the parking lot to complete their mission, Steve had switched the camera view, and the fake tips created hysteria on the other side of the mall. The Myrmidons had done their homework.

Many expected that Bruce and Michael were going to be committing beatings of those they suspected. They did nothing. Bruce added more Defense members to the parking lot at night, but he did nothing drastic, much to Perry's confusion. Bruce was calm and collected, ignoring the cries of the media and people who felt that the mall was not a safe place to shop anymore.

Michael Thompson had a closer eye on the inside of the mall. He suspected that members of his Defense had committed treason. The only person who was punished for Virginia's murder was the lucky member of the Defense whose ID Steve had used. Nobody in town was sure what happened to him. The police did not arrest anybody;

Bruce made sure of it. He wanted to be the one to enact punishment, but Steve did not see him at the mall anymore, and the rest of the Defense understood the message. They were being watched much closer than usual.

That was a victory that Perry wanted to take, because it could lead to more backstabbing against the Thompsons. Maybe some members of the Defense were going to be Myrmidons; there were now four of them. Shortly after their victory that summer night, Steve became a member with a unanimous welcome.

For the next couple months, the Myrmidons were growing, and the killings were growing. Perry, Freddie, and Chris were running out of room in their graveyard.

Perry and George saw each other every couple weeks or so. They were still hanging out, but their relationship was damaged. They were going in different directions. Perry never told him anything, and he did not intend to tell him anything about his life. Their friendship was becoming fake, because they knew nothing about each other. When they did hang out, they were reminiscing about the past, never making plans for the future.

Perry and Julia hung out a couple times by themselves, no Rose or Duane. After the incident at the mall, Duane and Julia broke up, but he was not in trouble because he worked for the Defense. Perry and Julia got the drink that Julia had promised, and dinner happened with a kiss to end the night, but they did not become a relationship. Julia was clear that she wanted to remain friends with Perry, and he made it clear that he cared for her but told her that he would rather have her as a friend in his life than nothing at all. He was full of shit.

He was not that upset about not being in a relation-ship, because he was seeing Tara. They continued their fling even when Perry took Julia out to dinner, but that was what their relationship was: a good time. He never took her in public. They went to a motel room for a couple hours. He told nobody about her, because she was still underage, something he was not proud of, but everything was consensual, and he did acts that were much worse.

His family was falling apart like everything else in his life. Laura and Leah went to college without Perry's help. He did not help them pack or unpack at their dorm. He was busy with his secret life. At his house, it was Perry and his parents, and his nightmare of living at home was becoming a death sentence. He barely said anything of any value to them, and when he did, it was because they were fighting.

Perry thought his life was becoming better because he was in control, but he was becoming less human by the day. Some of the murders were so brutal that there was not enough of the body to bury. Lost limbs, pulled teeth, hacked limbs, and decapitation were becoming routine in the shed. Although they were getting new members in their club, the only ones allowed in the shed were Perry, Freddie, and Chris. The new recruits stood outside, standing guard and wearing the lion masks.

The crying and screams were excruciating sometimes, but the Unholy Trinity seemed to get past it every time. They had a rotation for the one bringing customers and often members of the Defense to their salvation. After Virginia, it was Freddie's turn, then Chris's, and then Perry. Sometimes the three of them would be there. Once in a blue moon, Freddie and Chris were there with Perry's permission. They were discreet and careful, and Perry had nothing to worry about. As for the new recruits, that was all Freddie and Chris. After all, they were the ones who showed Perry the path.

Freddie and Chris found people like Perry—miserable with life and desperate—and there were a lot of employees at the Brine County Mall who felt that way. That was the only qualification to join the Myrmidons: working at the mall. Age did not matter, and two members were women. At the beginning of November, Perry had a new plan that would ultimately have Bruce and Michael lose complete power and authority of the mall and Brine County, but in the meantime, Perry wanted to have some fun.

One unlucky customer who insulted Chris at the start of September met a terrible demise. It was Freddie's turn for the kill, but Chris let Perry know the details and asked if he was allowed to pursue. The customer insulted Chris and had a good laugh at his expense with the Defense. He insulted Chris by saying, "Look at this employee you have with his hipster haircut." The icing on the cake for Chris was, "You clean like old people fuck—slow and sloppy." The customer was with two members of the Defense, and they were howling like hyenas when Chris was done. The customer placed his hand on Chris's shoulder. "Christ, boy, do I have to report you to Bruce Thompson?"

Chris stared at the customer and said nothing. Both members of the Defense pushed Chris back to his cleaning cart. Chris followed the customer home, not knowing of his affiliation with Bruce, and three days later, he was tied to a chair in the shed. The three of them beat the customer pretty severely, but he was still alive and could still talk. It was Freddie's turn. They all took the masks off; it made the job tougher. Freddie approached the man with a giggle, wiping sweat from his own forehead and deciding which weapon to use. Besides the knives, they had the baseball bat, a small hatchet, a circular saw that was used for special occasions, needles, a couple lead pipes, and a bunch of random gardening tools.

They often played music that made them seem more psychotic. They figured it would scare the people even more, and it worked most of the time. Some of the songs were "I Love You" by Barney and Friends, "Take Your Best Shot," and "Bye Bye Bye."

Freddie did not take a weapon yet, but he did something that scared Perry. He enjoyed it a few moments later. Freddie began to sing to the man, "I love to kill, long and clean and messy. I love to kill, it's getting worse every day!"

When Perry heard this, his blood froze, and he did not move. *Is he seriously singing that song from Mary Poppins? He changed some words. How the fuck did he think of that?* Perry was confused and taken aback, but he and Chris began to laugh hysterically. Perry had his hand on his stomach to stop the pain. This became a joyous occasion for them. Perry and Chris said, "We love to kill, slash, slash, and slash." Perry handed Freddie the knife, but he did not take it.

"Can you give me the hatchet for this one?"

"Why, Freddie it would be my pleasure," said a very chipper Perry. Chris was standing there rubbing his hands together like a kid on Christmas morning, waiting to jump into the pile of presents. Freddie had the hatchet in his hand, waved it over his head, and was about to drive it into the customer's head, but he noticed something. "Look, this little shit pissed his pants. Remember when he was a tough guy with you, Chris, making jokes at your expense?"

Chris said, "I sure do. It's moments like this that I truly live for, the small things, watching a grown man piss his pants before his demise."

The man began to cry. "You guys are really going to kill me over a joke?"

Chris yelled at him, "Who cares if it was some joke? You embarrassed the shit out of me in front of the Defense! You don't know what it's like to work at that mall with them and their rules and the Thompson brothers! Fuck you and your little joke. Now the joke is on you. We can't punish you in the mall for your actions, but we sure as hell can do it in these walls." Perry gave a nod. It was the first time he agreed with Chris.

The man had nothing to say. There was no talking to these three psychos. He was going to die, and he knew it.

Freddie said, "So is it all right if I continue?"

Perry said, "Put this asshole out of his misery."

Freddie drove the hatchet in the man's head, and there was a large mess that the new recruits would have to clean up. The recruits did not mind having to clean it up, but the Unholy Trinity would take the body outside, and the recruits would bury it. They were never allowed inside. Perry wondered if they heard anything from the outside, if the screams were heard, but the recruits never said anything, and he never asked, so he figured it could not have been that loud.

The killing that had a lasting impact on Perry was the customer who started it all, the customer who made him feel like he never had before. He forgot about her in the beginning, but he saw her in the mall. In September, Perry had not found a full-time job, but he was not looking for one.

He was leaning on the kiosk counter and noticed the customers. *I wish they could see themselves. They look like sheep being herded by the Thompsons and the Defense. They must really care about nothing. They notice nothing, walk-ing with their heads straight or many times looking at their fucking phones. They wouldn't even see somebody come up and shoot them. Honestly, what can they possibly be shopping for all the time? It doesn't stop, like the mail, but this is so much more bizarre. They will never stop coming here unless it is burned to the ground. All the years that I have worked here, the eight miserable years, nothing stops them, not snow or hurricanes, fucking nothing. They really sucked the life out of me, and it's one thing if they were at least nice, but it's the complete opposite. They have the biggest attitudes, and God forbid I don't have something they want. I tell them no, and they make a face like I murdered their families, but now, in some cases, I might have, and that keeps everything in order. A balance to their vulgarity.*

Perry was wiping the counters, making them spotless in case the Thompsons came after all. A dirty mall was a mall that the Thompsons would buy, not own.

George did not visit him for a while, and when he saw Julia, it meant nothing, not after she made clear her ambitions with him. They talked once in a while, and he still cared for her, but it was not the same. He knew there was no chance, so he remained friends with her. Working with Tara was not that awkward, and they had fun afterwards, but he knew she was too young to tell his family and George about her, so he didn't bother with it.

He was still watching the countless people walking up and down the mall. It was like he was in the middle of a zombie apocalypse. Freddie was working that night. He walked with his cart a couple times past Perry's kiosk. He still needed to empty the garbage bin behind the kiosk, but that would not be done until thirty minutes before closing time.

Nobody was working with Perry that night, just his lonesome self. Out of the corner of his eye, he saw something that made him excited. Not only was Bruce Thompson walking diagonally toward him, but he was with the woman who began it all. They were headed for the kiosk. Perry turned around and texted Freddie. *Holy shit, come to the kiosk. It's Bruce coming with the woman customer.*

Hopefully he knows what that means.

Bruce Thompson stopped at the counter and looked into Perry' eyes. Since the murder of Virginia, normalcy came back to the mall, but Bruce knew something was up. "Mr. Miller, remember my friend?"

"Of course I do, Mr. Thompson, and look, I would just like to apologize for how I acted. That is not a representation of me or this mall."

"Knock off the ass kissing, Mr. Miller. We all know you are not sorry, and that is a representation of you, but we are in a rush, and you could make up for it if you gave her some chocolate, if I remember." Bruce looked at the customer, and she nodded in approval.

Perry turned around, went for the machine, and saw Freddie standing behind it, emptying the garbage bin, making it look like he was doing work. He mouthed one word, hoping Freddie would understand. "Follow."

Perry had the chocolate ice cream in a cup, more than he was supposed to give. "Sixty cents."

Bruce Thompson laughed, thinking it was a joke, but there was no smile on Perry's face. He was watching the customer and looking in her eyes. Bruce took the ice cream, handed it to her, and winked at Perry. They both turned and walked away, and Perry could hear Bruce laughing. The good news that made Perry excited was he saw Freddie following them.

He saw that there was a message on his phone, and it was from Tara. *Hang tonight?* He shot back, *Yes, definitely. I was paid a visit from Bruce Thompson. I need to let off steam.*

Good, do your best with me, but honestly he's not that bad.

She's fucking amazing, but he's not that bad. I don't care what she says about him anymore. I think I'm actually starting to like her, but it could never work. She's still seventeen, and I will be twenty-six before she is eighteen. Jesus, she's still in high school, but she talks to me.

Perry texted her something that he did not regret at first but would over time. *I don't want to say this in text. I feel bad because I should say it in person, but I like you more than what we do, like I want to take you out to dinner.* After sending it, he read it over, hoping it would not sound too bad or incriminating. She might just be looking for a good time too, but she did not respond to him as quickly as previous texts.

He received one from Freddie. *Hey, so Chris came by, and he is following her home right now. Are we doing this tonight?*

Yeeesss!!! Finally I'm going to kill that woman!

No, we can't, because Bruce was with her. It will be too suspicious if they visit me and she goes missing the same night. We will have to wait until next week or so. We can get a member of the Defense tonight. I can ask Steve for another address.

Steve could get the address of some members of the Defense off the database but not all of them. Bruce Thompson made the wrong enemy, a friend of Perry. Bruce had two sets of eyes on Steve, but he was too smart to do anything that would break the rules. He never condoned violence, but when it was against the Defense or Bruce, he was all for it. He never told him about the random customers. Virginia was the only exception.

Perry began cleaning the kiosk, still waiting for a text from Tara, but Freddie messaged him instead. *Okay, get me an address.*

Perry asked Steve, and Steve delivered. Perry gave the address back to Freddie. *I'm going to sit this one out tonight. I have plans.*

Oh, really, with Julia?

No, unfortunately not, but you two have fun tonight, and eventually we are going to have to do more detective work. I think our guy is running out of addresses.

Okay, bro. Hear from you later.

Just like that, Perry signed the death sentence for a member of the Defense. In the past, it would have taken so much more work and thought, but his mind was so gone that he did not value human life anymore. He valued it less than the Thompsons.

He was about to close shop when an almost unfamiliar face showed up. "Hi, Perry. Long time, much too long."

"Hey, George. Do you want to grab dinner tomorrow?" Perry knew he was going to have to make more time for George or he would lose him completely, which he did not want to do. They were still friends but not as close.

"Sure. Is it all right if Lauren comes along too?" Lauren was George's girlfriend. They started dating about a month prior, and he considered it serious.

Seriously, man, she has to come along? Of course, the more the merrier.

"Okay, sounds good. I will let you know tomorrow about the details. I saw you here so it was easier to ask."

"Cool. See you tomorrow."

George was gone, but Perry did not really want Lauren to be there, because she was acquainted with Samantha. Not friends, but they were friendly. He was about to count the register when he saw a message from Tara. *Perry, I am very flattered, but could we talk about it in person?*

Are you fucking kidding me? A seventeen-year-old is

rejecting me now. She's not old enough to drive past midnight, and she has the gall to say no to dinner.

Sure. Want to make it the motel again?

Yes, please.

I will be there in thirty. I will call for the reservation in the meantime and text you the room number. Although she said no to dinner, Perry still wanted to have sex with her. She was gorgeous in his mind, and he was stressed out.

He counted the money, made sure it was enough, and left the kiosk. He noticed that Michael Thompson cornered an employee, and there was nothing to do for that unlucky person, just pray it ended fast. He had no idea who the employee was, just another countless face in the Brine County Mall. He made his way to his van and called the motel. He texted *Room 12* to Tara.

After they did the deed, they were under the covers, and Perry was looking up at the celling. The rush was not the same anymore for the two of them, not after Perry admitted to liking her. He could sense that she was uncomfortable. "Elephant in the room. So where do you stand for dinner?"

"Look Perry, I liked what we were doing, but…"

Liked what we were doing as in past tense. I fucked this up, and I do not trust that she will not tell anybody about this. Her father is friends with Michael Thompson. Am I supposed to take her out?

"Before you say anything, Tara, I really like you, not just hooking up or having a good time. I want to have a relationship with you."

"That is so sweet and cute, but our age difference bothers me. I'm still in high school, and you could be going to graduate school. I will not make it awkward when we work together, but I don't think we should do this anymore."

"You know what? I don't feel like fighting with you over this. You're right."

"Okay, good, we agree. You will make some woman very happy one day. You are too nice not to."

You obviously don't know me, sweetheart. I think I might have to kill her after all. Perry was trying to figure how to do the murder. He was not in his shed, there were no weapons, and there was no way to hide the body. He was thinking if he could take her body out of his room to his car or could do it at her house, but he was still unsure how well she knew the Thompsons.

"I have one question for you, Tara." They were both getting dressed, and he was looking for some blunt object to hit her with. The lamp on the nightstand might do the trick.

"Yes, what's your question?"

"How well do you know the Thompsons?"

"What is your obsession with them? I know they are power hungry, and they are rough around the edges, but they are just the owners of the mall."

"You didn't answer my question." He got closer to her.

She was becoming very uncomfortable. "Fine. My father is good friends with Michael Thompson. He might come over our house a couple times a year, and I never really met Bruce. I am not going to tell them about us, if that's what you mean. Jesus, what, are you going to kill me?"

Perry stopped inching closer. *What the fuck is the matter with me? She did nothing wrong, and anyway, I can't just start killing people.*

"You are right. I am so sorry, and I am not going to tell anybody either. Can I kiss you one last time?"

"Sure, but I better be going." As they kissed, he wanted to strangle her. He still did not trust her, but it took every fiber in his body to do nothing. After the kiss, she left the room without saying a word, barely surviving being with Perry.

The next week passed, and Freddie and Chris killed two more people. Perry sat both killings out, but he knew at night he would have the customer.

Freddie messaged him around ten o'clock. *We have the customer. Ready when you are.*

Perry had a great dinner, and the cherry on top of his night was going to be what was waiting in the shed. He pulled up to Freddie's house, noticed that Chris was already there, walked through the garage to the backyard, and knocked on the door of the shed.

"Who's there?" said Chris in a woman's voice.

"Open the door." Perry was overjoyed, but he did not want to sound like a woman. The door opened. She still had the sack on her head, barely making audible sentences. He threw his mask on. The two others already had theirs, and they waited about twenty minutes when she started screaming. He walked toward her but turned around to say to Freddie and Chris, "Thank you for making this possible, guys."

"Our pleasure," said Freddie.

Perry yanked the bag off her head and saw the face, the face that made him want to commit murder in the first place, and he slapped her as hard as he could. Freddie and Chris stood up. They never hit a woman before, none of them. They were used to beating men to death, but they killed women quickly, without torture. The customer screamed and started crying. That part was routine. He held his hand up high for Freddie and Chris and said, "I won't do it again."

     John P. Burdi

The customer managed to say, "Who are you guys?"

Perry took his mask off. "Remember me, you fucking bitch."

"No, please, let me go. I did nothing wrong. Please, I have a family. Don't let my kids grow up without a mother."

Perry said, "Let me enlighten you about who I am. Remember a couple months ago when my kiosk at the mall had no chocolate ice cream, but you would not let it go. You kept arguing with me, threatening to call corporate. You were making such a big deal that we did not have a product that you wanted, but you kept talking and making me feel like a little piece of shit. Well, in here, it's reversed. You are the little piece of shit, I am right, and you are wrong. I am God, and you are nobody."

"You went through all of this because we had an argument?"

"No. God dammit, didn't you listen at all? I am doing this because you made me feel lower than anybody before, you fucking fat slob. I am about to change that. People must be punished for their sins. In the real world they are not, but here they are! We are the real sheriffs of Brine County. We punish those who will not be punished in the outside. You see, out there, people of authority are not put in order, not like in here."

"I know Bruce Thompson. You can't get away with this."

"You think we are going to let you go when you mention his name? Now we have to kill you to save ourselves. You made that part easier to swallow, and I will sleep like a baby tonight." Perry took out a large Ziploc bag, the biggest you could buy. He walked closer to the customer and asked, "That day, why did you care so much?"

"Because it is my job. Bruce wanted me to get a rise out of you, because he does not trust you. I was supposed to act out, but you are a little piece of shit, so it made it easier."

Perry turned around to Freddie and Chris. They were captivated with all this. "You hear that, boys? Did you know Bruce did things like that?"

"No clue," said Chris. Freddie shook his head.

"That answer still is not good enough, which is why I am sending you to your salvation. Oh, and when you are in hell, Bruce will be coming soon. I can't wait until you guys meet down there."

Perry placed the bag over her head, and the bag closed around her neck. He placed a couple rubber bands over that, making it extremely tight. Freddie said, "Do you know her name?"

"I don't give a shit." She was not trying to fight it. She knew if the bag did not work, they were going to kill her anyway. Her tears were filling up the bag. He took a chair and sat in front of her, watching her suffocate slowly. He was looking in her big eyes, making sure the last thing she saw was his face.

After killing the customer, Perry felt that he was turning a new leaf and becoming the sheriff of Brine County. October came around, and with new members of the Myrmidons, he could make his move to end the reign of Bruce and Michael Thompson. Although killing Virginia only took about a day of planning, this took much longer, and he came to one conclusion: burn Brine to the ground.

Perry had the inspiration from Bruce Thompson himself. In the beginning of October, Perry was working one night when he saw Bruce walking the mall floors with people in construction helmets. They came up to his kiosk, and Bruce did the talking for his party. "Ah, Mr. Miller, give us a quart of the flavor of the day."

 John P. Burdi

"Want any cups and spoons with that, sir?"

"You fucking kidding me? You think we are going to eat that with our hands?"

The rest of the party was laughing, and Perry looked at Bruce. He turned around, cracked his neck, and pushed his glasses against the top of his nose. He filled the quart container with s'mores, the flavor of the day, and proceeded to check them out.

I wish I could throw it on the ground, and you and your little fuckfest can go and fight for the ice cream. What a prick this guy is. I am going to kill him someday, hopefully tonight.

"As a gift, I present you with our flavor of the day. Please enjoy."

"Finally, some hospitality from you. If you showed that in the first place, I would never have been suspicious of you."

Yeah, how's that fat asshole friend of yours? She's buried somewhere waiting for you. I saw her life leave her eyes, and I slept like a baby that night.

"I guess I am a slow learner, sir. Who are the people in your party?"

Bruce looked at Perry with the utmost disdain, but these people were not mall employees, not yet, so Bruce could not show his true colors. He said, "These fine people are contractors. We are adding some restaurants on the outside of my mall. Let's call it Restaurant Row, and these fine people will be building my restaurants. Sometimes it might be easier to burn something down to the ground before you can build onto it. This mall was built on uneven property. It is hard to add on, and that's why I am hiring the best contractors I can find. Now if you will excuse me, Mr. Miller, have a good night." Bruce and his party were on their way, once again not paying.

Burn something down to the ground before you can build onto it. I like that. It's the first thing he has ever said that I agree with, but he would never burn down his mall, not in a million years. He needs it to show off his power, but let him try and stop me from burning this hell hole down to the ground where it belongs.

Perry messaged Freddie and Chris the good news that he figured out a plan. Burn it to the ground. He saw a familiar person out of the corner of his eye, a person he thought he would never see in the mall again. Julia was walking up to the kiosk with Duane.

As they approached the counter, Perry made no movements. He was like a predator waiting to catch his prey. Even though Duane was much bigger and faster, Perry was smarter, and he knew at that moment that they would be getting into another altercation. Not that night but soon. He let Julia do the talking.

"Hey, friend, I know this is going to be awkward for you, but Duane wanted to stop by and apologize to you. We are not seeing each other, but he wanted to make amends, and he felt bad for what he did to you that night."

Felt bad for what? I was the one who beat him. I knocked him out, he gave me a black eye, and the only thing I regret about that night is that I did not finish the job, and this little fuck is still breathing. Why the fuck are you walking with him, Julia? This guy can hurt you.

Perry said, "Well, I guess everything is all right as long as Julia gets an apology. She was the one who was hurt."

By the way, Duane, we went on a date. It did not end like I wanted it to, but I bet she had a better dinner with me than anything you ever did for her. Why is he really here?

Duane began his pathetic excuse for an apology. "The first person I would thank would have to be Bruce Thompson. He told me the right thing was to come back here and apologize to you two. For everything I did to you guys that night, I am truly sorry, and I hope that it does not affect our future of working together."

Oh my fucking God. He is coming back to the Defense. Bruce has to have his hands on everything, and I guarantee his job is to watch me and Julia after that night that we did the job of the Defense. He thinks that's the reason why he is losing supporters. He's right about being suspicious of me but wrong in what he thinks. He has no idea the Myrmidons exist. Well, he will soon.

Julia said, "To be honest with you, Duane, I don't want to talk with you ever again. I don't care if you work here, but leave me alone. Can you handle that?"

She is amazing. She has more balls than Duane. Hell, she might have more balls than me. Maybe I should still pursue her.

"Yeah, that is understandable. You have my word," said Duane.

Perry did something that made him feel like he had won the fight. He extended his hand for Duane to shake it without saying a word, and Duane shook it. Not a word between the two.

Julia broke the silence. "Okay, well, I am going back to work. See you guys later. I'll talk to you later, Perry." She walked back to her store, and Perry and Duane both watched her. Then they had their real conversation.

"You know if you do something stupid inside this mall, I am going to have to punish you by the orders of Bruce and Michael Thompson."

Perry looked into his eyes and countered, "If you do something stupid in this mall or to Julia, I am going to have to punish you by the orders of God."

"What the fuck does that mean?"

"I wouldn't worry about it." Perry said nothing about the Myrmidons. Duane might tell Bruce, and he would be taken out. What he said was more than enough.

"Oh, I'll talk to you later, Perry. You guys going out now or something?"

"It's none of your business."

"It will be soon. In the meantime, we are always watching." Duane pointed to his eyes and the camera on the ceiling. Perry was not amused.

Yeah, I'm always watching too, you cocksucker.

About ten minutes later, Freddie came up to the counter and looked anxious. "Perry, my man, so you figured it out. Should I call a meeting of the Myrmidons? It will be the first in our short history."

"Yeah, you and Chris call it, but we must wear our masks, even us. Nobody is supposed to know who we are in case somebody is on the inside with the mall. Call the meeting in front of the shed at eleven. Tell people to carpool so it doesn't look like you are throwing a party. See you in a bit, Freddie."

Freddie turned and walked away, sending the message to Chris to send it to the others.

Perry had other news for the meeting. Not only was he planning to burn the mall down, but he wanted to do it on Black Friday when the most customers were there. He wanted the Myrmidons to crash a party. The Thompsons's third brother had a son shortly before his death, and the nephew of Bruce and Michael was going to be married. When Perry had dinner with George and Lauren a while back, she brought up the wedding, and the bride was an acquaintance of hers. *A small world,* thought Perry. The Myrmidons were going to crash the wedding shower. They were not going to be men there, which meant no Defense, and they would become visual to the public for the first time.

Perry arrived at Freddie's at around 10:50 and then went to Applebee's and had a drink with Julia. They talked about how they did not trust Duane and should watch him whenever he started at the mall. The night ended with a hug and nothing more. They were friends.

He put on his mask before he got out of his car, making sure nobody saw him. He walked through the garage and through the fence along the path, and he saw everyone—all twenty-one members of the Myrmidons, including himself. They built an army, an untrained one but an obedient one.

He walked to the front of the shed to complete the Unholy Trinity and took a seat. He pointed to Freddie and Chris, motioning them to begin. They were the only members who were known throughout the group. They had to recruit people, and they could not wear the masks in the mall. He was not sure if the other members knew each other, and he knew for a fact that nobody in the group knew that Perry Miller was the leader.

Freddie summoned the assembly. "Everyone listen, our fearless leader has come up with a plan to get rid of the Thompsons and the mall. Let's hear the leader out, and if we have questions or agree to it, let's do it."

Perry was unsure if Freddie was being sarcastic with "fearless leader." He knew that if Chris was speaking, he would be sarcastic. He did not care. He felt that everybody there respected him. He purchased a voice changer that fit in his mask to make sure that nobody could tell who he was, and the voice changer made him sound like a cross between Darth Vader and Bane, which he was enthusiastic about.

Perry told them everything about how he wanted to plan his attack on the mall during Black Friday of that holiday season. How he wanted to crash the bridal shower of the Thompson nephew to make the Myrmidons public. His end to his rousing speech was the name of the operation: Tis the Season. It was November 10, and Black Friday was fifteen days away. Everything had to be precise.

The Myrmidons in the audience began clapping and chanting. They were all in agreement and planning their move in November, the holiday season. Before the end of the session, Perry leaned over to Freddie and whispered, "I need you and Chris to get four new recruits, and they are going to be our guinea pigs for this party. Choose the biggest scumbags you can find. Any relation to the Defense would be perfect."

Freddie obliged, and everything was in order for the Myrmidons.

For the first time in his life, Perry knew his purpose: to end the Thompson's foothold on Brine County. The meeting was adjourned.

10.

THE SPREE

Perry was walking on air. He felt invincible, and he felt that he had all the power in Brine County. Fewer people were supporting the Thompsons, and he was a large reason why. The fake drug scene pointed a finger at the Defense, and now members of the Defense were disappearing, about two a week. Perry had a falling out with his family. George and Julia did not seem to matter anymore, he was not talking to Tara anymore, he was not applying for jobs anymore, but he was killing, and he was getting good at it.

Working at the Brine County Mall after November 1 meant that you had to work in a Christmastime nightmare. The mall had a gigantic tree up in the middle of everything. The kiosk was about one hundred feet behind it, so Perry had a view of the tree, and the only view he wanted was to see it burn to the ground. The mall and all the customers seemed to neglect Thanksgiving, which angered Perry to the extreme. It was one of his favorite days of the year, enjoying a dinner with family, simple yet powerful, but nowadays he did not have much of a family to enjoy a dinner with.

With Thanksgiving being treated like the orphan child, Christmas was coming like a freight train. There were more shoppers each day, and each shopper wanted a great deal from the store even if the deal was the same or cheaper online. More shoppers were more problems. More members of the Defense on shifts meant more eyes were watching Perry, Freddie, and Chris.

The hours were increasing by the day. Soon after Thanksgiving, the mall extended the hours every week. The week before Christmas had hours until midnight even on weekdays. Black Friday, the new Thanksgiving for retail, had the mall open for twenty-four hours with no breaks, and it opened on Thanksgiving at three o'clock. No Thanksgiving dinners for those unlucky employees. No seeing their families or enjoying good times, just being in a store and checking people out on useless items. The customers did not care. They did not apologize to the employees. In fact, the employees were treated much worse. God forbid if they did not have the item that the circular had, or the sale was over and the customer would fight to save five dollars. That was the norm for Perry, Julia, and other employees. The mall was closed the entire day only one day a year: Christmas. It used to be closed for Easter, but that was before stores signed a deal with the devil to be open during the holidays, because they believed people wanted to shop instead of spend time with their families. That was the paradox that angered Perry the most. People shopped for their families instead of spending time with them on holidays.

Music was played nonstop and not music that was enjoyable. Perry heard "Sleigh Ride" about fifteen times a shift, which made him angrier, more miserable, and have the beliefs of Ebenezer Scrooge instead of Tiny Tim. All day and night long he heard Christmas music, but he could not sit and enjoy it. He had to serve people. He supposed the music was for the customers and not the employees, and Bruce Thompson made it worse. Every Christmas in the mall, he wore a red or green blazer. He had the spirit out to the extreme, but he was playing for the masses. Hanukah was also celebrated but to a much smaller scale. There was a menorah beyond the Christmas tree. Michael Thompson dressed as Santa for all the children to take pictures; he fit the suit to perfection and had a voice like Santa's would be if he existed. Christmas was right around the corner at the Brine County Mall, but this year was different.

On November 15, Perry noticed something disturbing. A couple was holding hands in his line, but the girl was in a different league from the guy. The guy had a much worse physical appearance. He was shorter and heavier. The girl was drop-dead gorgeous, and Perry was single, like usual. No girls on the horizon, but he felt like he needed to figure out the mystery of beauty and the beast in front of him. Jealousy was not the word for what Perry was feeling. The couple made their order, and instead of turning around and retrieving it, Perry said, "Hey, let me ask you this question." He was only looking at the girl. The guy meant nothing to him, and he only wanted to show him contempt. "Why is a girl like you with that ugly, fat piece of shit?"

The girl looked bewildered and was insulted. The guy tried to jump the counter, which Perry wanted him to try, because he knew he could take him. The girl grabbed the guy at the back of his sweatshirt and pulled him back like a fisherman catching a fish.

"Not only was that one of the rudest things I have ever heard in my life, and not only was that one of the most inappropriate things I have ever been asked, but you could not be more wrong. My boyfriend is the nicest, most mature, and dignified person I have ever met, and if you are wondering why I am with him instead of being with somebody like you, don't look too far. You are not even worth fighting with, and fuck you!!!"

I was just asking a question. She acted like I killed the fucking guy, which to her surprise I just might. They all take me for some asshole, and pretty soon, I'm going to be running this county.

The girl's outburst caused a scene. Some onlookers watched and applauded her, but Perry was looking at the guy, the ugly, fat piece of shit. It was clear to him what he was going to do, and hearing "Silver Bells" made it easier.

It was near closing time, and he had a plan. The time was 9:24. Holiday hours were not in effect yet but would be next week. He took the keys out of the register and shut off the lights to the kiosk. He ran to follow the couple but stayed out of sight. He saw the guy's car. His girlfriend took a separate car for some reason, but he saw which car he went into and texted Freddie and Chris immediately. *Idk if you guys are working tonight, but some ugly, fat piece of shit got into a blue Elantra across from the Brine County Mall entrance. Please follow him, and update me on the whereabouts. Thanks.*

That should do the trick. That's what happens when somebody worse than me gets a girlfriend.

Perry ran back inside, and to his amazement, there was nobody at the kiosk, not even a member of the Defense. He put the keys back into the register and started to count it to make closing easier. There was a text from Chris. *Freddie is off tonight. I see him right now on the phone. I can follow. Do you want me to kidnap him?*

Stop asking these questions over text, you fucking moron. How many times do I have to remind him?

     J o h n   P.   B u r d i

No, I can take care of it myself. More discreet next time.

He knew Chris would not answer him until he gave him the location. He got insulted easily. He went into the back and started cleaning the spoons and containers. He dropped the money in the safe, went to his car, and waited for Chris. He started driving around the parking lot of the mall and noticed a lot more members of the Defense, which reminded him to text Steve, *Hey, it's been a while. I need you to get four members of the Defense who might turn on the Thompsons.* Steve did not help much since switching the camera view. He gave addresses to the database, but he did not even know about the shed. He was not at the meeting, but he was still important in the operations of the Myrmidons. Most important, he wanted to ruin the Defense.

Steve answered quickly. *I'm not really sure, but I can ask around carefully. When you need them by?*

The 20th. There is a wedding shower I want to crash. Could use members of the Defense with the expertise for this. Firearms are necessary. Although the Defense did not carry guns, Perry knew that Steve had some, with his background and experience.

I wish I had more time in advance for this. We need to talk in person or something.

Yeah, I'm sorry about that. I will call you tomorrow for the details.

Have a good night.

Perry loved working with Steve. He got to the point and was professional. There was no drama, not like Freddie and Chris, who still did not get back to Perry, who was starting to feel nervous about everything.

Twenty minutes later, Chris messaged him. *Found the address, twenty minutes away. He's hard to keep up with. Apartment. Nobody else there from the looks of it.*

Thank you, Chris.

Good luck. I'm getting high if you need me.

What a joke. I should have done everything with just Freddie. Where the hell is he anyway?

Twenty minutes later, Perry was in the parking lot of the apartment complex. He never went into somebody's home and killed them inside. He had no intention of bringing him to the shed. No lion mask for this particular situation. He looked around for cameras but didn't see any, and with his hood up, his face was unrecognizable. The only thing he had in his car was the baseball bat from the shed. He took that a week ago in case he needed it outside the shed, so with the bat, he walked up to the door. It was on the first level, easier to run away. He stared at the door, unwilling to do anything, but there was no turning back.

He knocked on the door with the bat, and it quickly opened. The chain was up, but when the door opened a couple of inches, that was enough room for Perry. He slammed the door with the bat, and it flew open. The chain broke, the guy fell down, and the door hit his lip. Perry ran in, closed the door, and hit the guy across the stomach with the bat. The yell as not as loud as he thought it was going to be. He grabbed the hood of the sweatshirt and picked him up. He had his arms wrapped around the giant torso and almost bear hugged him. He slammed him down on the coffee table. Perry thought he was dead. The table was sure as broken, and there was a lot of blood on the floor.

Perry was not hurt after performing the wrestling move. He quickly stood up and picked up the bat again. The guy was face down, his hands moving slowly. Perry began making his head into a smashed pumpkin. He was yelling, "And you get to have a girlfriend, are you fucking kidding me, you ugly, fat piece of shit? What a fucking

     John P. Burdi

joke." Perry stopped and realized he was talking to himself. The guy was long dead, blood was everywhere, and bone and brains were all over the floor. The scene was most unpleasant. He shut off the lights and made it seem like he had on the television on too loud.

Shit, I have to get out of here. I have been here for too long. Hope nobody heard. I was louder than he was. I thought he would cry like a girl. Good, well, now you don't have a girlfriend.

Perry opened the door and ran. He took the bat with him, and he was not wearing gloves. He did not want to leave it there or fingerprints. Granted, there was blood all over him and the bat, but he ran to his car. He got in and started driving casually. Nobody made a scene by calling the cops or screaming. He did not want to make a scene with his car. He began to laugh as he drove, laughing like he was reminiscing with old friends about good times.

He made it to the main road and knew he was in the clear. He had averted being caught and was driving home for a good night's sleep. He wanted to listen to some classic rock. He was trying to tune into Cream or Led Zeppelin when he saw two big, bright headlights in his rearview mirror. *Shit, that can't be the police. I'll be fucked.* There was all the blood on his shirt and some on his face, which he did not mind to clean off; it made him think of himself as some kind of warrior, a crusader. Not to mention the weapon he used was in his back seat. He did not think the car was the police, because he was doing about twelve miles over, and he still did not see blue and red lights flashing.

The car was getting closer, and he clearly saw that it was not the police. It was a Mercedes with new license plates. The driver wanted to see what he could do on the open road, but Perry had other ideas. The Mercedes was riding his bumper, and he slowed down to get under the skin of the driver, but it was to no avail. A driver was not going to bully him this time. Instead of braking and moving completely, he pulled over on the shoulder to let the car pass and counted, "One, two, and three." He slammed his foot on the gas pedal, and he thought his van was going to explode, but more miraculous feats had happened. The Mercedes was doing at least 60 mph, so he had to try and get his old van to 70 before the Mercedes was gone. He viewed his speedometer and increased from 20 to 30 to 40. "Please, don't shut down. I have to catch this prick." He had no plan but could figure out something on the fly. He seemed to get away with everything lately. When people were not expecting to see anything, a lot went past their eyes.

He was beginning to catch up with the Mercedes. He missed his turn about half a mile ago, but he did not care. Everything in Brine County seemed like a twenty-five-minute drive, and he was free that night. He wanted to prove a point. He thought of himself as the new sheriff in town, and he wanted other people to realize that too. He shone his high beams at the perpetrator and then made his move. He tried passing him on the left. He looked in the window of the Mercedes and saw that the driver was terrified. He was even with the car. He was playing a game of chicken, and he was lucky because no other cars were on the road. *It's like I really am supposed to be the guy in town. Let's see if this guy is going to stop me.*

Perry slammed his foot on the gas. He did it so rough that he was standing up. He saw the speedometer; it was around 80 mph, and the limit was 45. He drove in front of the Mercedes and slammed the brakes. He was now parallel on the road. He thought there was a good chance the Mercedes was going to pass him on one side, but the car had a problem. It was in a ditch and had rammed into a tree.

He parked his van on the shoulder of the road, got out, and took out his bat. He approached the Mercedes and was relieved to see that the driver was still alive, but the car was totaled. The tree was damaged too, but Perry did not care. He looked in the window of the Mercedes, and the driver had his head on the airbag. He chuckled a little and tapped on the window. He tapped to Beethoven's Fifth Symphony.

The driver, who probably had a concussion, lifted his head and yelled in pain. One of his arms were broken, and it looked like his nose was too. He was wearing a suit, his hair was in a business fashioned part, but now it was a mess. The driver was in his thirties, extremely slender. There was a lot of blood but not as much on Perry.

He tapped the window again, and the driver let out such a bellow that Perry wanted to run back to his van and drive home. Instead of doing that, he realized that the driver was not going to open the door, so he used his bat. He swung at the back passenger window, and it shattered. He reached in and used the power locks to open the door of the passenger window so the driver could not use the power locks to close them. The screaming did not stop so Perry tried putting an end to it. "Shut the fuck up. Jesus Christ." That did nothing.

Perry was on the driver's door and slowly opened it. The driver could do nothing, not with a concussion and a broken arm. Perry reached for the driver's seat belt and unbuckled it. "There, there, you're all right. Now calm down, I'm trying to get you out of this ugly heap."

The driver gave him his left arm that was not broken, and Perry pulled him out but threw him down in what seemed like one motion. The screaming would never stop. Perry had to make this quick. "You know why I tried to pull you over?"

The driver looked as bewildered as ever and did not understand the question but tried answering it. "What are you talking about? Why are you covered in blood?"

"Well, my affairs before this incident are none of your concern, so please do not worry about it. I will clean my clothes when I get home. The blood is not mine, and do not ask me that question again. Let's recap. I was minding my own business driving home, and I noticed your high beams were shining right through my car. You know they make them so illuminating these days. Those lights bothered me, and then you driving like a fucking lunatic practically riding my bumper. You might have even tapped me, and then you decide to pass me on the left. So not right, not even close, and for that, you must be punished."

"Are you fucking kidding me? I pass you, so you drive me off the road, my arm is broken, and my car is destroyed. How are you going to pay for that with that piece of shit van!"

"My payment is with my bat. You think you control the roads because you drive a Mercedes. Oh, excuse me, because you used to drive a Mercedes. It gives you no right to speed and drive that fast. It gives you no right to take advantage of people with vehicles like mine. I control the fucking roads, I control the fucking town, and it's about time people realized it. I am fucking God in here!" Perry knelt down in front of the driver, face to face, but the driver was looking down. Perry had the upper hand.

"Who the fuck are you? We both know the Thompsons run this place," the driver said with desperation.

Perry growled at the driver. He made a clicking with his mouth and began to touch his chin, thinking what to do. "You know what? I don't have time for this, and I'll tell you something else. Pretty soon the Thompsons are going to be powerless. They are not going to have a mall to run or anything, but too bad you are not going to see it." Perry held the bat over his own head and took a mighty swing across the driver's face.

"The Thompsons are fucking nothing compared for what I have planned for this crummy town, and fuck you and your Mercedes, you fucking sniveling little prick."

He was no longer kneeling, and the screaming stopped. He hit him three more times for good measure. He had killed two people on November 15 in the span of twenty minutes. Some kind of killing spree and no witness. He left the driver the way he was, ran back to his van, and drove home. This time, he was going to have a good night's sleep.

Perry awoke the next day and received fantastic news from Steve in a voicemail. He found four members of the Defense who would turn on the Thompsons. Better yet, Steve had two firearms that he could spare for this occasion. He needed to pick them up, but he would have to go earlier to the party. He forwarded the four members of the Defense about the plan and the four members who would convert thanks to Freddie and Chris. They had to make their fastest recruitment yet, so they had their work cut out for them.

On November 16, Perry had one job he wanted to succeed with: confronting Duane. Duane was an enigma. Perry trusted him less than Freddie and Chris. He did not trust him with Julia.

Perry knew that Duane's job after being hired by the Thompsons a second time, which was unusual, was to watch

Perry and, when the timing was perfect, eliminate him. That had been done before at the Brine County Mall; some members of the Defense were to watch specific employees and, when the time was perfect, strike like a lion attacking a gazelle without questions. He was one of the few who questioned why the police force did nothing when it came to the mall. He knew Bruce and Michael Thompson were involved, but he did not know how much and in what way.

Perry got the address of Duane's home from Julia. She questioned him, and he told her that he wanted to make it up to him and buy him a drink. Whether she believed him was another story. He planned the entire day. Duane was too strong and too fast, and he won the first time because he turned his head. That gave Perry an idea; he needed to distract him like he did the first time. Steve still had the guns, and Perry was not planning on getting them that day. He could not win a fight against Duane. He was not sure if he could kill him with the bat, like the boy and the motorist the previous night, but he did know that he was much smarter.

The best news was that there were no witnesses from the previous night. A few people saw a dark figure in the apartment complex but not enough to make an identification. The police were stumped when they saw the dead body of the motorist, his head bashed in, arm broken, and car totaled. There were no other cars in sight, so they figured it was an accident. Everything was going in Perry's favor, and he felt that Brine County was in his hands.

His neighbors were holding him down. The noise and the amount of cars were unbearable. Something had to be done. The planning was simple. He required only one item, and it was sold pretty much anywhere, but he needed somebody to drive him. The day flew by.

 John P. Burdi

Perry had time to grab a cup of coffee with George, although they did not speak much. Perry was thinking, and George was becoming more serious with Lauren. He wanted to tell Perry about it, but Perry was thinking about more pressing matters like how to kill Duane.

Dinner was even pleasant for Perry. His parents stopped questioning his career goals or where he was applying for jobs or anything of value.

Around ten o'clock, Freddie drove Perry to Duane's house with a bottle of Jack Daniels. Duane lived in a development with other members of the Defense in a neighborhood much nicer than Perry's. Perry he knew there had to be no scene, no running from an apartment with a bloody bat and bloody shirt, no car accident in the middle of the road with a dead body. He found the house with no problem. He hoped that there was nobody else in the house who would make everything difficult.

As Perry was getting out of the car, he said, "You know when to pick me up?"

"Yeah, in like an hour and a half," said Freddie.

"Good. I will be near the development entrance. Do not pick me up at his house, you understand?"

"Yeah, no problem, but are you going to be able to walk there? It's like half a mile from here."

"I think I can manage. Just remind me, okay?"

"Sure. You are like amazing with this kind of stuff."

"We'll see if this works, and then I will admit that I am amazing. See you in a bit."

Perry closed the car door and walked up to the front door of Duane's house. He rang the doorbell, then knocked four times, and the door opened, but Perry was not staring at Duane. He was staring at a girl he had not talked to in some time.

"Tara! What are you doing here?" To say Perry was surprised was not enough. This could ruin his blueprint for the night.

"I am kind of seeing Duane. What are you doing here?"

Seriously, is this some kind of a joke from Bruce Thompson? He knew she kissed me on the cheek. Is this his way of telling Duane to find out as much information on me as possible? And of course she's eighteen now.

"Well, Duane and I had an altercation a few months back, and he apologized to me, and I brushed him off about it. I was kind of hoping to smooth everything out."

After Perry said that, Duane appeared down the hallway. He said, "We'll let him in. Let's see what he has to say."

Holy shit. She has been telling him everything we did. This has to go faster than expected. Oh my God, this might fail.

Duane led Perry to his kitchen table overlooking the backyard.

Perry noticed an escape route, so he said, "Beyond your fence, where does that lead to?"

"What?" Duane looked at him, puzzled. This became an unusual night now for all three of them. Perry did not care that they were seeing each other. He was more upset about whether Tara was going to tell him anything.

"I'm just curious. This is a big neighborhood. Is this one big circle or something?"

"Yeah. You hop my fence and go right, it leads to the main road. To the left leads to more woods. You have any more questions on the geography of my development?"

Geography. That's a big fucking word for your vocabulary.

"No, not at the moment, but I have something I think you might like. A drink. Get three shot glasses."

Duane had a smirk on his face. He began to undermine the randomness of everything, and that made Perry hate him even more. *Just bring some alcohol, and he forgets that a complete stranger is in his house. Fucking moron.*

Duane motioned for Tara to go to the cabinet to get the shot glasses. He asked her, "You think you can handle Jack?"

"I can as long as your candy ass can."

Duane hollered, "This little fag can't handle Julia. Jack might be tougher for him."

I can't wait until like thirty minutes, you arrogant prick. Perry cracked his neck at the previous statement. If Tara had not been there, he would already be fighting with Duane. It was lucky for Perry that she was at his house.

"Okay. I can both take you assholes under the table."

Tara said, "I was just joking. Perry. You set yourself up for that one. You gave me no choice." She passed out the glasses, and Perry was sure not to touch anything except for the one he was using. He poured the first round, and he needed to make them feel comfortable.

"One, two, three, shot!" The first round was a triumphant affair, smooth, everything went down okay, even though Perry hated Jack Daniels.

Duane wiped his lips. "So you want to apologize about that cheap shot you used on me?"

Lord give me the strength not to do anything yet. This little rat is making it tough to hold back.

"Yes, I am. I have to say that I am sorry for what I did and not accepting your apology at the mall." Of course he did not mean one word of that pathetic excuse of an apology, but Duane was uninterested anyway. Tara was only concerned with taking selfies with the shots. Perry poured the second round of shots. He figured he needed about two more after the second round. The second round went down about as smooth as the first, and this time Perry was smiling. The conversation stopped after

Perry apologized. Duane could care less why he was there anyway.

Duane hollered, "One, two, three, shot!"

After the third round, Perry went to the refrigerator to see if Duane had any food. Duane did not oppose Perry looking in the fridge. Perry took the bottle of Jack Daniels with him.

At this point, Tara was tipsy, and Perry was having trouble looking at the food in the refrigerator and laughing a lot more than usual. Duane said, "Is there anything good in there?"

"No, not really. You need to go food shopping, man." Perry walked back to the table, bringing nothing except the bottle. *I might have to increase the amount of shots. Only one way to find out.*

Duane gave a sarcastic laugh, "This guy comes to my house with some booze, and he talks about how I need to go food shopping. You're probably right, but I don't need food as long as I have some Jack." Duane took the bottle out of his hand and began drinking out of it. He took a big gulp, much more than one shot, and slammed the bottle on the table. He took the bottle and poured shots for himself and Tara. Tara drank it right away, but Perry held the shot in front of his mouth but did not drink.

Tara stood up and went to the couch in the television room. She looked at Perry and lay down. Duane took the bottle once more and drank from it a second time.

Perry stood up and tipped the bottle, making it easier for Duane to drink. After his second gulp, Perry looked at Duane in the eyes.

Duane felt there was something wrong. "What did you do?" He looked at Perry in a pathetic and concerned manner. He grabbed Perry by his shirt, but there was no force.

"I gave you rat poison, you little prick. When I was looking in your refrigerator, I blocked what I was doing with the door. You did not look at me, and your only concern was getting more to drink. Most stores sell rat poison. It was easy to come by, and soon you and Tara will be dead."

"You son of a…"

Duane was already dead. He fell out of his chair and onto the wooden floor of his kitchen. Tara was dead on the couch.

Perry stood up and took the bottle and the shot glass he touched with him. He said his goodbyes to Duane and Tara and went out the back door. He hopped the fence and looked at his phone. Freddie had messaged him. *You ready? Is everything going alright?*

Perry struggled to text back. *Yeah. Be where you're supposed to be. I'll be there soon.* Perry took a right turn like Duane said and kept walking. He was behind the homes of members of the Defense, and nobody saw him. There was no struggle in Duane's home, just two dead bodies at Perry's hands. He knew that whoever investigated the murder scene would conclude that the deaths were caused by poison, but nobody knew it was him. He reached Freddie's car.

Freddie said, "Did you do it? Is he gone?"

"Yes, it was simple. I could not beat him in a fight again, but it was easy to poison him. Well, both of them."

"Both of them. Who else was there?"

"Some unlucky girl."

During the drive, Perry tossed the shot glass out of the car, getting rid of the evidence. He told Freddie to drive to a bridge, and there he tossed out the bottle of Jack Daniels.

I'm getting pretty good at this thing.

On November 17, Perry and the rest of the Unholy Trinity were planning for the following day when the Myrmidons would become public. They were planning to kidnap a member of the Defense, record their torturing, and send it to Bruce Thompson. As intricate as that plan might be, the kidnapping at the bridal party was much more difficult. This kidnapping would not take place in public, but nevertheless, planning was crucial. The three of them agreed who the victim was going to be, but the actual abduction was going to take the three of them. Nobody else in the Myrmidons was told. Chris had a camera at his house, so he set up the tripod ahead of time.

It was going to be done around ten at night. The three of them followed the schedule of the member of the Defense closely. They knew which nights he went home early and knew to make sure that Bruce Thompson was not going to be there. They had a plan for him during the night of the end of the revolution. Well, Perry had a plan for him. They made sure that they got plenty of sleep that night. This was going to be the most difficult plan they ever had.

Perry did not do much during the day of the eighteenth. There was not much for him to do. He was done applying for jobs and anything that was productive. He wanted to stop by the church to see the priest again, but he felt that bridge was burned, so during the day, he waited in his room until Freddie stopped by to pick him up around nine.

His parents were not concerned anymore. They were not sure about Freddie being a good friend to their son, but he was too old for them to worry about his friends, and they understood that concept.

When Perry was walking to Freddie's car, he felt doubts that he never felt when living this life. For the first time, he was unsure if this was going to work, but he did not have a choice now. It was too late. He opened the door,

     John P. Burdi

and they nodded to each other. Perry noticed Chris in the backseat. About five minutes into the drive, Perry said, "So how much did this car cost?"

"Fifteen hundred. Real piece of shit," said Freddie. The car was about fifteen years old and on its last legs, but this was going to be the last night that it was going to be driven. "I paid with cash a couple towns over, from some old guy, untraceable. The guy who actually bought it is some putz of the Defense that we are going to be using anyway. This checks out."

"Good. Any words, Chris?"

"No, except I did bring the masks, so when we pull into the driveway, we are wearing masks in a car that was bought a couple towns away by a guy who won't matter soon."

"See? You can teach useless pieces of shit a few things," said Freddie while laughing. Perry and Chris laughed too. The three of them were really coming together, forming some kind of serial killer team.

They arrived at the home of the member of Defense twelve minutes later. Perry had no idea how close this person lived to him. The house looked like a castle, and they knew the cameras were on the car, but they had the masks on, so it was impossible to tell who was in the car. "You two ready?" said Perry.

"Yes," they said in unison.

"Let's do this." Perry opened his car door, and one thought crossed his mind. *What if he is watching right now? He might have a piece on him.* There was only one way to find out. He ran to the front door and rang the doorbell. The two others went around and hopped the high fence. He jumped into the bushes, but he was not sure if the person was watching from inside. He was watching inside the bushes and, with the mask on, felt like a lion, hunting his prey, his behemoth prey. The door opened. The person looked around, stepped outside, turned around, and walked back into his house.

Perry heard the noise he needed to hear: a window breaking. He could tell the person was running to the back of the house, so he rang the doorbell again. Then he heard nothing. It was like existence ceased to exist. Nothing was happening. The waiting was agonizing, the unknown, the mystery. What was going to happen?

Silence fell to yelling on the intercom of the house that could be heard on the outside. Perry had no idea this home had that feature. He felt betrayed by Freddie and Chris for not finding out. This could draw attention from the neighbors. The man was saying, "Whoever the fuck is doing this, know that I am armed, and if you do not stop, I have every right to make you stop!"

Shit, everything is falling apart. I have to get in the house. Perry did the only thing he could think of. He rang the doorbell a third time, hoping that Freddie and Chris would already be in the house. He hid in the bushes again, but this time when the door opened, it was not a calm opening like expecting a package or knowing who rang the doorbell. This was violent, the door swung open in such a ferocity. The homeowner said nothing but was looking right at Perry. For the first time in Perry's young life, a person had a gun pointed in his direction. He was frightened, but the homeowner did not know about Freddie and Chris. The homeowner was walking closer to Perry, but then another glass shattered. The homeowner turned around and started running toward the back of the house.

Perry ran in before the door closed and yelled, "Behind you, you mother fucker!" He threw his mask off so the victim could see who was terrorizing him. The man turned around, and Perry knocked the gun out of his hand. Even without the gun, Perry knew he would never beat this behemoth in a brawl, but he did have Freddie and Chris.

Michael Thompson said, "Why, Mr. Miller, you little shit. You think you can invade my home? Hell, if I had known it was you, I would throw the gun away anyway, and with a little lion mask? Overcompensating for something. Oh well, let's see what you got." A fist the size of a shot put was coming for his head, and there was nothing he could do. Perry knew he was a poor fighter without having an advantage, and he had none. He fell, wishing the mountain of a man would not avalanche on top of him. He was getting destroyed, and the only thought he could manage was *where the fuck are Freddie and Chris?*

After blows to the head and stomach, Perry tried wiping his face, and to his amazement, there was not much blood. He noticed he was being picked up. Thompson held Perry over his head. "Mr. Miller, it seems to me that you have lost. Wait until my brother finds out about this surprise."

Perry now had the advantage. Freddie and Chris came running with frying pans. *Frying pans? That's the best these two could get?* Perry felt a release on his body, and he was making his way back down to the ground. Freddie and Chris were beating the titanic homeowner with frying pans. They hit him about ten times, and the homeowner was on the ground and was not moving. Perry raised his hand for them to stop.

"Where the fuck were you guys? He almost killed me, and I have no idea where he planned on throwing me."

"We needed to get something to fight him. We couldn't go against him with our hands. Hell, is that what you did?" said Freddie.

"This son of a bitch had a gun on me. I needed him to get rid of it."

Chris said, "All right, let's stop fighting. We need to bring good old Michael Thompson to the shed and tape this."

"For the first time, you are right, Chris. Sorry. Let's load him up," Perry said.

Chris looked at him with an "I told you so" look, and they began wrapping Thompson in a large carpet from his family room. They tightly tied it but gave him enough air. They wanted him alive when he arrived at the shed. Freddie said, "Are we supposed to drug him?"

Perry said, "Yeah but a small amount. We need to do this quick. We need to give the video to Bruce." They picked Michael Thompson up, threw him in the trunk of the car, and drove off as fast as they could. Freddie was driving with Perry in the front seat and Chris in the back, listening to hear if Thompson was going to wake up. They had kidnapped the most intimidating man in Brine County.

They arrived at Freddie's home in the beat-up car. They wheeled Thompson through the garage and backyard. Perry was walking the same walk that changed him—this time with a Thompson brother, his ultimate triumph—but he wanted Bruce more than anybody. At least that was what Freddie and Chris thought. They opened up the door to the shed, and Freddie and Chris tied Thompson to the chair.

"Make sure they are tight, as tight as you can make the knots, and put the sheet over him," said Perry. They nodded and made sure the ropes were very constricted. They put their masks on, and Chris went behind the camera.

Chris motioned with a thumbs up and said, "Action."

Perry and Freddie looked at each other, and Perry

began to speak in a clear, concise voice, a voice that was unknown with the voice changer, "Brine County, this is a message for Bruce Thompson and the Defense of the Brine County Mall. We are the Myrmidons, and we are the true saviors of Brine County, not you, Mr. Bruce Thompson. We see through you and your workers. We know the atrocities you and your little gang do to the citizens of this fine county. The employees you torture, the employees you humiliate, the employees you terrorize? I'm here to say that we are going to do that to the Defense. We are the Myrmidons, and in this county, we are God. This holy member of the Myrmidons is going to take off the sheet of his member of the Defense so the entire world can see."

Freddie stepped closer to Michael. They could see that he was moving slightly, so they did not drug him enough. The sheet came off, and Michael broke the ties on his feet and was up. None of them knew if he knew he was being recorded, but it terrified Perry, because Michael knew Perry was one of these people, and the entire plan would go out the window. Michael ran back to a wall, and the chair shattered. His hands were still tied to the arms of the chair, but he was standing straight up and looking at three people in lion masks, staring at him.

Michael was the first to pounce, and there was not going to be another member coming up behind him with frying pans. He grabbed Freddie by the throat, threw him against a wall, and started punching him, giving him body shots. Chris tried to stop him by grabbing his arm but with no luck. Michael kicked him in the knee, and Chris was down immediately. Michael left Freddie, and Freddie fell down with a few broken ribs. Now it was Perry's turn.

Perry was able to find a knife in all the chaos. He approached Michael with some knowledge from their previous altercation. He avoided the shot put fist coming for his head and ducked. He stabbed Michael in the side with the knife, but Michael grabbed him and threw him across the shed. As Perry landed, he severely twisted his ankle. He stabbed Michael and was still losing the fight.

Michael took the knife out of his side and threw it down. He yelled, "Three pussies down, and I'm still on top. The Defense will always win, and one member of this little fuck around gang is."

Perry hit him on the kneecaps with an old bat. The bat broke in half. Michael screamed in a way none of them knew he could. He fell on his knees, and Perry took the piece in his hand and stabbed Michael in the neck. He took the piece out and stabbed him in the forehead, and the third stab did the trick. Michael Thompson was dead.

Freddie and Chris were hurt but began to stand up. Perry walked toward the camera that was still rolling, but he was walking with a limp. He said to the camera, "The Myrmidons are always going to win. Your move, Bruce." He walked behind the camera, stopped recording, and said, "You guys all right?"

Freddie and Chris took off their masks with looks of amazement. Freddie said, "Perry, you killed a Thompson."

The thought still did not settle with Perry. One Thompson was dead, but he wanted the other brother. "No, we killed a Thompson, but we still have a lot of work to do."

Freddie and Chris knew what to do next. They put Michael in a hole and patched it up.

The three of them left the shed and the scene of the crime and enjoyed beer in Freddie's house. Chris said, "So we will see you at Mobile Diner tomorrow, right, Perry?"

"Yes, of course. You guys know what to do next?"

"Yeah. We need to do it now," Freddie said.

     John P. Burdi

The two of them went to torch the car on Michael Thompson's surveillance camera in another town over.

Perry went home, but this night was not over for him. A couple days ago, he gave a few members of the Myrmidons a task to see if they would comply and to see if he had as much power as Bruce Thompson. He went into his room to go to sleep and heard a car alarm coming from across the street. He looked through the window blinds. Four people in lion masks broke into the car across the street with bats and poured gasoline in the interior. The neighbor came running from his front door, yelling, "Please, stop! What are you doing?" The Myrmidons picked him up, threw him in the car, and lit a match. In Perry's eyes, the blaze was a fascinating sight. The Myrmidons ran back to their car and drove off.

Perry had told them to hit the address but did not tell them he lived across the street. He told the four this was a terrible customer, one of the worst, and they complied with no problem. He slept like a baby to the sound of horrific screams across the way.

11

JOY AND PAIN

ALL HELL BROKE LOOSE ON BRINE COUNTY. THE media had a frenzy the following day, but murderers in lion masks was the only thing brought up. Who were they? Where were they going to strike next? Perry had one of his minions deliver the video to the office of one of the news headquarters, and it was released immediately.

Bruce Thompson was not upset about the murder of his brother but more confused. Bruce watched the video with the police department, and no conclusions were made. All what was known was that three people in lion masks were in what appeared to be in an abandoned shack. The attack on Perry's neighbors was thought to be done by the same people, but there were four people in the attack, and Perry, Freddie, and Chris were not the ones doing it. They had a mob following.

The police were looking for seven individuals with almost no clues. The next town over found the torched car, but nobody knew who bought it. The ones who attacked the neighbors covered their license plates. The police, the Defense, and Bruce Thompson were stumped, and Perry could not be happier. He lamented in the moment he woke up on November 19. As far as he was concerned, he just earned the job of a lifetime; he was going to be the new Bruce Thompson of Brine

County. One man stood in his way. He lied, murdered, planned, and fought for this position, but he was more afraid of Bruce than Michael. With Michael dead, there was one less obstacle was in his way. He got rid of a Thompson, and that dream led to achieving another one. The nephew of Bruce and Michael was not in the loop of the mall. It seemed that his two uncles wanted nothing to do with him. Perry saw him a couple times walking with the two, but he seemed different to Perry. It seemed he did not want to hold Brine County in his hands. The irony of the situation was that Perry was more like a nephew to Bruce and the late Michael than their actual nephew.

The events of the night prior stung Brine County. Unlike the murder of Virginia and the fake drug scene, this was dangerous. For November 19, Perry had little planning to do. Everything was under control, but this was the first time he was going to use firearms. He was not going to be doing the kidnapping of the bride-to-be, but he would be using the gun for a later event, and he was nervous. The Defense did not use guns, at Brine County Mall anyway. Outside the mall, it was anybody's guess.

Perry started the day as every other. He lay in his bed ten minutes before he went downstairs. His father's newspapers were on the kitchen table. Nothing about Michael Thompson was in it, which angered him, but he understood it was printed before he killed Michael. Perry knew it was all over the Internet, which was what mattered.

He was drinking his coffee and reading in silence when his father walked in. "Pretty crazy with all of this, huh? The police will be here all day, trying to investigate."

"I know. A Thompson brother was murdered. Michael, I think."

A look of bewilderment was on his father's face. "What? I'm not talking about the Thompsons. Who cares about them? Our neighbors were brutally attacked last night. We were all outside, and your mom and I figured you were at George's last night. You slept through that?"

Who cares about the Thompsons? How about who cares about our neighbors? That was only a ploy, and besides, they were annoying with their fucking music.

"To be honest, I was so tired last night, I would have slept through anything, and my hours at the mall have been insane." His father looked at him with disdain. He knew Perry was lying, but he did not care anymore what the truth was.

"What the hell happened to your eye?" As a result of fighting Michael, Perry did get a black eye, and he was lucky to have no other scars. He walked to the sink to wash his coffee mug. "What happened? Why are you limping?"

"I fell at work. It happens a lot, but this time it hurt quite a bit. I'm fine though. I'm tough. I can handle it."

"You need to take better care of yourself. Pretty soon, your mom and I won't be able to look after you anymore."

Look after me, like not helping to pay for college, not helping me get a better job? What is it that they do? Have a roof over my head, which if I didn't, they wouldn't either. Everything is done for themselves. I'm just an extension.

"I know. You're right, like always." His father did not sense the sarcasm. "Where's Mom?"

"She went to church." Perry's mother was not very religious, but these were desperate times at Brine County.

"Oh yeah. That's nice of her. There is this interesting priest over there. I saw him at the mall. He was talking about those two motorists killed in June."

"You were talking to a priest at work?"

"Yeah. It was a while ago. He came up and wanted ice cream and asked if I knew the victims. One of them was my age."

His father wanted nothing to do with this story. He sat at the table and ignored him. Perry knew he stopped believing, so he stopped talking. He messaged Freddie. *Hey, you watching any of the news?*

Freddie messaged him immediately. *Hell yeah. Impressive, isn't it? The town is scared shitless. What happened at your neighborhood?*

I need to explain to you later. It all comes together. Word is the police are looking for people in lion masks. They think it's seven.

Let's hope the police find them all and everything is back to normal. Freddie was more paranoid than Perry when it came to cell phones.

Let's hope something gets done.

They kept their conversation short. They wanted no trail of evidence. Perry did want to catch up with somebody he had not seen in some time, Julia, so he shot her a message, *Hey, it's been a long time. Wanna grab lunch today?*

He ate his breakfast in silence with his father. There was nothing to talk about, and they had nothing in common anymore.

He went to the bathroom to look at his black eye and marveled at it in triumph. He had killed Michael Thompson—all the shots he took from him, and no cuts or anything except a black eye and a limp. It was his lucky day.

Perry went back into the kitchen. The front door opened, and his mother came back from church. "Hi, Perry. Do you have any plans today? They are having a memorial service for our neighbors and a couple of people who were murdered in their house. The authorities think they were poisoned. The entire town is up in arms. People believe there is a serial killer among us."

Fuck our neighbors and Duane and the little slut Tara. They really need a memorial service of some kind. I'm making these scumbags into martyrs.

His mother continued while he stared off into space. "Oh, and did you see what happened to poor Michael Thompson? He got tortured by maniacs in lion masks. The police assume they are the same people who murdered our neighbors and the other two. Apparently there was also some kid who was brutally murdered in his apartment, and a guy was found dead next to his crashed car. This town is losing it."

Perry had his hand under his chin, stroking it. "Well, desperate times, I suppose."

"Desperate times? People are getting killed left and right, and all you care to say is desperate times? What the hell does that even mean?"

"People are desperate for answers and control. Let's just say that Michael Thompson was not the most liked person in this county. He had all kinds of power and abused it. Don't believe whatever is being said about him. His brother fabricates the news anyway, and he has some kind of hold on the police."

Boy did I mess up. Michael Thompson is going to be considered a saint in this town. I have to kill Bruce fast and tell what they really did around the mall.

"Perry, what is your problem with the Thompson brothers? They are not that bad, and besides, being desperate does not mean killing innocent people. What if Laura or Leah got murdered because the person was desperate? What would you understand?"

His mother made a point that hit Perry hard. What if one of the Myrmidons went rogue and decided to have a

     John P. Burdi

spree of their own and Laura and Leah were victims, just like the motorist and the boyfriend and the neighbors and Duane and Tara? He knew his mother was right. "You have been changing and not for the better. You need to stop hating the world because it is unfair to you. Look at the people who died."

Yeah, I did look at them. I looked at all of them. I am the reason why they're dead, and to be honest, I don't care that they died. They wronged me. Not one of them was innocent. I'm only scared of what might happen.

Julia messaged him to say she could not go to lunch because she was working.

He left the house to get a haircut. He wanted it very short over his entire head. He made a generous tip to the barber and was going to meet Steve to pick up the goods to complete the operation to kidnap the bride-to-be. He arrived at Steve's a couple hours before it was going to take place. "So you gave the four assholes the shotgun?" Perry said.

"Yeah, I did, but it shoots blanks, so she will not die, and neither will anyone else. I told them to shoot it in the air and only once. Shooting once should do the trick and not have anyone try and be a hero. I'm not sure which one is going to do the shooting, but I only gave them one. As for the other three, I gave them real ones, like you asked. These guys are going to be our patsies."

One of them better not bring their own weapon and kill her. They did some number on my neighbors.

"Yeah, they're fucking morons. Great work, Steve, as usual. I could not bring down the Thompsons without you."

"Well, you did bring down one, but how will this bring down Bruce? He is worse than Michael ever was. Do you know how to handle these? I assume you are giving the other two to Freddie and Chris."

"All in good time, and besides, soon there will be nobody in lion masks. I know you are weirded out with this. Yeah, they will have them, and no worries. I've been reading up on how to use them, and every shot is going to be close range. Pretty much the gun will be in their face. It will be tough to miss at that point."

"Just a little, but this is causing real hysteria, and Bruce looks uncomfortable. He never got like this before. He thinks everybody is against him. Okay, so this is the Kel-Tec P-32, there is a ten-round magazine, and I am only giving you one magazine. These guns are not mine, because I don't want the bullets traced back to me. This gun is used by off-duty police officers and civilians. A lot of people use it, so there is no worry. The safety is on, so be sure to take them off when you use them. You don't want to embarrass yourself. I will see you later tonight. The truck is there, and I have everything I need. Pick me up and drop me off in the parking lot. "

"I'll be seeing you in a while. I have to get Freddie and Chris."

Perry left. Even though Steve was a significant part of the Myrmidons, he was never one. He never went to the meetings or visited the shed, but he was the second most vital person in everything. He went back to his house to get something of significance he was going to be giving back later that night. He ate a quick dinner although he missed it with his parents, because he had to pick up illegal firearms. He was all set. The masks were in his car, in the trunk so Steve would not see, with the voice modulator.

He picked up Freddie and Chris, and not much was said. They were on business. This was becoming routine for them, although they were sitting this one out. Steve came out of his house with a laptop, and it looked like he had a piece in his jacket. He was old and paranoid, being an ex-cop. He really felt like he was undercover.

The three of them drove to the nicest hotel in Brine County, of course the nicest hotel for a Thompson. However, Bruce was disconnected with his nephew. They parked in the far corner behind the hotel, too far for the cameras to see them. Technically, they were not even on the hotel grounds. Steve was going to walk a little, and as he got out of the car, he said, "Okay, so the cops will be with another call when the kidnapping takes place. I will make the distraction and kill the electric wires, so nobody will use their cell phones from the inside. The cameras will still be working, but considering this is a junker of a car, it does not matter if the plates are on camera. The two other cars will be parked right there. You guys are going to play the waiting game. Understand?"

"Yes, sir," said Perry. "Thank you."

Steve nodded, got out of the car, and walked toward the hotel. The three of them saw the other two cars coming and drivers with their lion masks on. Now there were seven people ready to be thrown under the bus. The first four got out of the car and ran toward the reception hall. Perry vaguely heard the music from inside, and there were plenty of cars in the parking lot. A light drizzle began to spill from the clouds, but the night was balmy for this time of year. He noticed his phone lost reception from the Wi-Fi. Steve had done his job. He heard one gun shot, and a bunch of screams followed. He saw people running out of the hotel, and people were trying to call the cops but no luck.

He saw the bride-to-be being carried out: one guy was in front and one behind. He told them how to put her in the car for a specific reason.

Perry, Freddie, and Chris got out of their car, and they were up. "Make sure to take off the safety, and do not under any circumstance use my name." They nodded and began to run toward the car. As they were running, he saw that she was safely in the car, and then he heard seven gunshots. The four people who kidnapped the bride-to-be were dead. They were wearing lion masks, and the three people who shot them were wearing lion masks. The three people were cheering but not for long. Perry ran behind one and pulled the trigger. A feeling of exhilaration exploded in him. The sensation of control felt nothing like this. The person fell to the ground immediately. He fired three more times. He got trigger happy.

Six bullets were left, and Freddie and Chris gave the other two two shots apiece.

Perry wanted more. He wanted to shoot more, and he felt invincible. Freddie and Chris reached in for the car, took the bride-to-be, and ran back to the junker. They yelled at Perry, "Christ, let's go!"

Just like that, seven people with lion masks were dead of a kidnapping, the same seven who were being searched for. The three people who killed them were wearing ski masks. Perry knew this was a triumph in itself. The police were going to be confused as anything.

Steve took a cab back to his house and destroyed the laptop.

As they left the hotel, the cops were just getting there. It was the perfect crime. Nobody expected it was them, and the bride-to-be was so scared, she said nothing. In the car, Perry put a sack over her head and said nothing. She was obviously crying her eyes out. He was eyeing her the entire ride. He wanted her then and there but knew he needed to resist. That was one of the rules of the Myrmidons: do not take advantage of women. He hated that thing. He was repulsed by it.

A couple minutes later, the car pulled into Freddie's garage. The three of them got out, and Perry opened the trunk to put on the mask for the voice modulator. "She is not going to be drugged, and I will carry her to the shed." The other two nodded and obliged. The walk was a strenuous one for Perry. The bride-to-be was doing everything in her power to escape, but Perry had her in a bear hug, carrying her, walking slowly. It was making him exhausted.

While the screaming continued, Perry dropped her. She tried running away, but he grabbed her by the arm and was pulling her like an animal. "Nobody can hear you, so save your energy and stop yelling. Your fate has been determined." There were a couple Myrmidons outside of the shed, and one of them, who was short with a Quicksilver sweatshirt yelled, "Yeah, boy, rape that bitch!"

Perry stopped in his tracks and eyed the kid, but with the mask on, there was no use. He yelled, "You say anything like that again, I will break your jaw. You understand? We don't do that thing, or do you need a reminder?" The boy said nothing more.

Freddie and Chris opened the door and tied her to their new chair with zip ties instead of ropes. They all knew she would not get out of the ropes but wanted to test the new system. He said, "Please leave us. No matter what you hear, do not come in until I come out."

Freddie said, "Have fun." He closed the door, and there was silence.

The bride-to-be knew she was dead. He approached her and took off the sack. She took in her surroundings. It was like she was on a set of a horror movie. Only one light bulb, weapons, and nothing else. He began the trial of sorts. "Why, hello there, good old Samantha."

Bewilderment was not the word that would suffice for what Samantha was feeling. It was beyond bewilderment. Just thirty minutes ago, she was having her wedding shower, and animals in lion masks kidnapped her, killed each other, brought her to an abandoned shed, and the ringleader knew her name. She had no idea who they were. The voice changer made it impossible to determine, and the mask revealed nothing, but Samantha asked the obvious question, "Who are you? What do you want with me?"

Perry answered in a talkative tone. "Why, you know who I am, but when I take off the mask, you might be surprised. Shocked, but you damn well know who I am, but I know for a fact, you have no idea what you did to me, because you think of nothing but yourself. Now do you want me to take off the mask?"

Samantha was stumped. The masked man gave her a riddle that only they knew the answer to. These two obviously had a history together, but fear was blocking her judgment. She thought of nothing else and screamed, "I don't care what you do. Just let me the fuck go, please!"

"Classic Samantha, not caring about other people, just her lonely existence. I will take off the mask, because I know you want me to, but you just don't know it."

"Fine, fine, take off the fucking mask. Are you serious right now! I'm tied to a chair in a shack with people in lion masks outside. Do you really think I'm concerned if you take off the mask or not? Do you realize I know I am going to be dead! I was supposed to get married, and what of Frank, are you going to kill him too?" She was crying hysterically. Her voice was cracking when she delivered the last statement.

 John P. Burdi

"Frank will be dead soon. After all, he is a Thompson. They lived life by taking everything from other people until I came along."

"Is this what this is about? I know his uncle recently got murdered. Oh my God, it was in here. What, are you going to record this?"

"No, not tonight. This is just for me."

"Frank has no ties with his uncles. He is different, and they barely saw him in his childhood even though his father died when he was an infant. All they gave us was money, not a family bond or anything like that. Just let me go, please!"

"I can't do that. I'm afraid you will tell people of this place and what we do. I like you tied to this chair."

"I won't say a thing. I promise."

Perry was nodding like a teacher determining if an answer was correct. "Well, I do want you to see me before we do anything."

"Yes, please. I want to know who is behind the mask." Samantha said it in the most obvious of sarcastic tones, but she just wanted to get out.

Perry turned around so his back was to her. He was getting more dramatic and loved the charismatic aspect of everything. He took out the voice changer and dropped the mask on the floor. He turned around and said softly, "Remember me?"

Samantha had a look of terror. In her wildest dreams, she had never thought Perry Miller was capable of doing this. They talked once after she ended the relationship, and that went as bad as the actual relationship, but she never thought he would kill her. "Perry!"

"Yes, Samantha, it is me, good old me, good old fat Perry who you don't give a shit about my opinion. Remember saying that to me? Well, with all due respect, you never called me fat to my face, just complaining to your friends and other people about my weight." He pushed up his glasses, trying to hold in his anger.

"I'm sorry, please, I'm so sorry. I should have never said that. I'm sorry for making fun of you."

"Frankly, that is not good enough. I don't want to hear you say sorry, which is bullshit by the way, but I want you to tell me to my face why you ended it with me. Not the political answer about you trying to find yourself but the real answer. The real reason why you did not like to be in public with me, the real reason why you hardly told your family about me. I want to hear it right fucking now!"

Samantha did not want to say what she was thinking, but she was tied to a chair in an abandoned shed, and she understood why she was there. Perry wanted truthful closure to their relationship, even as psychotic as he was. She did not want to tell him anything. She had moved on with her life and did not understand why he could not move on with his. They were in their early twenties, and this kind of thing happened all the time. Regretfully and nervously, she yelled out, "I was never attracted to you, and I never liked you, and I never want to see you again! Is that what you want to hear?"

Perry walked toward her whistling "Holly Jolly Christmas." He bent down and cut the zip ties from the chair, releasing her hands and feet. "That's a good start, Samantha." She began to stand up, but he pulled out the gun and pointed it at her heart. "I untied you mainly to make you a more cooperative witness. I wouldn't get up from that chair if I was you."

"Witness to what, Perry? What the hell happened to

you? Why can't you get over this whole thing? I broke up with you, get over it!"

He stood there with a grin on his face. He jumped into the second question. "You killed me when you ended it. Do you have any idea what you meant to me? You were my best friend, and you threw that all out the window. All the lies you told me over the years, all the lies to my face and behind my back. I lost track of all the lies you told me, and it made me question everybody. Because of you I don't trust anybody and probably never will. I might not have been the best-looking guy, but I have been honest with you, and I wished you were the same to me. And of course you broke up with me at the Brine County Mall, of all places. You think that plays into why I hate the mall so much?"

"I didn't want to hurt you. You were nice to me in the beginning, but I never felt the same. I wanted to give you a chance."

"Give me a fucking chance, like I'm a sheltered dog or something. You don't mess around with people like that. Honestly, did you think it was going to end well with that kind of commitment? And be honest for the first time in your pathetic life!"

"No, I knew it wasn't going to end well. I knew you were going to be hurt, but I thought you could move on from me and find a girl who cares about you." Samantha regretted saying anything. She was unsure what he was going to do, and she knew he was obviously not in a good mental state.

"You see, now you are finally truthful with me, and I might respect you a little more, but right now you are a piece of filth to me, nothing more."

"Why don't you just let me go if I mean nothing to you?"

"Because I am sick and tired of being pushed around. Now when people treat me bad, I am not turning my back on it. I am punishing people for it, and you were always first on my list."

"How did you find me? I haven't talked to you in over a year, and we don't have any mutual friends, and I know you don't do social media." She was trying to ask as many questions as she could to distract him.

"That's where you're wrong, Sam. We have a mutual friend. Your acquaintance, Lauren, who is in a serious relationship with George, whom you hated, told me you were to be married to a Thompson." *This little bitch. I'm the one asking the questions. She can't turn this around on me.* "A little over a year and you were to be married. Moving pretty fast, huh, Sam? I mean, are you guys even friends, like the way we were, and be honest, what's the difference between me and him?"

"I love him."

Perry twitched his eyes and cracked his neck to the side. He muttered, "How nice. It's a shame you are not going to marry him."

Samantha was crying uproariously. There was no tricking Perry. He made up his mind a long time ago.

She asked again, "What happened to you? Why are you killing people, and how do you have this many followers?"

These were questions that should have been asked many times in the last couple months, but nobody had asked them. He stood there thinking, still pointing the gun at her. "What happened to me? I began to take over this measly town and be the only one who would stick up to the Thompsons. I am a liberator for all the employees of the Brine County Mall who want to take matters into their own hands, and it is pretty amazing, isn't it? I show no physical dominance at all—barely five feet ten inches, overweight, can't fight, have no experience with firearms, and I am quickly becoming the most feared man in this county. I love the fact that nobody knows who I am, but when I have my mask on, they listen. Outside, a guy told me to rape you, and I said one thing to him, and it was over. You are looking at the new Bruce Thompson. Soon I won't have to say anything to anybody. I am going to look at them, and they will fear me. By using my brains and no conscience when I get my hands dirty, I am the combination of Bruce and Michael."

Samantha sat motionless and quietly said, "What drove you to start killing people? You were always smart, smarter than me, but I never thought you would use your brains to end people's lives. You hate the Thompsons and the mall this much?"

"Let's get one thing straight. I have not killed one innocent person, and it is not going to change tonight. Every person I killed did damage to me somehow, and this is my way of getting them back. I don't condone taking advantage of women. I don't break the law in any way other than murder. I don't steal, and I cannot stand public shootings. Honestly, those are the people who will rot in hell. I kill only for strategic reasons to try and stop the Thompsons. Most of the people I killed are members of the Defense and friends with Bruce, and do not get me started on the Defense. Those are the real criminals. I'm done being the doormat for society. In these walls, I am fucking God! I see the Thompsons as cockroaches. They think they are so powerful, but step on them, and they will be dead. Later in the week, good old Bruce won't know what happened. You see, nobody understands how bad they are, how they treat and manipulate people, how they think they walk on a fucking red carpet. I'm sick of them, and soon I won't have to worry about them, soon I won't even have to think about them. Did you know I saw Michael Thompson kill workers at the mall? One of them was a member of the Defense, but nobody knows about that, not to mention all the other people they killed over the years. They all think they help the town so much."

"And what, people just fall in line with you? They put on their toy lion masks and become a soldier for you, and you trust them?" Samantha ignored the part about the Thompsons. She'd heard the rumors since she was with Frank, but unfortunately for her, Perry was telling the truth, and nobody knew about it.

"When people are desperate enough, when they have nothing going on in their lives, they will listen and do anything to change that. I was desperate enough a couple months ago, but not anymore. The masks make the animal. We wear it because we want to be lions, not our former selves. You see, I am such an influence for these pathetic souls, and I don't trust one of these fucking psychopaths."

"What did I do to you? I broke up with you. It's life, Perry. I'm sorry I hurt you."

Perry laughed, but it was more like a bellow. "Stop saying you are sorry, and start telling the truth, goddammit. You didn't hurt me, you destroyed me, you killed me. I never told you this, but if you felt half of what I felt toward you, I would have asked you to marry me a long time ago. I loved you more than anything. You were my life, I would have given you anything, and you know we had great times together. Nobody could make you laugh like I did, nobody cared about you like I did, and nobody made you live like I did."

"You were never this full of yourself. I admit we had great times, and you made me laugh like no other person, but are you kidding me right now? Nobody made me live like you did? You still didn't answer me about why you started killing people. Because people hurt you, you resort to killing people? When life is hard and you feel like nothing is improving, you do not kill people, you try your best to turn things around. Perry, you are not telling the truth!"

Nobody has ever asked me that. I kill because I feel alive, good, I'll say that. This little bitch. I forgot how feisty she is. It's kind of turning me on, but she is aggravating me, like when we were in a relationship.

Perry could not hold in his anger much longer. "That's easy for you to say. What struggle have you ever had to endure? Having your beauty goes a long way, some intelligence, not more than me, but most importantly, mommy and daddy bought everything for you, and how is law school going? I wish I could go to med school or law school, but since my parents aren't moneybags, I probably will not go in this lifetime. I have nothing in this world, and you are a big reason why! I kill people because it makes me feel alive. I am good at it, and I don't mind getting my hands dirty."

"Of course I'm a big reason why. Everything bad that happens to you is because of me, right?" Samantha was sarcastic. "Killing people makes you feel alive? You are so full of shit. Do you ever think that this is beyond wrong? What about the families of the people you kill? You destroy people's lives, and not just the people you kill."

What the fuck is she talking about? Why I would think of the families? "I never thought of the families. I try not to think of the people I killed."

For the first time since Perry began going to the shed, he felt nothing—no exuberance, no dominance. He knew Samantha was right. Not one person had questioned his actions, and for the first time, he started really thinking about what he was doing.

Finally he told Samantha the truth. "Fine! Fucking fine. I could barely sleep sometimes. I think about the people I killed all the time. I keep telling myself that I am taking over, but soon there is nothing that will need to be taken over. It will all be destroyed like me. You happy, Samantha, seeing me destroyed?" He was crying. He knew he should have turned down Freddie and Chris's offer to bring him to this place on the night that seemed such a long time ago.

"You wanted me to tell you everything I did to you? How about you tell me everything you did to all the people?" Samantha knew he was vulnerable at this point. She wanted to try anything, and now Perry was in the hot seat.

Perry stood there shocked. He made a clicking noise, squatted to eye level with Samantha, and looked her in the eyes. "I forgot how beautiful your eyes were. The first person I killed was in this shed, and his name was Calvin. I never met him before, but he complained about my two partners to Bruce Thompson, and they got in trouble, so they kidnapped him and brought him here. They knew I was desperate and mad at the world so they invited me here to watch, but you see, I stepped up and killed him myself. They buried him in the back, where you will be soon. Then I kidnapped this older woman who did not want to have a sexual relationship with me, and we made a fake drug scene at the mall. You might recall that in the news in the summer. Then we recruited new people and started kidnapping and killing a lot. I suffocated a woman

     John P. Burdi

with a plastic bag in here, used a saw, bats, and knives. I had a sexual relationship with a minor and killed her, poisoned her with a member of the Defense. I killed Michael Thompson, a driver who cut me off, a guy who had a girlfriend and was much uglier than me, and my asshole neighbors." Perry was wiping the tears from his eyes. Saying everything was worse than thinking it. "It all started with a car accident that I caused that killed two people and that woman I killed with a plastic bag."

Samantha thought there was still a way to talk sense into him.

After the confession, Perry stood up and walked toward the door. Samantha said, "You trust these two people who talked you into coming here in the first place?"

Perry laughed. "Freddie and Chris? I trust them as much as I trust you, which is pretty much absolute fucking zero. They showed me the way to relieve stress, but they didn't say it was going to be this hard. To think I used to be a good guy."

"I knew you weren't like this. You are still good. Maybe you can still make a good decision, and what are you feeling now?"

Don't listen to her. She is only trying to talk you out of killing her. She could care less about the other people. Perry ignored his thoughts for the moment. "Honestly, ever since I started doing this and wearing the masks and starting the Myrmidons, I felt joy and pain. The joy comes from killing the person, feeling in charge for the first time in my life, feeling like nothing can overtake me. The pain comes soon afterward, the pain I will have to deal with for the rest of my life. Unfortunately, I have to live with it. I don't want to kill you, I don't want to kill anybody anymore, and I am the one who is dead."

"See, you are not a bad person. Please let me go."

"You interrupted me, and for the last time, I'm not finished. The person I kill feels the joy and pain but in reverse. They feel pain, when I beat them, torture them, and take over them. The joy comes when it is all over, when they see nothing but black, when they are nothing. I assume it is a better feeling than getting tortured. You are going to be feeling that soon. Joy and pain coincide with each other. I will be feeling pain for most of my life, but the joy helps, even though I know how bad the pain will be. I can't let you go. The Myrmidons would kill me if they knew that, and what they would do to you would be worse. We have big things planned for later in the week."

Samantha thought she was talking her way out of this but to no avail. Perry was gone. He cared more about covering up his mistakes than trying to correct the wrongs. "Perry, please, don't do this! Please don't hurt Frank!"

"Besides, you would tell the police on me and everyone here, and if the decision is to be in jail or kill you, I would have to pick kill you. No matter how much pain there is, there is still the joy of not going to jail."

"I won't tell anybody, I swear, just please don't do this, I'll do anything!"

"After all the years of lying to me when we were friends when we were in a relationship as boyfriend and girlfriend, when we were lovers, now I know when you lie, and I have become as good a liar as you. I learned from the best." Perry aimed the gun at her throat. "I'm sorry, but if I don't kill you in here, they will torture you out there. I'll always love you." Perry fired the gun, shooting her in the throat. Her hands held in the blood and pain. He walked toward her, put the gun against her head, and fired again. She fell out of the chair, Perry being the last thing she saw.

He wiped tears from his eyes and put the mask back on with the voice changer. He opened the door and proclaimed to the Myrmidons, "We need to plan for Friday."

12.

BLACK DAY

Bruce Thompson held a press conference during the week of Black Friday. It was his busiest day of the year at this mall, and the people of the entire town were terrified to leave their homes. He was declaring that Brine County was safer than ever, and the three people who kidnapped Samantha had lion masks, the same masks that were in the video of killing Michael Thompson. He declared the Myrmidons dead, just like Perry imagined it. They did not find Samantha's body, which Bruce could care less about. He hated his nephew, Frank. He knew he needed people to believe him. Perry hurt Bruce where it counted the most to Bruce. He was going to lose money this Black Friday if people did not shop.

Thanksgiving was approaching on the 24th, and at midnight on the 25th, it was his time. Perry never referred to the day as Black Friday because he hated it so much, but this time, he planned on making it Black Friday so he would love that day in the future. He thought about Samantha saying he was still a good guy. Maybe she was right, but he still had to make his own decisions. He thought she was right, and this must stop. Deep down, he regretted killing her.

She almost broke me, but she did make some good points. She made me realize how little I trust Freddie and

    John P. Burdi

Chris. I have two bullets left, and they are both for Bruce, my last kill.

Perry had one thing left to do: the attack on the Brine County Mall on Friday. Everything was accounted for, and all the strategies were going to be enforced. He needed Steve one last time, and then Steve would go into early retirement as well as Perry. Their plan was made for the two of them. As for Freddie and Chris, he had no idea what they were going to do after, and he did not care. Killing Samantha was going to be the last time he would step into the shed. He had no use for the two after Friday. He supposed they would go their separate ways.

He had lunch with George during the week. They talked, and Perry warned him, "Do not under any circumstance go to the mall at midnight on Friday."

"Why? I thought Bruce said everything was taken care of."

What, are you listening to the enemy instead of me?

"There have been many threats when I have been working recently, and the mall does not want us to tell the outside. Please, do not go there. I am not even working."

George was unsure if this was a real threat or not, but he had every reason to believe Perry. "Sure, I won't go there on Friday." They ate their lunch and agreed not to go to the mall on Friday.

Perry also warned his family not to go there, and they agreed, although he was concerned about Laura and Leah. He thought they would still go, so that was something he was going to have to look out for.

His numbers going into the attack were twenty-seven Myrmidons, counting himself, Steve, Freddie, and Chris. Steve told them there would be fifty members of the Defense there, and Bruce would be in his office and walking around. He always did that the day after Thanksgiving.

Police officers would not be there per Bruce's wish. He did not want the customers to feel uncomfortable, and besides, there were probably more members of the Defense than police officers in the town.

Perry had a quiet Thanksgiving with his family—no arguing or fighting. As he was eating pumpkin pie, he decided to message Julia. *Hey, Happy Thanksgiving, hope all is well.* He put his fork down to take another piece and saw that she had messaged him.

Thank you, Happy Thanksgiving. Are you working tonight?

Perry quickly typed, *No, thank God. You shouldn't go shopping there. The shit is going to hit the fan with all these murders in this town.*

No worries. I won't be shopping, but I will be working.

It was as if a knife had stabbed Perry. All this planning, all the strategies, and he did not even ask Julia if she was working that night. Now he felt that it was his obligation to protect her from his plan. He typed, *Okay, if you hear any loud noises, any screaming, you run out the back door of your store, go to your car, and drive as fast as you can. Do not look back.*

This got her attention immediately. Instead of texting back, she called him, sounding frantic. "Perry, what the hell are you talking about?"

"Just be careful. I worked earlier in the week, and there were threats." He sounded as calm as possible even though he was as nervous as she was. He did not want her to be harmed under any circumstances.

"Really? I heard nothing. There were no meetings or anything in that regard, and I'm sure there will be a big number of the Defense there unfortunately. The only good thing with them is that they will not want to let the mall get damaged."

She's amazing. She hates the Defense almost as much as I do.

"I didn't want to alarm you. Just be careful, okay? Who knows, maybe I will bump into you tonight and keep you company."

"I would like that. The overnight gets pretty dead around three in the morning."

"Enjoy the rest of your day. See you."

"Bye, Perry."

Hopefully that was not the last time he was going to speak with Julia, but with the events later in the night, it seemed possible. He thought of the priest when he visited the church to see if there was evidence against him in the car accident. His prayer still resonated in his mind, especially, "When the shadows fall, you do not walk alone." His shadow fell, but he was alone. He had no faith. He was not sure he had a friend. He felt that Julia talked to him more because she felt obligated to after the incident with Duane. She knew how much he cared for her, but her feelings were not of that kind. He had alienated himself from George and his family, and Freddie and Chris were not his friends, but after the night's end, he did not need to worry. He knew Samantha was going to haunt his memory forever, but she made him realize how unhappy he was, even though the only purpose was to make him relieve some stress. At the beginning, it did bring him happiness, but not anymore.

The day after Thanksgiving was Perry's least favorite day of the year. He could not stomach the people shopping for hours on end. The demand for insignificant items blew his mind. He would see the bags the people were carrying like bags of gold. He would see the lines forming for his measly ice cream stand and not understand why people would wait in a long line instead of leaving after making their purchases. He would see the fights between customers, fighting over items like there was a food ration. It was an ugly scene for humanity—the same when people rushed to the grocery store during a snowstorm. Last, he would see the Defense in all their glory. Bruce Thompson was at every Black Friday and loved walking around during the graveyard shift, making sure not an item was left in his mall. Very rarely did the Defense break up fights between customers on that day. He almost watched it as a gladiator match in his arena, and they would end it if it was more than two animals trying to kill each other for a comforter or a thermal shirt. He just stared. It was not worth fighting with them that day.

Each year, the day started earlier. Now stores were open on Thanksgiving, but the attack was not going to be until midnight.

Freddie picked up Perry, and he told his family not to go to the mall on his way out. He told them he had to go into the store because there was an emergency. He realized he could still make the decision of not going, but he had to make sure the last deed was done. He carefully hid his gun in the back of his pants, opened the door of Freddie's car, and said, "Where is Chris?"

"He's meeting us there. He is driving some Myrmidons. Where is your mask? You are not wearing it for our biggest night?"

"No, I can't. Remember I have to finish the last part on my own, and I cannot wear a mask, because it would draw attention. The rest of the Myrmidons are pawns. You and Chris shouldn't be wearing them either, and besides, I left my mask at the shed after I killed the bride. Hiding the gun was enough. Hiding the most notorious mask in this town is asking too much."

"So what will happen after this is completed?" said Freddie like an eager student asks a teacher.

"I assume we will all go on our separate ways. The town will be liberated, and there will be no need for us." *I will be long gone. Maybe move out west.*

"As long as there are customers shopping for products, there will always be a need for us. We will always need you," said Freddie in a sincere way.

"You and Chris can overtake everything. I might retire after tonight. Just keep driving, my friend, and we will get there soon." He saw no need to elaborate on tonight. He was playing things close to the chest.

Freddie ignored the last statement and thought Perry winked after he said it. The rest of the ride was silent on a night that would not be. They pulled up to the Brine County Mall in the same place where Perry witnessed Michael Thompson commit murder, and he saw the rest of them. The rest of the Myrmidons were wearing lion masks but did not need the mask to show how animal they became. He came to a pack of wolves, waiting for their prey. This was the first time that he feared them. He knew there was no more trying to control them. He also knew that Steve must have killed the cameras, because if the Defense saw this from the outside, they would have been stopped. As for the customers, Perry knew they would not notice anything. They were too busy shopping. The parking lot was as crowded as a presidential inauguration. The people still trusted Bruce.

Perry and Freddie remained in the car. They were not going to participate with the rest of the Myrmidons, and they had jobs to do. They left the car slowly so they would not be seen by the rest of the Myrmidons. The order was to attack everyone and anyone. Perry and Freddie slipped in a side door and went their separate ways.

Perry ran down a hallway and past some bathrooms that would lead into the food court, next to the carousel with the portrait of Bruce Thompson. As soon as he stepped into the food court, he heard "Carol of the Bells" end and "Christmas Canon" begin precisely at midnight. He saw the herd of Myrmidons running through the doors: the Myrmidons with knives, the Myrmidons with pipes, and the Myrmidons with bats, running like a stampede. He did not recognize one of them. They were all different in size and stature. One he believed to be at least six feet six inches tall. He thought there were a few women in the ranks, but they were all wearing their masks and looked as one being.

The killing started; innocent customers, innocent workers being slaughtered like cattle, blood pouring everywhere, limbs flying everywhere. The screaming was atrocious, and the laughing was worse. He heard, "Please don't!" "Please help me!" "Call the police!" "Where is the Defense?"

He witnessed people's throats being slashed. He saw the life leave people's eyes. The Defense was not coming. Freddie did his job of locking them in the meeting room. Nobody was going to be coming to help the innocent. He doubted Bruce would call the police. Bruce did not like the law being implemented in his mall by people other than the Defense, even if it meant innocent people died, as long as he remained in power.

The Myrmidons became killing machines. None of them had remorse. They moved to the next customer or

 John P. Burdi

worker, anybody who did not have a lion mask. They were killing people easier than Perry or Freddie ever did in the shed. He was sure he was not seen as he watched the dismay. He drowned out the rest of the noise, and all he heard was "Christmas Canon" while watching the bloodshed. People were begging to be spared but to no purpose. The Myrmidons were doing no such thing. It looked as if fifty strong were doing the killing. Only twenty or so showed up to the meetings, and there were new recruits. It was appealing to people as desperate as Perry. He was petrified that there were that many people as despairing as himself.

The Myrmidons were leaving the food court and were moving to other stores in the mall. It was clear nothing was going to stop them or get in the way. *On this night, on this night, on this very Christmas night.* It felt like it was being sung about one hundred times. That was all Perry could think about, as everything else was obstructed. *What have I done?* Perry no longer felt anything about a revolution. He no longer felt in power. He was destroyed by his own creation. He stood at the carousel, watching, wincing on the inside. He created this death and destruction, but he had a choice to make, a choice that could lead to salvation within himself. He felt the gun in his backside with two bullets left, both for the same man, and he was close to his office, but he thought about something else. *Julia is working. What if they decide to kill her and they know she is not on their side?* Kill Bruce or save Julia? He made the choice quickly. He ran as fast as he could though his ankle still hurt from Michael Thompson, running past the massacre, not hearing what song on the sound system or anybody crying for help. He managed to run past the Myrmidons, and they did not harm him. They were too busy going into stores, and the store Julia worked in was still down a bit.

The Myrmidon was looking right at Julia and slowly approaching her with a knife in his hand. Julia screamed and looked for a blunt object as a weapon, but none were close by other than the cash register, and that was heavy. She tried to pick it up, and to her amazement, she had in her hands and yelled at the Myrmidon, "Don't come any closer!" He kept approaching, so she threw the register at him. There was not enough velocity, and he managed to avoid it easily, but he was off balance.

Perry ran into the store and grabbed the guy from behind, picking him up by the legs and slamming him into the glass fixture. The glass shattered and fell like a light rain on a summer night. Perry turned him over onto his back side and ripped the mask off, and to his shock, it was a guy he worked with at the ice cream kiosk. He punched him three times, picked up a piece of glass with a sharp edge, and held it against his neck. He saw his own reflection in it, and the monster looked back at him. He dropped the piece of glass and punched him again for good measure. He threw the mask back on him in case the police came. He stood up and calmly said to Julia, "Get out of here."

Julia was on her way. She went through the back door, and Perry realized she would be safe. The Myrmidons were working on the inside of the mall, and soon it would all come down. He was praying that nobody else he cared about was in here.

As he stood up, he realized this Myrmidon was the one who told Perry to rape Samantha when he was dragging her to the shed. He got back some composure and started running to Bruce's office, but it was too late. To his astonishment, he saw the Defense approaching. They were marching like a well-trained army. His soldiers in the revolution were like barbarians against an empire. Hope dwindled away rapidly. The Defense began firing back with guns.

What the fuck? How did they get guns? They are just shooting into this mess. What if they kill innocent people? What the fuck happened to Freddie, Chris, and Steve?

The fighting in the next couple minutes was entirely Perry Miller's fault. The Defense was looking for anybody with a lion mask and shooting to kill. He noticed they had handcuffs, and if one surrendered, they were going to take him into custody, but the police were nowhere in sight. The Defense was effective. They were picking people off like flies.

Perry was extremely lucky he was not wearing a mask. He ran through the same door that Julia left. He knew it would lead to the office of the Defense. He would try and find Bruce, Freddie, or Chris, but he left to excuse himself from his massacre. He ran past the custodian's closet and thought of rubber gloves. He took a pair and threw them on. He wanted the gun to be untraceable. He ran down the abandoned hallway and stood face to face with the Defense's office door. He peeked in and saw two members looking at cameras that were still operating. What he saw seemed like a war movie with a disappointing and despairing ending. His revolution was becoming a colossal failure.

Did they get Steve? The cameras are still on, and what happened to Freddie? One of those questions was answered. Standing behind Perry, Freddie tapped his shoulder.

Perry jumped and turned around, pointing the gun at Freddie's head. "What the fuck happened? You were supposed to lock them on the inside and throw the grenade that Steve gave you. How the fuck do they have guns?"

Freddie said, "Lower the gun, cowboy. I couldn't lock them in, because there was no meeting, and they were all standing outside the door with guns in their hands. They almost shot me but saw my custodian's uniform and told me to get lost. I found Chris though." Freddie sounded more disappointed than Perry, and Chris walked out of the shadows. Perry began yelling at him and put the gun near his backside.

"Where the fuck were you? You were supposed to help Freddie. He couldn't do this by himself."

"I drove some fellow Myrmidons to this shit show and couldn't find you guys. Stop yelling at me. Did you kill Bruce? What the fuck happened to that?"

Perry knew Chris was right. He did not do his due diligence, but he was not going to tell them he saved Julia instead of killing Bruce. He did not trust what they would do to him. "Bruce wasn't in his office. I think we have a mole on the inside. The Defense knew too much. They never have people on the outside of the office. Bruce not being here, and the guns? Somebody flipped."

Chris said, "I think you're right. We have to get the fuck out of here!"

Perry was unaware of what happened to Steve, but the more he thought about it. He knew what he had to do next. The three of them were walking through the same hallway to get out of the mall, so Perry took out his gun and fired at the back of Chris's head. He fell immediately.

Freddie quickly turned around, and Perry whispered, "Sorry" and shot Freddie in the face. They were both dead within seconds. No bullets left. Bruce was going to survive the night. The revolution was dead, and the Unholy Trinity was no more.

Perry ripped the gloves off and began running into the mall. Maybe the Defense could save him, especially since he was not wearing a mask, and the blood on him made it seem like he was injured.

He ran into the center of the mall. The Christmas tree display was down. The Myrmidons at least did that, but there was no fire. None of them were left. The Defense and Bruce won. Perry ran to a member of the Defense and yelled, "Help, help, I am injured."

One approached him and threw handcuffs on him. "Mr. Miller, you are under arrest through the Defense of Brine County for conspiracy to endanger the Brine County Mall."

Is this real life or something? They can't arrest anybody, and conspiracy to endanger the fucking mall? How about you guys with guns firing into crowds of people?

"Where is Bruce Thompson, and what did he do with Steve?"

"Those questions are irrelevant. We are taking you to jail, and we know that is not your blood. There is no wound."

Perry was not going to fight with the Defense, because there was no point. He wanted to hear what the police were going to say, and at least he was alive, for now.

13.

THE VISITOR

Perry sat in the cell. He was taken prisoner at ten past midnight. Ten minutes, and his revolution was in shambles. He was unsure what happened to Julia. His phone was confiscated, and he had not made a phone call yet, although the authorities told him that his family knew where he was. He thought they would storm down to the station with a lawyer, but he thought they were so saddened by his actions that they would leave him to rot. The most mysterious aspect of everything was that he had no idea how much the police or the stronger branch, the Defense, knew, so he sat quietly.

He had been in his cell around seven hours, saying nothing, only being told about his parents knowing where he was. He sat on the uncomfortable cot and was looking at the bars in front of him. A sense of loss took over him, and he could care less what would happen to him. The only thing he cared about was the information people knew. As far as he was concerned, his life was over. He did not sleep, did not eat the filth that was presented to him, did not go to the bathroom even though he had to. He just stared in silence. He thought about how different everything could have been if he had not gone to the shed with Freddie and Chris the first time. They would be alive if they had never taken him.

    John P. Burdi

He wanted to apologize to his family for everything that had happened. He was still unsure if Laura or Leah went to the mall and, if they did, if they were unharmed. He wanted to make sure that Julia had made it home, and he wanted to tell George everything. The only true friend he had, and he hid his life from him, but he could not do anything. He was powerless. *It's over. I'm done.*

He pondered all the lives lost. The customers, the workers, the Myrmidons, the Defense—they were all the same to him now. He thought about Samantha the most, and thinking of her made him realize she was absolutely right. The families had it worse than the people who had fallen. Samantha could have lived. That was one of the most unstrategic kills of all. That was Perry flexing his brain muscles.

Perry still did love her. He was not lying when he told her before he pulled the trigger. *I did save her in a way. If I didn't kill her, her fate would have been worse, but it was my fault she died in the first place. I killed her because of how much she hurt me.* Perry placed his hands on top of his face to prevent anyone from seeing his tears. He still did not make a sound. He did not want them to know he was a prisoner. The least thing he could be was a martyr, but his people were dead, and so it would just be for himself.

Around nine in the morning, the guard came by and said, "You got a visitor, fuck face."

"How lovely," said Perry in a mundane tone.

The person standing in front of the cell looking at Perry with a slight grin began the exchange. "Mr. Miller, leader of the Myrmidons, we meet again."

"Why the fuck weren't you at the mall last night? How did you know everything? And what happened to Julia?"

"I'm the one who asks the questions. You ask another question, and you know what will happen." Bruce pulled out a gun and pointed it at Perry. "You think anybody will blink if I kill you in here? That's not the point. The last thing I want to do is kill the great Perry Miller."

Perry wished he would pull the trigger and end everything, but he still wanted some answers.

"You like being in here, Perry?"

"Is that a serious question?"

"I'm trying to lighten the mood, and I am not sure how else to start this proposal, but yes. Do you like being in here?"

Seriously? You little grinning prick, you think I like being locked up? I'm going to answer this without answering it. "It beats being dead."

"So no, but maybe you want to be dead. I'm not sure. You have a most unusual psyche, Mr. Miller. I can't figure you out. I know you trust people too much. You want to know how I knew your plan of attack, but more importantly, little Romeo, you want to know what happened to your lovely Julia?"

"Yes. Honestly, that is the only answer I want that will stop you from pulling the trigger, and what's with the Defense and guns?"

Bruce cocked the gun. "What did I say about questions?"

"That wasn't a question. It was more of an observation, Bruce."

"I like you. You know that, the fight in you, the balls you have, but most importantly, that brain you have. Your plans and schemes, your ideas, and getting people on your side—they only rival mine. Julia is fine. She escaped because of you."

"Oh thank God, and thank you. With you gushing over me, it doesn't seem like I am in trouble, but please continue."

"Knock it off with the manners. I know you hate me, I know you want to kill me, and you went into my mall last night intending to kill me. I mean, you killed my brother, and you hate my control, so I don't blame you."

He knows I killed his brother, and he does not want to kill me. He's more fucked up than I am. Perry said nothing. He trusted Bruce the least and knew this could all be a trap.

"But most importantly, I know everything you did, Mr. Miller. You and the other two, you brought customers and some members of the Defense back to that little shithole of a shed and buried the bodies in the field beyond it. You know, that's the problem with the youth today. You guys are so angry, because you don't like authority, and you think you're entitled to everything. My fortune and way of life took years to get, not months, so when you youngsters don't agree with something, you whine and cry and try to take what isn't yours in the first place. Don't ever try and make people feel sorry for you, because in reality, they could care less. Take this as a life lesson. People only care about themselves. You think when people go to bed that they really pray for the lives of others before they sleep? Or they think about starving children? They only care about themselves."

Is this philosophy class or something? What the hell is he talking about?

"Now excuse me for getting off topic. This is all about you and what I do and do not know. Well, I know everything. I have a question. Why did you kill Freddie and Chris?"

"Because I did not trust them. They could tell the police everything to save themselves, so I saved myself to be sure, and I am pretty certain one or both of them told you or made a deal with you."

"It's a fucking shame we hate each other, Perry. I like you. You remind me of myself when I was your age. More importantly, you are right. That little fellow Chris, he told me everything, and we did have a deal. I want to say I loved the theatrics of everything, the masks, pure genius. Killing people with masks to make me think your group was dead was even smarter, but you made one colossal mistake. You didn't buy the masks—you let Chris, and he was not as smart as you. He used a credit card. When you made the video of killing my brother with those masks, I investigated, and even though he bought them out of the county, he still used a credit card with his name on it. You see, Perry, when you try and take something that is not yours, in this county, you need to do it yourself, because everybody else is incompetent. You trusted Chris to do that, and he failed. After I found out it was him, I made a deal with him. He would be high up in the Defense, and he told me your plan of last night, but you killed him, so his plans went out the window. He told me all the people you and Freddie killed. It's a dishonor you killed Freddie. He did not say a word to me. He was trustworthy, but who knows, but Chris was an animal."

This maniac knew about the plan last night, and he let innocent people die.

"I know what you're thinking. I let innocent people die, including my brother, but he was not innocent. Michael helped me in the beginning, but he was too headstrong and violent. He killed in broad daylight in the parking lot, for heaven's sake. He wasn't the first brother I let die. See, you can't trust anybody, even brothers. I don't want to open that can of worms, not yet at least. I heard his son's fiancé

     John P. Burdi

was murdered—you probably did that as well—as well as a motorist, some slob in his apartment, and neighbors. Yes, I know where you live, young man. Back to last night. I said to the county that since the police force is so scarce and more young lads want to fight in the Defense, why not let them carry firearms and make arrests? They were unsure until last night when they stopped the massacre and made arrests. I had to let people die for my greater good. More power. It's ironic that you tried and stop the Defense from having any power, and now because of you, they have more power than ever. For that, I thank you."

Please kill me.

"What's wrong? No quick comeback? Oh yes, and Steve. Chris told me he was working for you, and when he was working last night, and it looked like he was trying to destroy the camera feed. We caught and killed him. Heard you two were trying to steal my money from my safe and have an early retirement. This is the kicker. You might be asking yourself is there any evidence against you, or is it Chris's word against yours? Last night, I was in my office, waiting for you with a gun pointed at the door, but you never made it. You saved some girl and killed your partners to cleanse yourself. As I was watching the cameras, I saw you limp with the same limp and sweatshirt that you had in the video of killing Michael. I knew it was you, and bravo for another mistake." There was a long silence. "Anything on your mind?"

"I'm going to fucking kill you one day, and you wipe that grin from your fucking face."

"There's that spirit. My last inquiry is the reason why I am here. Why wouldn't I tell the police? As far as they are concerned, the only thing you did was punch one of those Myrmidons. They know nothing. You and I are the only ones who know the truth about everything. The entire county thinks the Myrmidons are no more, and they are right. There are a few survivors, but they are locked up. I am here because I have a job offer for you. Work for me, and kill the people I say to kill, because frankly, you have a talent that most people never have. You kill without remorse and leave no evidence. I mean, look at what you accomplished with the other two: change. The county changed because of you. You put fear into everybody's head. You are short, overweight, and probably can't fight worth a lick, but you still managed to kill members of my Defense and Michael. I do need to punish you, so if you refuse any killings, I will murder your entire family. I know where they live and who they are. Laura and Leah and your parents, and that Julia you are crazy about. If you refuse any of it, they will be dead because of you. If you die on the job, you are released. Oh, and if you try and kill me, your family will be dead. You have no choices. If you decide to rot in here, your family—you can guess—will be dead."

Perry sat there in agony. He had no choice, and he was not going to let Bruce know that he regretted killing people. His conscience or lack thereof was one of the things keeping him alive. "I don't have a choice."

Bruce smiled widely. "Not at all, because the mall owns those who work in it, and I own you, my little slave. I bid you farewell. Your past will always be with me unless you give me a reason to shout it out. The police will know nothing. You will be released later this night, and I suggest you eat something. You can't kill on an empty stomach. When you make your killings, you need to be discreet. I will not protect you, and if you get caught, well, you know the rest. Remember, I have the power. You aren't even close. You will hear from me soon. Goodbye."

     John P. Burdi

As Bruce walked away, Perry did not watch him leave but was brooding over the job offer he had just received or the job commitment he needed. Kill people at the behest of Bruce Thompson, and if he did not succeed, his family would be dead. Even though Samantha made him realize the errors of his ways, he had no choice but to ignore them. He needed to kill again. Even though he was efficacious at it, he was killing himself more than anybody else.

He sat there on the cot, waiting to be released, but he had more disdain for himself in these moments than he did when he met the customer who changed his life. He was thinking about the chain reaction of meeting her, talking to Freddie, that car ride home, and so on. He pushed his glasses against his forehead with such animosity that they almost broke in half. He sat there more puzzled with his life and the world than ever before. He had become like the lifeless drones he hated and feared so much when they shopped at the mall, but this time, his mall was Bruce Thompson, the man who owned him. He stared straight ahead into the abyss that had become his life.

ACKNOWLEDGMENTS

Writing this book was not an accomplishment for myself. It was an accomplishment for the people in my life who aided me every day along the way. So, I would like to start by thanking my parents. My parents are the most hard-working people I know, and the most valuable trait they taught me about was perseverance—not just for writing this book but in life in general. I couldn't do anything without you guys, and I am always looking to make you proud of me even though I make as many mistakes as I do triumphs. Thank you Danielle for everything you did for me, even getting me a job at our mall to help me get inspired to write *Joy and Pain*. You are not only a great sister, you are a great friend. Thank you for always being there, whether it be watching the same episodes of *Breaking Bad* or going to lunch. To the rest of my family: aunts, uncles, cousins. Thank you.

Thank you Mike, Marissa, Pat, and Dan; you guys have always been there for me even if I was not. You guys are the best friends anybody can ask for. You guys are my brothers, and Marissa, you're like another sister. From kindergarten to half-price apps to our weddings, all of the memories will be cherished and never forgotten. But, most importantly, you guys always make me happier when we are together. You make me laugh when I need to, and you listen to me when I talk. Thank you now and always.

Thank you Anthony and Michele, my mentor and my drinking buddy. You two have always been there for me, always and without any hesitations, no matter how much I screw up with everything. Since I make the same mistakes, you guys help tremendously. Anthony, you were the first person to read my book, and thank you for your insight and helping me with ways to improve with my writing. Michele, oddly enough, I think we became very good friends after you hit my car. Thanks for letting me drink at your house when I need a drink.

Thank you James, because without you this book never would have been written. Thank you for working with me at Sears. It might have been the only reason I worked retail in the first place; you made it worthwhile. All the drives we went on and will continue to go on never went unnoticed, because you might have written a few lines in *Joy and Pain*. You are the unofficial co-author.

Thank you to Luminare Publishing for making my dreams come true—especially Patricia, Jamie, Lori, Kim and Melissa. Thanks for making this process as easy as possible. Without Luminare, this book would be a story on a laptop.

A special thank you is in order for Franchesca Malaga for creating my cover in such a short period of time. You are going to have an amazing future in art.

Thank you Tim Anderson Jr. for making me look somewhat decent.

And to the reader, thank you.

DEARLY BELOVED

Richard parked his car in front of Stephen and Michele Lynn's house at around 7:30. He was exhausted for this was his second week of starting a new job, a new career. He was twenty-four years old, four years younger than Stephen and two years younger than Michele Lynn. Richard was a modest man. He hardly wore his glasses even though he definitely needed them when he drove. Richard had a buzz cut with a very long and skinny face. People would mistake him for being droopy, but that was his face. He never forced a smile or laughed if he wasn't amused; he hated being fake. Richard wore his work clothes, a buttoned-down shirt tucked into khaki pants. He did not have time to go back home and put on some comfortable clothes, or in his case, nylon shorts and a T-shirt that desperately needed to be ironed.

He was very quiet, rarely spoke his mind, but grew up with Stephen in the same neighborhood, and they formed a friendship. Stephen was mentor to Richard, and Stephen had zero trepidations putting him in his wedding party despite being the youngest person in it and Richard did not care for a specific reason. He was fond of one of Stephen's friends. His relationship with Stephen's wife to be, Michele

Lynn, was a strong one. She would always welcome him in their home and never made him feel like a third wheel. Richard and Michele Lynn would make fun of Stephen at his own expense to form a strong friendship, and Stephen did not mind. Richard stepped out of his car and began walking up the driveway.

He rang the doorbell and began wiping the sweat from his forehead. It was a particularly warm day in September, extremely humid. Stephen opened the door like a madman and shouted, "Hey Rich, come on in, what are you waiting for?" Stephen was very tall and skinny, and clean-shaven with black hair that was a little longer than Richard's. He had an abnormally large nose, which Richard loved to point out. Stephen did not mind.

Richard looked a little confused but blamed the volume in his voice for being nervous, for the next couple of days would be the most important for Stephen and Michele Lynn in their young lives. Richard did not answer to the question posed by Stephen and walked in. He slipped off his shoes and placed them on the carpet by the door. Richard followed Stephen into the den of his house, a cozy television room. Richard slumped in his favorite chair in their house and reclined to relax a bit. "Where is your fiancée?" he finally asked. Richard always made himself feel comfortable in the home of Stephen and Michele, and there was no reason not to.

"She's out with her mother, buying some last-minute things for the weekend. How did the tux fit? I think they did a pretty good job." Stephen was pacing around the room very nervously. He actually made Richard a little nervous doing so.

"Yeah I guess, it definitely fit, and I was pretty comfortable. I'm not sure how they can really fuck something

     John P. Burdi

like that up. You measure a chest and arms and find the jacket. You measure the waist and find pants. Sounds pretty easy. And dude, fucking relax man. You're making me sweat." Richard ended his tuxedo shop rant with a long and exaggerated yawn. He took a tissue out of the box on the coffee table to wipe his eyes.

"You would be nervous too. Wait until the time comes. So, how was your first week teaching?" asked Stephen.

"The time won't come any time soon. Believe me on that one. And for the week, it was fucking long, too long, and I still have tomorrow, which, by the way, I might be a couple of minutes late to the hotel. I looked how far it's going to take me to get there from my school. It was like a couple of hours."

"Haha, and you haven't even finished your first full week yet. Wait until you get to, like, March. Remember how slow that went during school. Okay no problem, I know you will be there."

Richard nodded in approval. "So is Timothy going to be prepared for Saturday. If he's not, I can handle the job, you know."

Stephen quickly responded, "Yeah, he's ready, although Michele keeps changing the script on him, though. I know he's very nervous, but he was the first one who volunteered. He's a good public speaker when he's not talking about himself for too long, and the script is built around us."

"I mean, cut him some slack. Can you officiate a wedding when you are a complete moron. I know he's your friend, but he's not mine, so I really don't care. I probably won't see him after the wedding anyway," responded Richard.

Stephen laughed at the complete moron comment, "Yeah, he is a moron, but he helped me out with a few things when I needed it. He has strong family connections. His family was friends with mine, and he helped me get into the fire department. Why he's not a firefighter, God only knows."

"Don't say that expression in front of him; he will probably say, 'Well I know because I can officiate now, you know word of God, fucking putz.'"

"Take it easy. As stupid as he is, he can kick both of our asses, except if Sam was there."

"You're right," Richard quickly answered. "Sam will kick all our asses. I guess dumbest person means best fighter."

"Sam is a good fighter, but he's also a good brother, believe it or not, and he did help us with a few bullies when we were younger."

"I know, he is better than Timothy on the power rankings, I guess. He's not that bad once you get to know him."

Stephen was pouring coffee in mugs for the two of them. He followed up with what Richard said, "You know he actually likes you. Sam doesn't like many people, but you he doesn't mind."

"Well isn't it obvious, I am pretty awesome when I'm not tired. Sorry about the insults to Timothy."

"You can call him Tim. He won't mind. All his friends call him Tim."

"Exactly, he isn't my friend. Who knows, maybe one day."

"Here, have some coffee, on the house."

"And this, my friend, is the highlight of my day, as pathetic as that sounds. Thank goodness for this coffee," Richard stated.

"Well, how are you doing on the lady market?" asked Stephen.

This was a complicated question for Richard, for he really liked Katie, who was the same age as Stephen and a good friend of his. Stephen and Katie went to school together, and they had been good friends for a good seven years before Richard met her at a barbecue and was infatuated with her ever since. They hung out a few times, but she made it perfectly clear that they should always be friends. She did not like him for a boyfriend. Richard did not want to hear any of that and was hoping to make her change her mind during the weekend, but he did not tell anybody, not even Stephen.

Richard finally answered the question after a long pause. "I'm not doing too well in that department, like with everything else in my life right now, but who knows, maybe that can change this weekend."

"Yay, that's the spirit from young Richard Lionheart. Why don't you try to pick up one of Michele's friends. A couple are single, you know."

"Yeah, maybe. You know that might be the best advice you have given me in a while. Go into teaching, yeah that was pretty sound advice, you little prick."

"Haha, take it easy over there. You have a good job. Why don't you wait and see it play out for once in your life instead of shooting things down the second they happen when it is not the exact thing you want."

"Thanks doc, you know you don't have to solve all my life problems. I can figure out some too, once in a while," answered Richard.

"Yeah I know, but I want to help."

"You're going to make me throw up. Relax with the sentimental attitude, I don't want any of that garbage."

"Just drink your coffee and relax. Michele texted me, and she should be back in like ten minutes."

"Is that my cue to leave? You guys want some alone time or something?"

"No, you can stay a little. I think we are both too nervous to fool around anyway, and we don't really have the time, and there is so much work that needs to be done."

"Blah blah blah, I really don't care about all the work that needs to be done. You think you can handle it without telling me. Just let me rot here, alright."

"Sure thing, you can rot all you want for another like fifteen minutes or so," quickly answered Stephen, who just finished his coffee and washed out his mug. Richard was savoring every moment of his coffee and checked his phone to see if somebody messaged him. But there was no notifications.

"So, you think Sam has his best man speech written? I know he won't memorize it," said Richard.

"Oh, not a chance in hell for memorizing it or writing it. I'm not sure if he even picked up his tux yet. He's probably eating dinner at some bar right now by himself trying to pick up girls."

"And that older brother of yours gets a lot of girls to fall for his bullshit. That might be the only way he is smarter than me. Did he ever have a long-term relationship?"

Stephen looked perplexed by the question, and poured himself another cup of coffee after taking another clean mug. It didn't matter because Michele didn't drink coffee anyway. After pouring himself a second cup, he began to answer, "There was this one girl, Joan. They never dated, but he was crazy about her. He was completely different around her too. He restrained himself from acting like himself, and I know that's not prime for a good relationship, but he changed for the better. I know they talked a lot. I never saw him smile like he did when she messaged him, and he lied about where he was going when they hung out because he didn't want the family to know about her. To be honest, I'm not sure what happened. I think she wanted to be friends, and he couldn't handle it or something. I know he hasn't talked to her since, and if you bring up her name, he kind of stands there frozen."

Richard stared off in the abyss. Stephen was unsure if he was listening and took a big gulp from his mug. "You know, a yes-or-no answer would have worked."

"Yeah I know, but not many people know about that. I'm sorry I made his confession to you. I'm not sure why I did that." Stephen was very confused and a little worried, but Richard did not really care. He worried about his own problems.

How does he like his new job? What is he doing again, installing solar panels or some shit like that?" asked Richard to avoid the shear awkwardness of the situation.

"Yeah, the solar panels. I think so far so good for him. He told me that he likes the hours. I'm not sure if he was telling the truth, but he's getting some of his responsibility back."

"I'm not sure he really had any, but he has a good heart, still kind of dumb though," answered Richard.

Michele's car pulled up in the driveway, and Stephen ran to the door. Richard followed in a very lazy manner, almost tripping on his way to the door. Richard continued, "You know, you don't have to run to her all the time. I think she is going to marry you at this point, but you know, happy wife is happy life, right?"

"You'll learn someday, hopefully very soon," answered Stephen quickly. Richard did not have an answer for Stephen's statement. He stood behind Stephen, waiting for Michele.

"Hello girls, you guys get your nails done?" asked Michele. Richard was finishing his coffee. He did not have the energy to answer with a quick comeback.

"Of course we did, with your money. We switched it around this time," responded Stephen. Richard almost dropped his mug with the stupidity of Stephen's comeback. He knew his friend had messed up the second he mentioned money. He ran to wash the mug in the sink, and now this was his cue to leave their home.

Michele Lynn, blond with an extreme expression of intelligence, simply pointed towards the sink, indicating that the garbage was waiting for Stephen to take it out. Richard was putting his shoes on and quickly said, "See you tomorrow at dinner, Michele."

"Have a good night Rich, but your friend might not be at dinner tomorrow."

Richard laughed and said, "And I have a lot to learn. Come on, I'll throw out the garbage with you." Stephen was gathering the garbage from the can underneath the sink when the bag ripped and it all fell on the kitchen floor. He covered his face with his hands in frustration, but he was more frustrated with his idiotic answer. He finally managed to put all the garbage in a bag that was not ripped without the help from Michele and Richard.

Stephen stepped out of the kitchen. "Okay, let's go Rich." Richard and Michele hugged, and he stepped out of the door, barely holding it for Stephen. As they were walking to the garbage cans on the side of the house, Stephen asked, "What do you want to ask me?"

"What makes you think I want to ask you a question. Why don't you worry about not insulting your wife-to-be a day before your wedding."

"Fine, then I won't answer your question. See you tomorrow."

"You think Katie would get a drink with me if I asked her this weekend?"

     John P. Burdi

Stephen carefully placed the bag in the garbage can and looked at Richard dead in the eyes. "I would not ask her if I was you. Didn't she say she wants to be friends?"

Richard looked right into the ground, the hole that he was going to dig for himself. "Yes, but I might be able to convince her otherwise this weekend."

Stephen wanted to head into his house and try to receive forgiveness from Michele. He began walking backwards. "I can't tell you what to do, but don't do something that you'll regret doing, or something that you won't do and live a life of regret."

Richard began walking to his car, cursing under his breath as he got to the door. He shouted back, "Thanks fortune cookie, see you tomorrow for dinner. The shit will hit the fan this weekend." Richard got into his car and drove away almost in one motion. Stephen waved to him and shook his head in anguish. He was thinking his good friend might make a terrible mistake.